Destiny of a Shield Maiden

T. Karr

GOLDEN CIRCLE PRESS

Anmore, British Columbia

Canada

ISBN-13: 978-0995251007 (sc)
ISBN-13: 978-0995251014 (e)

For my children

Who shared this journey with me

Special acknowledgments to

Amy Karr, Cathy Mogus and Brad Craig

CHAPTER 1

Tomorrow, I will risk my life at the festival. I pull my hand from the green waters. The sea is still cold, making the game more challenging than it already is. My heart begins to beat faster, and then I hear the familiar voice.

"Red!" he shouts. "What are you doing up so early? Did you miss me?" I now see Erik on the *outside* of a nearby dragon ship, effortlessly jumping between the fastened-down oars. He races around the vessel as if floating in air. The Jarl warrior puts his forearm across his face. "Look, with my eyes closed!" he dares with a huge smile.

"My name is Livvy, not *Red*, for the hundredth time!" I shout back.

"With hair as bright as earthfire, can you blame me? And just so you know, I preferred it long!" He pauses on an oar while waving his arms to keep his balance.

"Don't kill yourself showing off!" I yell.

Erik laughs as he reverses direction and races towards the stern, jumping in long strides. "And I'm going to win this year!" he hollers. I watch as he rounds the ship out of view.

"You always win!" I yell back, unsure if my voice reaches him.

Erik is not just any noble. He's the son of Godi, our chieftain. Although the Jarls choose our chieftain every spring, Godi is the only one we've had since coming from Norseland. I

1

am just a Karl, and like the other commoners, I don't get a say in who rules the clan. But I think I would pick Erik if asked.

Here he comes now, roaring down the far side of the ship and stopping on the final oar. "Enough practice, start counting, Red!" He dives into the water and is out of sight before I can protest. I sigh loudly and do as he says.

Erik is the defending champion of the oar race, one of the festival's oldest games. He has a natural advantage over most Norsemen in the clan. Erik is tall, with broad shoulders and big arms. At eighteen, just one season older than me, he has already fought in a dozen battles. With his blond hair and muscular body, the girls whisper and laugh that he's a descendant of the gods.

I reach one hundred and thirty when the warrior pops his head out of the water in front of me. "I believe that's another record," Erik boasts, pulling his long, wet hair behind his head. I'm tempted to tell him I can break two hundred, but he's having too much fun for me to spoil it.

"Watch out for my cousin in the dunking game," he says while treading water. "Thoren competes as a warrior. I worry she doesn't know how strong she is."

"Really? If you say so!"

I know all too well how Thoren competes, and I'm quite certain she means every bit of the pain she inflicts. Thoren is Godi's niece, the daughter of Bryanjar, the mightiest warrior in the hamlet. It's with this birthright, that as a girl, they allow her in battle – or at least no one will dare challenge her father otherwise. The chieftain calls her a shield maiden, a woman who fights as fierce as any man and more so than many. The tale is a Shockhead froze when he saw her, and she just walked up to him and drove her spear through his heart. She then took his sword and cut his head off with it. Although I'm not looking forward to competing against her, the image of her striking down a Shockhead does make me smile.

Erik interrupts my thoughts. "If you're doing this contest for the silver, I'll make sure Olaf is paying you what he should," he says, swimming effortlessly towards shore.

I call out, trying to sound serious, "He gives me *at least* half of everything he earns!"

"I forgot how generous Olaf was! Very well then, my maiden!"

"Oh, now I'm a maiden, am I?"

Erik waves goodbye, and I do the same. The truth is, I hate the dunking game and am competing only for the silver. I have little chance of winning, but any chance at all is one I need to take. A piece of silver is worth more than six months pay at the smithy, and I'm running out of time to save.

Erik reaches the shore and picks up his clothes before walking towards the hill. The hamlet will awaken soon, and I make my way towards the meadow, passing a dozen blooming sod houses along the way. As I reach the plateau, I stop and turn back to look at the sea.

Godi proclaims our fiord is the greatest in all Iceland, and although it's the only one I have seen, I can't imagine there could be one more magnificent. Its waters are deep and wider than I can swim. With a westerly wind and our strongest oarsmen, the dragon ships take a half day to reach the end where the big sea begins. The great mountains surround the fiord on both sides, dropping steeply into the sea's depths. It will be almost winter again before the snow at their peaks disappear.

All of the dragon ships are in the harbor today, as the Jarls will be racing them tomorrow in the summer festival, and their colored sails are casting dancing pictures on the water. I count twenty-two ships in total, each with a prow and stern in the likeness of a dragon's neck. The rectangular sails aid the rowers in crossing the vast sea and are already hanging from the tall masts anchored to the center of the hulls. A red dragon marks the sails on all our ships, a symbol of Fafnir, the greedy dwarf-turned-dragon, who guarded his hoard of glittering gold and gems. The sail warns the enemy that our army, like the dragon which breathes fire, will slay them without fear and mercy.

I often dreamt if we were born Jarls, with nobility and wealth, that Grim and I would sail a dragon ship in search of the rainbow bridge, and not even the giant sea serpent would stop us. The rainbow bridge connects our realm to Asgard, the home of the gods. We wouldn't be able to cross it, as the bridge is on fire and well-guarded to keep out the giants, but it would be a sight to see. My little brother, though, is more interested in wrestling the older children to submission than he is the sea.

I make my way back to the kot to check on Grim. In the far distance, the smoke rises in the southern sky. The elders say it's a sign the giants will soon attack Midgard, the kingdom of humans. I've never seen a giant or met anyone else who has, but I'm told they're bigger than ten men tall and eat people just to fill their bellies between meals. Loki, one of the most powerful giants, is bound in Asgard with Odin's ropes. The ground has been shaking a lot more lately, which means he's getting close to breaking free.

I approach the kot through the meadow. Although small, our home is well-built, and I'm very fond of it. The sod walls are almost six feet thick to fight the long, cold winters and stacked on stone footings to keep away the rot. The roof is thatched with thick branches and a grass covering, which in the spring becomes alive with green grass and wildflowers. We even have a wooden door with an iron key, although we have never locked it. Inside is a single room with a dirt floor and a hearth in the middle. A bench lines the back of the room where we sleep.

"Hi, Disa. Are you hungry?" Grim asks excitedly as I enter through the door. Grim is warming up yesterday's stew in the iron cauldron.

"Yes, I'm hungry, too," I say. "And thank you for starting the fire. You're getting good with the flint." Dis means guardian spirit and is a nickname the priest had for me when my brother was younger. Grim picked it up, pronouncing it Disa, and has called me it since. I don't mind, but there's nothing spiritual about protecting a child from starving or freezing to death. And it's not like they gave me a choice.

My brother is changing so quickly with each season. He's now seven winters old but can throw a spear farther and swing an ax harder than most children two winters older. Few would think that Grim and I were siblings from appearance alone. His eyes are much bluer than mine, like the winter sky, and his hair is as golden as Thor's. I have stopped growing and am almost halfway between my father's spears, five and six feet in length, whereas Grim is already up to my shoulders. I wouldn't be surprised if he's heavier than me by next winter. If born a Jarl, I'm sure Grim would already be a young apprentice destined to be a great warrior.

I unwrap some dried apples and take out the last of the skyr. I mostly make the creamy curds when the snow begins to fall and before the goat's milk dries up for the winter. It's Grim's favorite so I made some for the festival, but that was a week ago, and now, not surprisingly, it's all gone. I scoop what's left into a bowl for us to share.

"I heard this is our last summer in Iceland," Grim says.

"Who did you hear that from?"

"From the Jarl children. They said the war with the Shockheads is coming."

I learned long ago to speak with Grim as a brother and not as a child. How else will he become a Norseman? "Yes, Grim, the war is coming. The Shockheads took everything from us. But our army is getting stronger, and by the spring they should be ready to sail to Norseland and take it back."

"But I like it here," he says.

"You will like it there more. I promise."

"But you have never been there. How can you make such a promise?"

"In Norseland, we will feast on honey and buttermilk, and live in a rock castle, like an earl and maiden," I say. "And you can be anything you want to be there."

"A warrior like Erik?" he says with a smile.

"Anything you want."

We sit down together on the bench by the small table. "Can you help me practice for the battle of Ragnarok?" Grim asks.

"I was hoping you would ask. Let's eat and then head to the field right away. I need to be at the monastery before midday, and then I must work. But we have time."

We finish our meal, Grim dresses, and I unwrap the sheepskin by the bed. I pull out the weapons and lay them on the floor. My father didn't own a sword, but his weapons are strong and are my most cherished possessions.

I pick up the spears first. One is five feet long and the other six. The spearheads are made of iron, each with winged tips, and fastened to hollow shafts made of ash wood. I take out the battle ax next. Its head is shaped like the crescent moon, and its handle is three feet long. The weapon is heavy, but not too heavy that I can't throw it with two hands.

I pick up my father's shield and set it against the wall. It's round and made from linden wood, is light for its size, and reinforced with iron around its rim. It covers me from my shoulders to my knees when held up for battle. I like the shield exactly how it is, but Grim says it looks funny and needs paint. All the nobles paint their shields with swaths of black and yellow, made to resemble the sails of a dragon ship, but Grim wants to paint on a creature like a dragon or wolf. I promised him we could do something with it this summer but need to convince him it's best to avoid anything that draws attention in battle.

Lastly, I take out the knives. I have two with straight blades, but my favorite is the seax. The seax is curved and heavy, and is the length from my fingertips to my elbow. The blade is attached to a strong wooden handle. The seax fits tightly into a leather sheath, which I attach to my belt, and I sharpen it at least once a week. I'll never own a sword but train with the seax as if it were one, imagining it at times to be Sigurd's blade which slays the cursed dragon.

Grim picks up the shorter spear and runs to the door. "C'mon Disa, grab the shield and spear. Let's go!"

I pull a sandy tunic over my head and slip into my worn boots. I pick up the weapons, and we head out to the fields, a short walk away. The battle of Ragnarok is the prophesied final battle between the gods and the giants. When the giants rise up against the gods, Odin will select the greatest warriors in Valhalla to join him. Loki will escape from his ropes and will join forces with the other giants, attacking the kingdoms, including Midgard. At the festival each year, the children act out the final battle in a play down by the shore. They display their fighting skills, and the clan chooses the best young warrior with their cheers.

We arrive at the fields, and Grim immediately springs into action. He drives the spear towards me, and I defend with the shield. He swings the knife while evading a gentle thrust from my spear. "Disa, like you mean it! You always say you fight like you train. Do you want me to be killed in battle?"

"Okay, you asked for it," I warn. We practice long after the hamlet wakes up. It amazes me how fast Grim is improving. We will have to start using wooden sticks soon as I can't afford to be confined to my bed, tending to a spear wound.

Grim is hungry again, and we go back to our kot. I wrap my father's weapons in the sheepskin, except for the seax, which I keep on my belt.

"Do you feel that?" Grim asks nervously.

Standing quietly, I hear a humming. Suddenly the ground shakes, growing increasingly violent. A roaring growl as if from the land of the dwarves follows it, echoing through the kot. I fall to the hard earth, unable to keep my legs beneath me. Grim is crawling, reaching for his knife. I pull my seax from its sheath, rolling to my back.

"It's the giants! Grim screams. "They're here!"

CHAPTER 2

The walls sway from their footings as if threatening to bury us alive. I want to curl up on the earth but then see the look of fear on Grim's face. I manage to get up and stumble to the door. My legs wobble as if I'm balancing on a log in the sea. I push the door open and search the horizon for the enemy, but there is no one. I look south towards the smoke, but there isn't any sky fire either. Grim is now behind me, his arms around my waist. The shaking stops completely as fast as it arrived. The sea is angry, but the rest of the hamlet is quiet again.

"It's Loki. He's still bound," I say, trying to sound calm.

"The shakings are getting worse," Grim stammers. "Maybe it's not Loki but the gods who are angry."

"Our gods have no reason to be mad at us," I say. I don't admit this thought, too, has crossed my mind. Loki is a giant, but I can't imagine him big enough to shake all of Midgard. But these are the stories told by the elders, and it's best not to challenge them.

I check if the kot is in need of repair. The sod walls aren't leaning any worse than they were before the shaking. A few pieces of driftwood fell loose from the roof, and I quickly put them in their place. Grim is now back in bed, already falling asleep. I want to lie down with him, but I'm late. I leave, quickly making my way to the monastery to see Papar.

Our kot is on the northern edge of Papar's land, closest to the shore. The monastery is but a short run across the barley fields. The grass is still green and soft, but will soon turn a golden brown. Once the spikes become brittle, the grain will be harvested and used to make bread, feed the livestock, or make malt for brewing ale.

I sprint across the fields on the path flattened by my many crossings and approach the monastery. I knock quietly on the wooden door as I have done every week since last autumn. I step back to look up at the grand structure. The monastery is made from wood, just like the Jarl houses on the hill. Its walls are shaped like a ship with oval sides, and there are dozens of driftwood poles supporting the roof.

The monastery was built many years before Godi and our clan arrived, and Papar says the trees were much bigger then. It's the largest home in the hamlet, and all the monks sleep here. I think there are almost twenty Saxons still alive but most are getting very old. Many Norsemen wanted to take their home from them, and many likely still do. But Godi ruled to leave the monks alone, and in exchange, they would make the nobles ale and wine. As long as he's chieftain, Godi has the final word, and his men will obey him.

The door opens. "You are late," the old man says, smiling.

"Sorry, Papar. I had a bit of a mess to clean up in my kot after the shaking."

I enter the monastery. The fire is lit, and the smoke is finding its way to the opening in the roof above. Three monks sit quietly in the back of the room, writing on their skins as they often do. A cross, as Papar calls it, is mounted to the wall behind them. There used to be a stone one erected outside the walls, but it was destroyed years ago. Godi allows Papar to display offerings to his god as long as they are kept inside the walls.

I sit on the long bench which runs end-to-end along the wall. Papar takes a seat next to me. Even sitting, I feel as though I tower over him. Perhaps he was taller in his youth. His gray hair is cut short, and his eyes look tired.

"It is good to see you, Livvy," he says softly in his strong accent. "Did you feel the ground roar?" At first, I found his accent so funny that I would sometimes laugh out loud, often uncontrollably, and I would apologize repeatedly. But he would laugh with me, so I think he understood. Now I can mostly keep my laughter inside.

"Yes," I reply. "The great battle is coming soon. What does your god say?"

"The beginning of sorrows is near. But I am here to live in peace, not to battle or conquer."

When I ask of his gods, where they live, or what strengths they have, his response is always the same. *The monks do not battle or conquer.* Yes, the monks don't train and don't have weapons. How can they conquer anyone? But I love Papar no matter how small and weak he is. He gives me more than any of our mighty warriors do.

"How is Grim's training coming?" Papar asks.

"He is getting stronger every day."

"To grow strong, he must eat. Are you getting food enough?"

"Are you getting *enough* food?" I say softly. I don't feel right correcting an old man, but this is what he has asked me to do.

"Yes, of course. Are you getting *enough* food?"

"Yes, Papar. We are eating well." Papar always asks first about Grim and then if we have enough food to eat. He has been my spiritual guardian, my Dis, since my father died. He treats me like a daughter despite my loyalty being to Odin. I'll miss him dearly when I go back to Norseland. I glance at the monks at the back of the room, writing on their skins. Who will read their symbols once they're dead?

Papar notices me looking. "Next season, I will teach you to write Saxon," he says. "But first, I must learn to speak better Norse. Should we start?"

I smile, for it seems Papar can sense my thoughts, although I know only the seers are granted this kind of magic. "Yes, Papar. That's why I'm here. Again, I'm not learned in language, and I'll teach you all wrong. But I don't wish to sleep with the Thralls again, so I'll repay my debts as we agreed."

"I want to learn it wrong, and no one better to teach me the wrong way than you," he says with a grin.

Papar took pity on Grim and me, and gave us the kot we live in, provided I repaid the gift by working for the monastery one day a week for a year. He told the other monks the trade was fair, knowing very well I had the better side of the arrangement. As far as pity, I needed none, but the longhouse where they put Grim and me was crowded with over twenty, and I was afraid I might drive my knife through the throat of the next man who tried to get in my bed. Actually, I was quite certain of it.

We begin as usual, with me reciting stories of the gods and kingdoms, of what has happened, and what is to come. After every pause, he repeats my words back to me. And, as with each lesson, it feels Papar is captivated by each word I speak, like a child hearing a saga for the first time. Perhaps I would be equally fascinated by hearing the stories of his gods if he would ever share them. I start with the story of how Odin lost his eye.

"Odin, the father of all gods, sought wisdom above all else," I begin. Papar says the same words slowly, doing his best to sound more Norse than Saxon. I tell of how Odin learned that Mimir, the guardian of the well of Urd, had knowledge of all things in the cosmos. He was granted this power by drinking water from the well. Odin searched for and eventually found the well of Urd and asked Mimir for a drink. The guardian knew how great this power was and refused Odin a drink unless he was offered an eye in return. Without hesitation, Odin gouged out one of his own eyes and dropped it in the well. Mimir stayed true to his word and dipped his horn in the well and gave Odin a drink.

Papar repeats the story's ending after me. "Odin knew there was no sacrifice too great for wisdom and used this wisdom to rule the cosmos."

Papar stands and pours water from a jar into two horns. "That is an incredible story, Livvy. Can we do another one?" The way he says it makes me feel like he is teaching me something, not the other way around.

"How about I tell you the story of how Loki tricked his way into Asgard?"

"Oh, sounds exciting. Please!"

We finish today's lesson and step outside. The sun is high, and there's a light wind blowing off the sea. I can taste the salt in the air. "We have been busy preparing the apple wine for the feast tomorrow," Papar says in quite good Norse. "Over twenty jars. Tomorrow, I will celebrate solstice with you."

I haven't seen Papar drink wine or mead, but he has surprised me many times so perhaps tomorrow will be another. "Your Norse is improving a lot, even if you sound like a poor blacksmith," I say.

"This is good news. I am getting old, so I must learn quickly before I die."

Why would he want to learn our language before dying? I can't think of how to respond, so I smile and say goodbye for now. I quickly make my way to the smithy at the far reaches of the Jarl village.

I work as an apprentice to Olaf, the Jarls' smith. In addition to a small wage, the job gives me the opportunity to practice with the weapons I work on. Training with steel is something girls don't do, unless you're Thoren. But it never seemed fair to me. I've seen the stares from both the girls and boys, but if they don't like it, they can try and take the weapons from me.

The smithy's location was chosen to provide close access to wood for charcoal and away from the longhouses so that the loud hammering would not disturb the nobles. It's a simple, single-room structure, about three times the size of my kot, with a furnace outside for smelting and a hearth inside for forging.

The wooden door, blackened by the smoke and heat, is open, and Olaf is inside stoking the hearth. The man is the same age my father would be but looks much older than he should. He's missing the long finger on his left hand from an errant swing of his hammer while he was an apprentice. Fortunately, I still have all my fingers and try my best to keep it that way. Olaf used to keep the hair on his face long until an ember got caught in it last spring. It was then that I chose to cut my hair short. I got funny looks from just about everybody, but Grim says he likes it.

Olaf and his son Volund are the only blacksmiths in the hamlet. They have more work than two men can handle, but they hide the secrets of their craft and get paid very well as a result. Many Karls believe their work must be of sorcery. How else could one turn stone into a gleaming sword?

Olaf only offered me work because my father, too, was a blacksmith. And I'm sure he thinks a girl will not be a threat to his trade even if she knows the secrets of his magic. And truth be told, he's partly right in that I have no intention of becoming a blacksmith in Iceland. I'll be back in Norseland before the second winter arrives.

"Start the furnace. We need to smelt more iron," Olaf bellows without looking up. "The nobles want all available ore and steel made into swords and axes before the winter starts, so there is going to be little time to play with your Christians."

My weekly visit with Papar is a regular point of discontent with Olaf, but I'm learning to shrug it off. I work hard, and there are many days I'm not paid a full wage. What copper or iron I do make, I save a portion which I hide in the back wall of my kot. I'll use it to start a new life for Grim and me when we return to Norseland. I'll never again be at the mercy of another for food and shelter, or worse, forced to marry just to stay warm.

"Do you think the gods approve of this nonsense, teaching them our language and ways?" Olaf asks, not letting up. "The monks should be slaves. Instead, Godi invites the priest into his home, and they drink wine together."

It's best I keep quiet. It always blows over.

Olaf mumbles a few more words under his breath before looking back in my direction. "Volund is at the bog to see how much ore is left to harvest," he says. "So I'll need you to help with forging today until he returns. We have a sword to craft."

I load the furnace with charcoal and light it with the flint, unable to conceal my smile. It's rare that Olaf gives me the opportunity to forge steel, and never when Volund is here. Volund wants to ensure no man, *or girl*, poses a threat to his future, no matter the likelihood. My labor is mostly tending the fires, filing, and sharpening the forged tools or weapons. I have learned to cast shoes for horses and tips for arrows, but hammering, bending, and punching ore into a weapon, let alone a sword, is the work of a master. A single sword costs sixteen milking cows to purchase, and only the wealthiest Norsemen can afford one. At this price, the weapon needs to be perfect.

After a quick lesson, I spend the rest of the day hammering on the hot iron and steel to draw the bars into length. Olaf does the twisting and bending to give it shape, and I watch carefully, trying to remember as much as I can. He shows me how to read the color of the fire and when to quench the metal with water, so it cures hard and sharp but isn't brittle. By the end of the day, my arms are tired and sore, but I'm very pleased with what I learned. A few more days like this and maybe I'll know enough to make Grim a sword – not that I'll ever afford the steel.

Leaving the smithy, I remember I'm out of meat and will need to go fishing if I'm to have strength tomorrow. I retrieve my long spear and net from the kot and head north towards the sea. I have a spot in a hidden cove below the cliffs which is only accessible at low tide. It'll be ripe with clams this time of season, and I'll go there if I fail to spear a fish. And tomorrow night at the feast, Grim and I will eat until our bellies hurt. I start into a light run with a sudden burst of energy.

CHAPTER 3

My brother's small hand is lying still on my shoulder as it was when he fell asleep. As the ground tremors have become more frequent, Grim has slept much closer, pushing me off the bed onto the hard earth more than once. The truth is, he's much braver than I am, and I need him there next to me as much as he needs me. I locate the sun through the small holes near the ceiling. We've slept in!

"Grim, wake up," I say, shaking his shoulder. "We're going to be late." Grim instantly jumps out of bed in a panic, crawling over me.

"Why are you still in bed then?" he cries. "Let's go, Disa!"

We quickly dress and eat the remaining bread and fish from yesterday. We are soon out of the kot and run down to the shoreline. The crowds are already amassing near the black stone, mostly gathering on the grassy slope.

The two hundred or more nobles live at the top of the hill in their wooden longhouses. There are three times as many kots in the hamlet, but the longhouses are much bigger. They need to be to have room to keep all their things. Two towers are perched near the crest where the watchmen can gaze down the fiord for enemy ships.

Although we were born Karls, Grim and I once lived with the Thralls in one of the longhouses. Grim was happy to stay warm at night and to have bread and fish to eat, but to me this arrangement was unbearable. The Thralls are either slaves or bondsmen. If a Karl can't pay his debt, he or she becomes a bondsman and works for their debtor until their dues are paid. But without a family to feed us, Grim and I became bonded to the clan, unable to cover the debts of a simple meal or warmth of a fire.

Grim sees his friends and darts off, likely to put some final planning into the great battle that will conclude the festival today. Soon Godi and Erik arrive at the plain below the hill. Godi is taller than most men in the clan and was one of the greatest warriors in Norseland. He looks older than when I saw him last and his white beard longer, but they say he can still beat the younger warriors in battle. He is wearing the long, red cloak which he wears to all public gatherings, and a large pin made of gold holds the garment in place on his right shoulder. The chieftain stands up on the black stone and waves his arms. Silence comes over the hamlet.

"Welcome, my fellow Norsemen," Godi calls out in his slow but commanding tone. "The gods continue to be good to us. We prospered through the long winter, and the sea is abundant with fish, and the crops with grain and fruit."

Godi welcomes the visitors to the hamlet, vowing to treat them as guests of his house and telling them that we must stay united against the Shockheads. As custom at each festival, the chieftain tells our saga of Iceland, to remind the elderly and to teach the children, such that our stories will never be forgotten.

"Norseland was ruled by many kingdoms, and the kingdoms lived together in harmony, and they prospered," the chieftain begins. Usually, Godi starts with how Fairhair ruled the small

Kingdom of Vestfold in Norseland. But this time, he skips the story of Harold Fairhair's rise to power and goes straight to the part where Fairhair's army began its onslaught on the lands.

The full story goes that Fairhair was an average man in an average kingdom, and although most knew his name, it was because his father was a beloved chieftain, not because he was. Fairhair fell in love with the beautiful princess of Hordaland, a kingdom bordering his, and proposed to her in marriage. However, the princess only laughed and said not until he ruled all the kingdoms of Norseland. Fairhair went mad with resentment and killed her father and forced the princess to be his wife. He grew thirsty for power and built an army, promising his warriors women and treasures from their raids. He vowed he would conquer all of Norseland, and his army would not cut their hair until he was victorious. It's from their tangled hair, which often went down to their waists, that his ruthless warriors became known as the Shockheads.

Godi tells the crowd how he took our clan to Iceland to save us from certain death. Our warriors have since returned to Norseland many times. And although we lost men in the battles that ensued, we killed far more of theirs. And with each fight, our warriors become stronger and more determined. The people around me nod their heads and shout out, "Death to the Shockheads!"

Godi finishes the story by raising his sword in the air. "Our children will die as old men and women in Norseland, and we'll kill any Shockhead who gets in our way. We'll sail soon and will be victorious!"

We cheer loudly, standing up and raising our weapons high into the air. Then out of the corner of my eye, I see Quibly barreling towards me. I brace myself as he hits and hugs me at the same time, lifting me well off the ground. My body is touching nothing but his belly as he spins me twice in a full circle before setting me back on the ground.

"You're lucky I saw it was you and didn't swing my seax at your head," I threaten. The big boy is breathing too hard to counter and just laughs. I laugh, too, and pretend to do just as I said with my weapon.

"Are you ready for the dunking game?" he asks. "Thoren is."

"I'd like to see you out there! Can you even swim?"

"Remember to fight and not just pull each other's hair," Quibly responds with a wide grin. I punch him in the shoulder as hard as I can, but he doesn't flinch. Next time I'll use a rock.

Quibly is my closest friend in the hamlet. We have known each other since before we could talk. Quibly's father owned the farm next to ours, and we spent countless summer days exploring the forests in search of elves and dwarves. In the winter, we made snow caves to hide from the trolls and carved out secret tunnels to escape if discovered.

I was actually heavier than Quibly at one point and maybe stronger, but that time has long passed. He's half a head taller than me and must be twice my weight, mostly carried in his belly. Perhaps it's all the cream he sneaks while milking the goats. His face is round, and his hairy jaw is far too short and sparse to be called a beard. And he wears his wool cap no matter the season, which doesn't help with his sweating. But somehow Quibly's strength has matched his size, as he can lift stones heavier than most two boys can do together. I always feel safe with Quibly next to me, but maybe that's because I know I can outrun him if a troll attacks us.

We sit down together, and Godi continues the festival proceedings. "Today, our warriors and those aspiring to become one will compete in the games," he says. "The games celebrate the strengths of the clan and what makes us Norsemen."

The crowd cheers and both Quibly and I join in. "This year, our games include the dragon ship races, wrestling, oar jumping, rope pulling, stone lifting, and for the girls, dunking," the chieftain continues. Quibly looks at me and shakes his head when Godi mentions the dunking. I shrug my shoulders, but my heart begins to beat faster.

"The final games will be the warrior battle of Knattleiker and the children's battle of Ragnarok," Godi proclaims, raising his sword again to the sky. "Then the great feast will begin, and we'll eat and drink until dawn!" We cheer loudly one last time, and the crowd quickly disperses as people race to their favorite competition to get a good viewing spot.

"Livvy, I need you to walk on my back," Quibly pleads as he plunks himself down on the ground. "I must loosen up for the stone lift and don't want to damage this beautiful body of mine. I would ask Thoren but I'm afraid she won't be able to keep her feet off me."

I take a deep breath and slowly inhale, then jump as high as I can, landing on his wide torso.

Quibly whimpers, "I said to walk on it, not destroy it." I give him a light kick to the side of the head and jump off. "You and Thoren need to get along. I can't have my best friend and my future wife trying to kill each other," he says while getting to his knees.

Quibly has been obsessed with Thoren since he noticed girls

for the first time. I don't count as we never look at each other that way. And who could blame him? Thoren is striking to look at. Her skin is the color of bark from a birch tree, and her black hair is curly, unlike any maiden in the hamlet. Her breasts are full, and her legs are thick and strong. But it would be kind for Thoren to at least acknowledge Quibly's existence one of these days. Maybe then the tormented boy could move on.

We find Grim and watch wrestling and the rope pull, and then go to the sea to watch the oar jumping. Erik's vessel is the closest dragon ship to shore. I hope to sail on this mighty ship one day, preferably back to Norseland. There's no one I would feel safer sailing the great sea with than Erik. His vessel is the finest in the hamlet and can carry over thirty warriors. It's long and light, and with a shallow hull, it can navigate waters only one fathom deep. Erik says it's the fastest ship in Iceland, maybe in all of Midgard.

The rules of the oar race are simple. Two opponents start on adjacent sides of the ship and race in the same direction, jumping across the oars which are tied down to the hull. When reaching the bow or stern, they must quickly move to the other side of the ship, again leaping across the oars. The opponent who either catches the other or lasts the longest without falling into the water, wins. The first three matches end with both opponents falling into the sea before they make it past fives oars. Now it's Erik's turn to compete. He waves to the spectators while pretending to lose his balance.

Quibly tilts his head towards me and whispers, "I look like that with my shirt off but can't stand the cold." I roll my eyes and slap him in the belly.

Erik's opponent loses his balance, plunging into the water

almost as soon as the horn blows. Erik stops, raises his arms in frustration and hops back into the ship. One by one, Erik defeats his opponents. He catches up with one warrior and runs past him like he isn't there. To no one's surprise, it isn't long before Erik is declared the champion.

"How are our warriors to take back our kingdom if they can't jump on a few wooden sticks?" Quibly says, shaking his head. "Do I need to show the boys how to be men?"

"You would break the oar and fall into the sea the moment you stepped on it," I say, laughing.

"Are the girls still jealous that you and Erik have this thing?" Quibly asks, as if in rebuttal. It's not like he hasn't teased me before about this, but it's been a few weeks. I want to punch him again.

"There is no *thing*!" I snap back. "We talked a few times. The girls just waste their time dreaming of dreams that won't happen. Jarls do not marry Karls, and certainly the sons of chieftains do not."

"Whatever you say," he says, grinning.

I shift my back towards him and watch the girls ogling at their chieftain's heir. I recall when Erik first spoke to me. I spent two weeks sharpening weapons for the Jarls as part of my yearly payment to the nobles. Although Erik inspected my work every day, we spent more time talking about Norseland than of iron and steel. It's not like he invited me into the longhouses for wine, but he told me wonderful stories of the Jarls who live in castles made of stone. The hives in their gardens make an endless supply of honey, and buttermilk flows like water at the weekly feasts. The horses are tall enough to ride into battle, and the cows are fat enough to feed an entire hamlet.

"It's time for me to go to the stone lift," Quibly says, getting to his feet. "I'll see you at Knattleiker."

I forgot for a moment I wasn't alone. I turn and give my friend a hug. "Good luck, Quibly."

"Thanks, but I think you'll need more luck than me."

I can't argue with him on that.

As Grim and I walk to the seaside for the dunking game, my brother reaches up and takes my hand. "I love you, Disa. Don't die."

CHAPTER 4

My opponents are at the shore when we arrive. There are eight of them. Although the game is open to all girls, both Karls and Jarls, I'm the only non-noble standing in the group. I'm suddenly aware of the Jarls who have gathered around to watch their shield maiden make short work of the rest of us. I even see wagers being placed, most likely not on *if* she will win, but on *how fast* she will do it. I tell myself I have trained hard and what is destined to happen will happen. I unlace and take off my boots, and remove my seax and sheath from my belt, setting them down on the pebbled earth.

The gamekeeper, a small man with a whiny voice, recites the rules. "You play on your own will and can quit now or at any time during the game by shouting surrender. Your life and health are your responsibility, not of any opponent. Weapons are not allowed. We need more girls at the hamlet, not fewer, so if you have to kill someone, make sure she isn't one of the pretty ones. Thoren, do you understand me?"

The gamekeeper chuckles and the crowd joins in with him. I think of how easy it would be to drown this little man.

"You will compete in waters two fathoms deep, next to the marker," the gamekeeper continues. I look out to the sea and spot the red-painted driftwood with a knot of twine around it. The marker is tied to a stone on the sea's floor and looks to be forty or fifty strokes away from the shore. "You will use the water to force your opponent into quitting," he says. "The last girl remaining wins a piece of silver. If there are no questions, we will begin."

Drown or be drowned as Quibly puts it. I glance at Thoren, and her dark eyes are staring back at me as if I'm her prey. She isn't doing this for the silver, for she has plenty. Her arms and shoulders look much stronger than last year. Her black hair is tied in a single braid, and the bones in her cheeks are moving in and out as she clenches her teeth. At least she can't bring her sword with her. My heart is beating out of my chest, but there is no more time to strategize or think. The horn sounds, and we race into the icy water and swim towards the marker.

An elbow immediately strikes me on the side of my head. The sky goes black, and I choke on the sea water as I cry out in pain. I swing my arms with clenched fists, but they only hit air. The world comes roaring back into focus just as two hands push my head underwater. I try and take a breath of air, but it's too late. I desperately kick my legs, trying to surface, but a girl is gripping my hair and pushing down with the full weight of her body. I reach up and grab her wrists but can't break them free. I was so focused on Thoren, I forgot about the others! My foolishness may cost me my life. My lungs are burning and swelling in pain. I resist the urge to breathe – I have only moments left.

Thrusting up with both hands, I find a single finger gripping my hair and pry it free. I pull on it as hard as I can and hear muted screams come from the surface. Pulling harder, I feel the finger snap. She releases her hold, and I kick to the surface, gasping for air.

"Surrender!" a girl screams, turning to swim to shore. "You will pay for this, Karl!"

I quickly catch my breath. There are now only three girls left. Thoren is about ten feet away behind a girl half her size, with her arm wrapped tightly around the little girl's neck. Taking a deep breath, I dive under the sea. The frigid water tries to squeeze the air out of my lungs as I swim towards the throng of limbs thrashing in the water. I realize I don't have a plan, other than hope to take her by surprise.

As I reach the mob, I spot the twine that holds the marker to the sea floor. I reach and grab the closest ankle with my hand, pulling it tight into my chest. I swim downwards, kicking with my legs. Grabbing the twine with my free hand, I yank myself down farther, taking the girl with me. I close my eyes and count. Her free leg strikes me in the head, driving a sharp pain down my spine. I hold on.

One, two, three...

At one hundred, I open my eyes and look up. A blinding light surrounds me. For a brief moment, I wonder if I'm traveling to Niflheim, already dead. Then through the light, I see the terror on Thoren's face. I close my eyes tight as the twine rips through my skin. Her legs weaken and soon the kicking stops. I let go of the ankle and surface, filling my lungs with air. Thoren is floating motionless on the sea. I spin in a full circle. We are alone.

The goddesses who decide the afterlife must not be ready for her death, for moments later the shield maiden sputters back to life. She shoots me a long, perplexed glance and swims slowly back to shore, fending off all who approach her. I also swim back and am greeted with muted cheers from the crowd.

28

Although I'm happy to be alive, I'm exhausted and just want to see Grim. I soon spot him running towards me, his arms cradling my things.

"Good, you didn't die," he beams, handing me my seax and boots. He hugs me tight. "Quibly smells and snores like a troll. If you left me with him, I would kill him in his sleep."

It hadn't occurred to me Grim might be fearful of a life without me. My brother has no memories of our parents. Papar says I'm his guardian spirit. I guess Grim has no other, at least not in our realm. The elders say the goddesses of fate spin our destinies when we are born. But just as the battle of Ragnarok between the gods and the giants is destined to come, so is our future. I wish the gods would tell me my destiny so I can get on with it. I can understand why Odin gave his eye in search of wisdom. I suddenly feel lost.

"Grim, I love you," I say.

"I know, Disa. I knew you would beat Thoren. I dreamt it."

"You dreamt it?"

"But in my dream, you were also walking on water and dressed in armor," he says, laughing. I laugh, too, and give him another hug. A few Karls congratulate me on the victory. Thoren and the Jarl spectators are nowhere in sight.

The children gather on the field by the large, black stone beneath the grassy hill. The battle of Knattleiker just finished, and the wives are nursing their husbands' wounds. Knattleiker is a game played by both the Karl and Jarl Norsemen, and involves a lot of tackling and beating to take a leather ball from one side of the field to the other. The game is customarily played on the ice lake in the winter but is also the highlight of the solstice festival. I don't understand the complete rules, but wooden sticks are used to hit the ball across the field, and from there it seems there are no rules at all. Most of the damage comes from swinging the sticks as swords, not at the ball but at each other. I'm not sure if that's in the rules, but no one seems to care if it is or isn't. Quibly made an honest effort but spent most the game kneeling on the grass gasping for air.

Grim runs onto the field, waving his knife and spear, both too big for his frame. "Kill the ugly giants!" I yell, just as Quibly plops himself down next to me, his plump face dripping in sweat.

"And watch out for Loki, for he's a sneaky bastard!" Quibly bellows in support. Quibly wraps his arm around my shoulder and jerks me in. "I heard you beat my love today. Everyone in the hamlet is talking about it. They're saying you were under the sea for a half day and you saved Thoren from the mouth of Midgard's sea serpent."

"Oh they do, do they?" I muse. "I've been waiting for her to come thank me for that."

"Well, here she comes now," Quibly says, standing up. "Now remember you're her hero." Unfortunately, Quibly is not joking, and she's coming my way. I stand, slowly feeling for my seax just to make sure it's there. Thoren, her long curly hair now flowing past her shoulders, is marching towards me. Her sword is in its leather sheath stretching across her back. At least she doesn't have it out.

She stops in front of me, ignoring Quibly as if he isn't here. "I died. You killed me," she states bluntly.

I stutter, "I—um—don't," before she interjects.

"The gods willed it," she says. "I saw the Valkyries in Asgard. There were three goddesses riding on beautiful white horses. One took me by the hand to the great hall of Valhalla. A golden tree stood before its gates, and there were golden shields covering the ceilings. The hall was filled with ten thousand fallen warriors preparing for the final battle. The goddess told me there are battles still to fight here on Midgard and my time is not now, but knowing death will give me new strength."

I'm waiting for when she says she needs to kill me now. Quibly is in a sorceress' spell and isn't going to be of any help if a fight ensues.

"You were part of my destiny, Livvy, so thank you for doing your part," Thoren says. She abruptly turns and walks off.

Quibly's spell comes off. "See, you're her hero," he stammers.

I let out a deep breath and look back towards the field to locate Grim, confused as to what just happened.

The horn sounds, and the children's enactment of the Battle of Ragnarok begins. I search the crowds but don't see Erik. I can't help but wonder if he saw me compete in the dunking games but then realize how silly those thoughts are. Why would he be there? Erik is a great warrior and would be in the dragon ship race, sailing across the fiord as he does in battle, not watching a blacksmith's apprentice try and push a girl's head under the water. Still, I think he would be impressed I beat his cousin, with or without the help of the gods.

I put my attention back on the field. The children, the

supposed chosen warriors from Odin, are launching their fight against the giants, played by warriors from the clan. There's the fire giant who destroys the rainbow bridge, the wolves who swallow whole the sun and the moon, Niflheim's dragon, the sea serpent, and of course, Loki, the sorcerer. Godi is standing on the black stone in his red cloak, observing the battle while yelling, moaning, and cheering. Grim and the other children perform well. In the final act, the realms are destroyed, and the youngest children race onto the field, representing the birth of a new world.

Godi raises each child's arm in succession, and the crowd cheers. It's Grim's turn. With his spear thrust towards Asgard, I yell until my throat and chest are raw with pain. Grim looks my way, unable to conceal his smile. He doesn't win, but it doesn't matter to me as a Karl never wins. It doesn't seem to matter to him either.

Grim runs over, and with him, a small group of children. "What did the sea serpent look like?" they ask excitedly. "Was the maiden, Thoren, in its teeth? Did you kill it?"

"Well, he's bigger than the gentle giants of the sea—much bigger," I say, with eyes open wide. "But I swore to Odin I would not speak of what happened for fear it can hear and take revenge on us all!" The children run away with glee, and Grim rolls his eyes at me. Quibly wasn't kidding.

At the kot, I wash and get ready for the feast. The bleeding on my palm from the twine has stopped, but my ear is still ringing from the hit to my head. I try and ignore it. I think of putting on my mother's dress, the one she was married in, not one of her working dresses. The dress is green, stops at the ankles, and has straps for the shoulders which are held up with oval brooches made of iron. My father crafted the brooches for their wedding, engraving them with bell flowers like those from the meadows that he said my mother loved. I tried the dress on once when Grim was gone and was surprised how well it fit.

My last memory of mother is fading, and I try and think of it often so I don't forget it completely. As I swaddled my brother for the first time, my father knelt down and told me I must fetch fresh goat milk three times a day. I rushed to the barn to proudly perform my new duties, too young to comprehend the true meaning behind his words. The next day I built my first boat, surrounding my mother's grave with stones in the best shape of a dragon ship I knew how to make. My father said the ship would give my mother safe voyage down the ice river to Niflheim, and if I failed her, she would be alone forever.

I wonder if I would do more the things that girls are supposed to do if she were alive. I'm sure the boys must think I would be a terrible wife, and they would be right. I cook, but not very well, I don't wash our clothes as much as I should, and I would rather practice fighting with Grim than weave or sew. And as for dresses, they are uncomfortable, and I would never wear them to work as forging iron in one is a good way to catch on fire. I put on clean trousers and a tunic, and make my way to the hill.

CHAPTER 5

The feast looks magnificent. There are pits of water filled with hot stones and boiling fish, and spits roasting horse and sheep. There are tables of seabird eggs, barley bread, apples, berries, and bowls of honey. And as with every feast, jars of mead stand on every table, with more underneath. Our mead is made by fermenting honey with water, and it's both sweet and strong. I can feel its effects on one horn alone, but that's never stopped me from drinking three or more if offered.

I visited the hives a few times as a small child and even saw the keepers smoke the bees into a trance to extract the honey and wax. The keepers say that bees are almost as smart as us, and maybe more so. They are the only creature that searches out a king to take care of an entire clan. They follow their king wherever he goes and carry him when he tires and can no longer fly. If a bee becomes lazy, the others will gather together to kill it, for it will use more resources than it produces. But it's also possible the beekeepers tell the children such stories to keep them from being mischievous.

The Jarls are feasting at the tables by the longhouses, and the Karls are on the grass near the crest of the hill. The music has already begun, and drunken men are singing the clan's favorite songs to horns and flutes. Grim runs off to gorge himself, and I go to do the same but am blocked by a small man carrying large jars. He looks like a child on his first day milking goats.

"You are going to have wine with me," Papar announces, much louder than in his usual soft voice.

"Yes, I will!" I laugh. I join him on the grass but not before filling two wooden bowls with meat. Papar pours me a horn of his apple wine. It's not as sweet as mead, but it's quite good. I drink it down, and he pours me another.

"Do you see the nobles gathered there?" he asks, pointing to a table away from the others. Godi, his brother Bryanjar, and the elders are huddled together.

"Yes, Papar. Why?"

"They are preparing for battle," he whispers. "Many ships were spotted by the scouts in open sea, heading west. The Shockheads are not in Norseland. Godi says their defenses will be weakened and that our warriors should sail soon and not wait for spring."

"How soon?" I ask, my stomach turning.

"I do not know. Godi is a friend, but I am just a priest, and he shared only enough so I can prepare for what will come. I think they will sail soon while the days are long, but this is only guess for me."

"I don't see Erik," I say, looking around the feast. "Shouldn't he be at the table if they're preparing for battle?" I actually started looking for Erik the moment I got here. I'm hoping he gives me the silver for winning the dunking game.

"Erik took his ship and a few men with him, for fear the Shockheads are planting a trap. They are going to scout the northern shores before the warriors sail for Norseland. They just left."

It won't be Erik giving me anything then. For him to leave before the feast, there must be something greater happening than scouting. Why couldn't he wait just one day? I wonder if Papar is telling the whole truth. I think back to Erik's stories of Norseland. I'm both anxious and excited. It won't be long now.

"I have never understood the Norseman's need to battle and raid," Papar says, looking out to the sea. "It not my place to judge, for that will come after death, either by your Valkyries or by God, but it is a way I do not understand."

"The gods look favorably on warriors," I say, taking another sip of wine. "Those who die as warriors will go to Valhalla."

"Your mother and father are in Niflheim, not Valhalla, is that right?" I nod yes. I'm usually very uncomfortable talking about the death of my parents, even with Grim, but tonight I don't care as much. "Is this a place you want to go when you die, to Niflheim?" Papar asks.

"It doesn't matter if I want to or not, it's where I'll go when I die. That's just the way it is."

Papar takes my hands in his. "Why can't you choose Valhalla? It's much nicer, is it not?"

"Because I'm not a warrior and I'm a Karl.

"And a girl?" he says, more as a statement than a question.

"Yes, and a girl. Why do you ask these things?"

"I don't see those as reasons," he says. "Are there not girls in Asgard? Goddesses like Freya? And Thoren is a warrior, a shield maiden as you call her. The same warrior who you beat in battle today. Will she not go to Valhalla?"

"It was not a battle, Papar. It was a game."

"From what I saw, it was a battle."

"You were there?" I ask, surprised.

"Of course, I was there. I prayed to God you didn't get killed," he says with his funny laugh. "Livvy, I'm not permitted to talk to you, or any of the clan, about God. But I'm old and don't think Godi will kill me now. Christians have a place in the heavens like Valhalla. But to go there after death, one must choose to go there when alive."

"Why wouldn't all choose to go there then?" I question.

Papar smiles and shrugs. "The decision may seem like easy one, but the path there is difficult and not well traveled. Why doesn't everyone choose to be a warrior? Perhaps they don't want to train or they fear death. Or perhaps, Livvy, they don't think they are noble enough to be one."

"Norsemen believe our gods weave our destiny," I say. "Our fate is sealed the day we are born. It's not ours to choose. You are born a girl, a boy, a Jarl or a Karl. I suppose some are born Saxons."

"Maybe you are right," my old friend smiles.

Godi is up from the table and walking towards us. I hope he didn't overhear us talking. I've never spoken to the chieftain, and I don't feel ready to start right now.

"You must be Livvy," Godi declares as he approaches. He's still wearing his red cloak and is carrying a horn filled with some drink. Papar stands, so I do as well, but I trip over my own boots and almost fall into the chieftain. I can feel my face go warm with embarrassment. Godi smiles underneath his white beard. "Papar has mentioned you often. Come to think of it, so has my son. I understand you are the one responsible for Papar's improvement in Norse."

"She has been a tremendous help," Papar says.

"He is easy to teach for an old man," I say. They both

37

laugh.

"Well, as per the rules, you earned a piece of silver for winning the dunking game today," the chieftain says. "I'm just sad to have missed it. Earl Bryanjar has asked to meet with you sometime. Would you be willing to do so? There is nothing to fear. He's not upset you beat his daughter. Quite the opposite I think."

"Yes, Chieftain. I would be honored to meet with Earl Bryanjar. Thank you."

"Very well then, I will let him know. And here you go." Godi places a piece of silver in my hand. It's much lighter than I imagined it would be. "What do you plan to trade it for?" he asks.

I hesitate, then say, "I'm saving for a goat."

He, too, hesitates. "Good choice, Livvy." He touches Papar on the shoulder and walks back to his table, greeting the clan as he goes.

I didn't like lying to Godi about the goat, but not even Quibly knows I've been saving my earnings for Norseland. I don't want anyone telling me I'm foolish to save and should be purchasing farm animals instead. Coins will be much easier to carry across the sea, and metal doesn't die unexpectedly. I put the silver in my pouch.

"Why would Bryanjar want to meet with me?" I ask Papar.

Papar smiles. "Perhaps he wants to arrange a re-match?"

I smile back. "I need some more wine."

"Then more wine we will have!" He pours me another horn full.

The clan is getting louder and more drunk. When we go to war, the gods will decide the destinies of the men around me. I hope they're on our side. If our warriors are victorious in Norseland, they will come back for the rest of the clan. If they aren't, then the Shockheads will come for us instead, and we can only pray to Thor we are killed and not captured.

The sun is behind the mountains, and the gray sky is at its darkest. The men, both Karls and Jarls, are still singing but most are passed out on the grass. Papar and the monks left some time ago, most likely to avoid being collateral in a drunken brawl. Grim is wrestling with the Jarl children, wagering with silver he doesn't have. I take a break from dancing with Quibly.

I drank way too much wine, along with a considerable amount of mead, but it's worked to clear my mind. I lie down and look up at the stars, far too many to count. I'm very drunk but don't care. Quibly lies down next to me. I wrap my arm around him, my head on his chest, and fall asleep.

I hear screaming. Loud piercing cries are coming from every direction. I jolt awake from a dream, but the cries don't stop, they only get louder. I jump to my feet and try to focus in the dim light, my legs wobbling underneath me. Quibly is now up. I'm in a horde of chaos. The horns are blowing. I try to make sense of what is going on, my head pounding. We're under attack!

I pull out my seax and gather my bearings.

"Grim! Quibly, help me find Grim!" I yell. Quibly is frozen. "Now!" I scream.

He pulls out his knife and takes off.

I run across the plateau, hollering Grim's name over and over. I race to the crest of the hill and look below. I stop breathing. A wave of warriors is charging up the slope. They're wearing fur over their backs, swinging axes and swords, and moving faster than any men I've seen.

I turn and run. The warriors pour over the hill like a rogue wave, chopping our people down like twigs. They swarm the plateau, swinging their weapons at everything that moves. Grim is nowhere to be seen.

"Grim!" I holler again, but my voice is lost in the screams of death. I stop and turn. A warrior is hurtling towards me, his battle ax raised, roaring like a wild animal. I grasp my seax as he charges out of the shadows. His head is covered with the face of a wolf. His eyes, red as blood, pierce into mine. He isn't human. Today I die, but I die fighting. The beast suddenly crashes to the earth, and a large stone lands at my feet.

"Livvy, you have to get out of here!" Quibly shouts.

I'm struggling to get air into my lungs. "Did you find Grim?"

"No, check your home. Go!"

I run towards the kot. There are bodies everywhere. I tumble down the hill and sprint along the shores towards the sod houses in the meadow. The hill behind me is now ablaze. They're burning the longhouses. Soon I'm at the kot and swing open the door. I see it coming but can't react in time. I fall into blackness.

CHAPTER 6

The light is blinding. The world around me is swimming and then it bursts into focus. Thoren is staring down at me, and the sky above her is slowly rocking back and forth. I see fear in her eyes. I'm on my back, lying on something hard, and my head is throbbing in pain.

"Don't—move," Thoren whispers. She's deliberate with her words, almost threatening. "We've been taken."

The intense pain in my head is overbearing, and I'm struggling to think. I see Thoren clearer now. She's hurt. Her face and arms are badly bruised, and she's wearing nothing but a white tunic. Her arms are bound to a wooden pole. She looks like me, not like a noble.

"You were in a deep sleep," Thoren whispers. "They put us on a ship and are leaving. Do you understand me?"

I suddenly remember opening the door. Grim! "Where's Grim?" I say in a panic.

"Keep your voice down. They have him, on another ship, along with all the children who survived. If you want to see him again, you need to listen to me."

I'm suddenly dizzy, and my mind's in a fog. I'm going to throw up. This can't be happening! I look around me. Men are boarding the ship, their weapons clanging against their armor as they move. A large, black bird is painted on the wool sail above me, fluttering in the wind. It looks to be a raven with the sun painted behind it – the bird of Odin. At the bow of the ship, there are two girls, curled up and tied. They're both Jarls. No one resembles the beasts with the eyes of blood. Did I imagine them? Over the hull, I see an army of ships. Round shields line the sides of the vessels, and the oars are in the water. The shields are painted with the same bird as on the sail.

"You're not bound yet, but you will be," Thoren says, pulling my eyes back to hers. "When that happens, it's over. You need to tie yourself to the mast. Make it look real. There's a rope a few feet behind you. Slide yourself back and get it when I tell you." I slowly move my hand and feel my forehead. It's swollen and soaked in blood. "You must not let them know you're awake. Do you understand?"

I look into her dark eyes. They are intense and angry. Even now tied up, Thoren is fighting. And I don't have the strength or courage to utter a response. I need to see Grim.

Thoren darts me a warning glare. Someone is approaching, and I close my eyes, trying to hold my tears in. I can smell a man's breath. His face is next to mine. The whiskers of his beard are scratching up against my lips. He runs his hands through my hair. I hold the air in my lungs, afraid to breathe. He stops. Is he gone? I don't dare move.

"Now, Livvy!"

I open my eyes.

"Quickly!" Thoren commands. I take a deep breath and slither my body towards the rope. I grab it and move back to the mast. My head is pounding much harder now.

"Tie your hands to the mast. Make it look like they did it." I try and do as she says. My hands are shaking and not working right. I fumble with the rope not knowing how to do it. Eventually, I manage to make a knot. I can't see how it will fool anyone.

"Lie still," she orders.

I close my eyes to try and make sense of my racing thoughts. I must get to Grim to see that he's alive, even if I must endure what these men will do to me. Godi didn't allow slaves to be mistreated, but this isn't the usual way. For the first time, I can understand why my father took his life. If Grim is dead, there's nothing I would want more than to join my brother in Niflheim. The men shout in unison, and the oars splash as they hit the sea. We're leaving.

I go in and out of consciousness, only to wake up each time to the reality that this nightmare isn't a dream. The hard planks are digging into my back, and the pain in my head is only getting worse. I slowly open my eyes. The sun is behind the mountains, and the sky is gray. The clouds open, and heavy, cold rain falls from the heavens. I curl up to keep warm, being careful to go unnoticed. The oarsmen stop rowing and take the sail down, wrapping it over the hull to shield the rain. Soon they are eating and drinking as the ship sways in the rising waves of the sea. They pass Papar's jars of apple wine around as their voices get louder. Papar must be dead – and Quibly, too. I can't bear to think of them. I must keep focused on Grim if I'm to keep it together.

"The fiord is narrow here," Thoren whispers. "We can

swim. We'll escape when they're drunk and asleep."

"I can't do it," I utter.

"Then you will die. I'm leaving. You will soon regret you didn't do the same. I need you to untie me."

Thoren lies down and curls up, resting her hands against the wooden planks. I slowly work one of my hands free and start on her rope. At first, it's impossibly tight, but I eventually manage to loosen it. Thoren sits back up and looks away.

The waves are slapping against the side of the ship as if daring me to jump in. Maybe my fate is to die in the belly of Midgard's serpent. The drunken men are now laughing and singing. They speak Norse, but with an accent I haven't heard before. If they aren't from Norseland, they can't be the Shockheads. Who are they?

I can hear one man above the rest. His voice is deep, and when he shouts, the others stop talking. He's clearly the leader, at least on this vessel. He says what sounds like *Westman*. Yes, he says it again. I'm now certain of it. I've heard Westman mentioned many times by the elders in their sagas. It's an island in the south of Iceland. I don't know where it is, but it's a long sail around the island. Maybe Grim and I will drown at sea going there, and he can meet his mother. I suddenly miss the woman I can barely remember.

Most of the men are asleep, but a few are still drinking. I look underneath the sail at the pelting rain. Through the darkness, I spot the shadow of a ship near the shore. I strain to look for any signs that Grim and the children might be on it. There's a man on the bow. I squint my eyes. Is it Erik? He must be coming for us! The current or wind turns our heading, and I lose sight of the ship.

Papar said Erik had but a few men with him. They couldn't possibly defeat this army, but at night they could sneak up on a single ship. He must know Thoren is here. I look over to tell her, but one of the drunk men is coming. He wants her. He grabs Thoren, and she spits in his face. He turns her around and slams her into the mast. But Thoren's hands are now free, and she's reaching for the knife on his belt. I release my own hands and dart under the sail as fast as I can. I spot the ship, but my hope quickly turns to horror. What have I done?

The vessel isn't Erik's! A black raven flies on the sail and on the shields that hang from the hull. I can't go back. I dive head first into the darkness. Just as my arms hit the frigid water, I hear a man scream. Thoren got the knife.

I surface from the blackness and tread water for a moment, thinking of surrendering. But they'll kill me if I return. I go under the cold water and swim as long and hard as I can away from the boats. My boots are pulling me down, but I don't dare stop to remove them. I swim below the surface until my lungs are screaming for air. The men are yelling and searching the water, but the heavy rain hides me well. I take a deep breath and go under the water again.

By the time I reach the shore my body is shivering, and I'm too exhausted to look for warmth. The rain has stopped falling, but I don't care. Grim is gone, and I'm alone. In the far distance, the ships are bobbing in the sea. I see no signs of Thoren. I take off my wet clothes and curl up against a fallen tree. I cry myself to sleep, praying this is all a horrible dream.

Grim and I make the long walk to our parents' grave. The ship stones are where I placed them on the ground when I was a little girl. Grim sits on the earth and begins to cry.

"We should go," I say. "It's getting late." He ignores me. I decide to leave him be for a while.

Grim gets up and begins to gather stones, placing them in a pile next to our parents' grave. I want to help him, but it seems this is something he needs to do, so I just watch. It isn't long before he's gathered all the stones nearby. He takes a large one from the pile and places it on the ground. He does another, placing it next to the first.

"What are you doing, Grim?" He still ignores me.

I can see now that he's making a ship just like the one I made as a little girl. I sit on the ground and watch him carefully put each stone in its spot. When finished, he lies down next to his ship. I stand and walk towards him. It's getting late, and we need to go. As I approach, I see his ship surrounds a hole in the earth. How did I not see this hole? I look inside it. A girl with red hair, in a green dress with oval brooches, lies at the bottom.

"I love you, Disa," Grim cries.

I awake to the sounds of the sea rushing against the sand. The water is lapping at my feet. It takes me a moment to realize I'm not dead. I roll onto my stomach and get to my knees. I'm alone. I look up and down the fiord. The green water is still. It strikes me that my little brother is now a slave, and my body begins to tremble. I look to the sky and to the gods in Asgard. They won't lift a finger to help a Karl and her little brother. They may even be on the other side. "Why have you done this to me?" I scream. My father left me because he couldn't handle this pain.

There is nothing left for me in Iceland. I lay my head on the rocky sand and stare at the sea. A black raven is circling high above the water. Two of these birds sit on Odin's shoulders. Every dawn, Odin releases them to fly over the realms, and they return to him each day with knowledge of all that is happening. Perhaps the bird flying above is one of them. I wonder if she will tell Odin that the army was victorious, destroying the hamlet according to plan.

I close my eyes and again see my brother crying by the grave. Grim is alone too, tied up in the hull of a ship. I don't want to do to him what my father did to me, but what choice do I have? Even if I can find him, I can't save him. I'm not a warrior. I make arrow tips and shoes for horses. If the gods wanted me to be a warrior, they would have made me a boy and a noble. I wish Quibly or Papar were here with me. The thought of them dead wrenches at my stomach, and I don't know how I could bare knowing for certain they are gone.

A bird's caw echoes over the water. I stand and look up at the sky, squinting to see through the bright light. The raven is back. She flies towards me and lands on a small rock not far from my feet. Her black eyes look into mine, and we both stand motionless.

"What do *you* want?" I say. She cocks her head before flying south towards my home. It's as if she wants me to follow her. I watch her until she shrinks into nothing.

I hear Grim's words again. "I love you, Disa." They begin to ring over and over in my head. I am Grim's Dis, his guardian spirit. I don't know if I'll see Grim again, but I can die trying. The alternative is to just die.

I think back to the ship. The man with the deep voice said

Westman. They must be going there. The army will most likely make further stops, to raid or to gather supplies. I don't know how long the voyage takes by foot, but if I can make it there by land, maybe I can find a way to rescue Grim from a life as a slave. I remember the silver given to me by Godi. My pouch is still on my belt. I reach inside and find the coin with my fingers. It's a start.

I squeeze the water from my clothes and get dressed. I take a long drink from a pool of water on top of a big stone. I find some clams, and despite not feeling at all hungry, I get them into my stomach. Grim is waiting for me. There's no one else to save him. I begin the trek along the shore towards home.

The steep cliffs, caverns, and streams force me away from the shore and into the dense canopy, hiding the warmth of the sun and playing tricks with my sense of direction. I spend more time going up and down than forward. By nightfall, my feet are blistered, and my legs are cut up from the sharp underbrush. But the pain takes my mind off Grim and helps me focus on getting home. It's almost an entire day before I see the hamlet, at least what's left of it.

I thought I was prepared for the carnage, but it's much worse than I imagined. There are dead bodies everywhere, their stench filling the air. Blackened wood and debris are strewn across the shores. The enemy burned what vessels they didn't take. My hunger and aching legs now mean nothing. There is something on the commanding black stone between the shore and the hill. I hobble across the plain, drawn towards it. A man in a red cloak is lying face down on the rock. I get sick. Godi's torso is cut open. I don't understand who would do such a horrific thing and why.

I trudge up the slope to where the Jarl settlement once stood overlooking the sea. The longhouses on the hill are now nothing but smoldering ash. Flies are swarming the dead, and the grasses are red with blood. A few old men and women wander the plateau weeping, most likely looking for the slain bodies of family. I don't dare look at the dead faces for I'm far too afraid of what I'll find. One old man notices me and hobbles my way. His leg is wrapped in a bloody cloth, and his eyes are hollow as if his spirit has already left our world.

"Young maiden, how is it that such a pretty girl is not enslaved?" he quivers, embracing me with his frail arms.

"The gods are good," I lie. "Can you tell me who did this to us?"

"The Berserkers," he wheezes with his eyes wide.

"The what?" I ask.

"The Berserkers," the old man says again. "They look more like trolls than men, and they fight like the ugly beasts, too. The Berserkers are the witch's army, you know. They brought the bastards with them to ensure victory."

"The Shockheads brought them?"

"No, my maiden. The Danes." The old man coughs and places his palm against my face before turning back towards the death. The Danes? What fight do we have with Denmark?

My thoughts are interrupted by a shout. "Livvy, is that you? Livvy!"

I look up in disbelief. Quibly is running towards me! I jump into his arms, breaking into tears.

CHAPTER 7

I fall to my knees in exhaustion, taking Quibly down with me. We cry together and hold each other tight. Pressing my hands against his scruffy cheeks, I look into his big eyes. "I never thought I would see you again," I whimper.

"Are you hurt? I thought they took you," Quibly stammers.

"They took me—and Grim. I never saw him. I don't know if he's alive."

"I'm sorry, Liv."

"Thoren was with me. She was badly hurt." I wipe the tears from my eyes and tell my best friend how Thoren helped me escape and the last I saw of her.

"How did you survive?" I ask. "What happened?"

Quibly's demeanor quickly changes, and he looks at the ground before finally speaking. "I ran back to the farm soon after you left for Grim, to find my mother and father. They killed them. My parents did nothing to deserve this! I ran. Like a coward, I just ran. I hid in the mountains while our friends were murdered, while you and Grim were taken, and while the hamlet burned to the ground. Odin will surely punish me. I should have died in battle. I wanted to fall on a spear, but I didn't even have the courage to do that."

I don't know what to say. What he did, or rather didn't do, would be punishable by death if ever brought in front of the

Thing. The Thing is the assembly of the clan elders who appoint our leader, but they also decide our laws and the punishments for breaking them. Quibly may not be a Jarl warrior, but he's able to fight, and he's expected to do so if a battle comes to us. But the Thing, along with the chieftain, the elders, and the longhouses, are all gone. And Quibly is not just my closest friend – he's the only friend I have who isn't dead. I take his hands in mine.

"Quibly, the ambush was a battle we couldn't win. The gods spared you for a reason. A dead warrior can't fight again."

"There are no more reasons for me to be alive," he says under his breath.

"You can fight again," I say. "You can fight again with me. Help me find Grim. Show the gods that you're a warrior."

"There's no one left to fight with or against. It's over."

"No, there's hope," I say. I stand up and look around the plateau. "An old man told me it was the Danes who attacked us."

"Yes, that's what they're saying," he says. "Their ships were hiding in the shadows of the cliffs. They waited for us to be drunk and asleep."

"The old man also said they brought *Berserkers* with them. Something about a witch's army?"

"Warriors under a seer's spell or something," Quibly says.

"Do you believe that?" I ask.

"I saw the blood in their eyes and the power with which they swung their weapons. They weren't like any warriors I've ever seen. The Danes really wanted us dead."

"I don't understand what fight the Danes would have with us," I say. "We have done nothing to them."

"We know they wanted the monks," Quibly says. "I heard them yelling out *Saxon* myself."

"The monks are old and feeble, and not a threat to anyone, anywhere. It makes no sense they would send an army to kill them."

"Some said Ragnar Lothbrok himself was here."

"The King of Denmark, here? Isn't he dead?"

"Yes, but the old see what they want to see and hear what they want to hear. He's a legend, alive or dead."

I remember back to the stories I've heard of the Danes. Denmark is south of Norseland, a two-day sail across a small sea. Ragnar was their king for over twenty years. His army was infamous for their raids that plundered distant lands for silver, gold, and slaves. But the Norseland armies were as strong as his, and this equality averted a war between our kingdoms.

"So, you said there is hope?" Quibly asks, bringing me back to the present.

"Yes. There was a man on the ship. I never saw his face, but he mentioned Westman a few times. I'm quite sure he was talking about Westman Island in the south. I think they're going there."

"And that gives us hope, how?"

"I'm going there to find Grim and I'm going now. I want you to come with me. Help me rescue Grim and Thoren."

Quibly looks at me like I've gone mad. "The Jarls, other than the old, are either dead or enslaved. Godi and Bryanjar were killed. Did you see what they did to Godi?"

"Yes, I saw him on the rock."

"And you didn't see any signs of Erik while at sea, right?"

"No."

"Erik and his warriors left only shortly before the attack," he says. "They would have encountered the Danes in the fiord. I'm sure they're dead, too. Livvy, there's no one left who can fight."

Nothing Quibly is saying is wrong. Our army was destroyed, and the Danes left with everything we had – our weapons, our livestock, and our children. But we are still alive, and until we're dead, *we* can fight. I must convince Quibly to come with me.

"We need to find Grim and leave soon for Westman," I plead. "We can cross the mountains to the hamlet in the valley and ask for directions there. Quibly, *please*."

"Livvy, he's gone, we are—"

"We are going—I am going to find him, with or without you."

"It's a long journey, Livvy. We don't know how long it'll take, and it's very unlikely they'll be there. You just heard a man say Westman. It could have meant anything."

"They'll be there and so will Grim," I say. "I can't explain how I know this but I do. I can't live the rest of my life knowing that I just abandoned him. If my destiny is to die, then that's my destiny."

I think of what else I can say to convince him. He would do anything for Thoren. "I will let you cut off the head of their leader, for Thoren, if you come," I say.

This image seems to appease him. "How about I hold him down, and you sever his head?" he half smiles.

"Agreed! You will come?"

"I didn't say that."

"You killed one on the Berserkers with a stone!" I say,

remembering the beast charging towards me at the feast.

"He got back up."

"But you saved me. I would be dead if it weren't for you."

"Let me think about it, Livvy."

"Thank you." I reach my arms around his belly as far as I can and rest my head against his chest. We get up and make our way back along the shore towards the meadow, avoiding going too close to the black stone. Soon the monastery roof is in sight.

"They didn't burn it down?" I question.

"Maybe they didn't bring fire with them to the meadow. The sod houses were looted, but most stand as well, including yours."

"I still don't understand why they would come all the way to Iceland to kill the monks," I say. "They're weak and no threat to them. The Danes were here for another reason. They had to be."

Quibly just shrugs. He looks as exhausted as I feel. We stop in front of the barley fields that encircle the old monastery. Although many of the green stems and their spears are trampled to the ground, most still stand, swaying in the wind like nothing has happened.

"No one will go in there for fear they'll be cursed," Quibly says. "I don't think you should go in either. You won't like what you'll find. Papar is gone. It's best to just leave it at that."

"Maybe," I say.

We part ways near the farm, agreeing to meet later after I gather supplies. Quibly will give me his decision then, but I'm going to Westman no matter his answer. As I approach my kot, it looks eerily untouched, except for the wood door which hangs ajar from a broken hinge. Inside, the hearth is broken, and my father's weapons are scattered on the floor. The spears, ax, knives, shield, and my seax are all here. Why were they not taken? The weapons of a Karl are petty compared to a warrior's sword, and most likely they weren't worth the effort to carry them. There's plenty of that night I'm learning I don't understand.

I fasten the seax to my belt, pick up the shorter spear, and step outside. The monastery stands tall in the distance. I walk slowly towards it, crossing the trampled green fields of barley. I stop at the wooden door as I have done so many times before. It is closed and looks undisturbed. We were attacked by these Berserkers, our clan was slaughtered, and my little brother was stolen. I decide I'm already cursed. I open the door and step into the dark room.

The putrid smell of the dead fills my nostrils. My eyes adjust, and I recoil at the sight. Most of the monks are still in their beds as if slaughtered by a nightmare while they slept. I look for Papar, but the bodies are unrecognizable. I run outside and get sick. I miss Papar deeply but can't look any further. I wonder if he's in the Christian heaven, feasting with his god. I return to my kot and lie down on my bed. I need to go and find Grim but can no longer keep my eyes open.

For a moment, I'm lying next to my little brother, my greatest worry being whether we'll be eating fish or clams for dinner. But the nightmare rushes back, reminding me that the world I knew is gone forever. I don't know how long I slept but fear it was a long time. I quickly gather what food I can find and make a sling for the shield to carry on my back. The small spear can be used as a walking stick, and the knives are easy enough to carry. I'll give Quibly the longer spear and the battle ax if he comes. I check within the back wall, and my copper and bog ore pellets are still there. I put them in a leather pouch, along with my silver, and pack a skin bag with my food and a few clothes.

At the shore, I find Quibly standing quietly, kicking stones into the water. The sky is dark with clouds, and a light mist wets the air. Across the plain, the black stone is empty.

"I buried him this morning," Quibly says. He doesn't turn around. "There are no boats left, so I made a stone ship, just like the one you did for your mother and father, to guide him to Valhalla."

It's our custom that a chieftain, like Godi, would be buried in a ship with his most prized possessions, to take with him to Valhalla. The clan would then celebrate his departure from Midgard, for in Valhalla he would feast, drink ale, and prepare for the final battle of Ragnarok. The gods will be pleased that Quibly buried him.

Quibly wraps his arm around me. "Liv, you are the only one I have left. Let's go find Grim and Thoren. We all die eventually, why not a few years earlier."

I smile in relief. "Thank you, Quibly."

We approach the pool of fresh water on the hill. It's fed from the river that stretches up to the snowy plains high in the mountains. We'll track the river up, as it follows the shortest path and will give us water to drink. The farthest I've ventured up the mountains was a full day's walk with my father when we went to gather wood from the linden forest. Linden wood is strong, light, and doesn't split easily like oak or birch, making it the perfect wood for shields. My father made the very shield I carry on my back from the wood we gathered that day. I've never been back, as it's not safe for a girl to wander the hills and forests alone. And Quibly prefers rowing to walking, and he hasn't been any farther than me.

"It's a long way up there," Quibly grimaces.

"Do you want me to carry your fat ass on my back?"

"Yes, that would be great if you don't mind," he says, as he fastens the battle ax to his fur pack.

I look back at the hamlet, at the hope that's now lost. Without our chieftain, I don't know how Grim and I'll get back to Norseland, but we'll find a way. The night of the feast wasn't a battle between warriors – it was an ambush from cowards. I'll find Grim, and the answers to the Berserkers and the Danes, even if I die doing it. I look upwards at the rising mountain, the meandering river, and the dark clouds. I don't look back again.

CHAPTER 8

The fire cuts through the dense fog that's settled over the forest. Although it's not raining, the damp air feels just the same. Quibly fell asleep the moment he laid down, before I even started the fire. I was at this forest once before, but it looks much different now than through the eyes of a child. A land lurking with trolls and dwarves is now a cluster of dark trees where the fox and mice hide. It took a half day to reach the forest, much longer than I had hoped, but it was the steep terrain and river crossings that slowed me down as much as it was Quibly. We saw no evidence along the way that the Danes or the Berserkers were here. The mountain air is much cooler than at the sea, and I move closer to the fire and lie down for a quick rest.

I awake to a rustling that doesn't belong here. There's someone or something in the forest. It moves too quietly to be a fox. I draw my seax and sit up, straining to hear over the rush of the river. I listen carefully for some time but don't hear it again. It knows I'm awake or it's gone. I fight to stay alert but fall in and out of sleep, unsure at times if I'm in a dream or awake.

After a restless night, dawn arrives and it's time to go. I search the forest for any signs of the enemy. The trees here are much taller and thicker than any we have in the hamlet. At home, the larger ones were cut down to make houses or to burn in the fires. I see no one and only hear the gushing river and the leaves rustling in the wind. I wake Quibly, and he's not too happy about it, but there's no time for sleep. We have some stale bread to eat and continue our winding hike up the steep mountain.

The river thins into a creek, and the big trees are far behind us. The air is now cold. The earth here is rocky, and the sky brightens as we climb above the clouds. At midday, we crest the mountain and enter a realm unlike any I've ever seen. I've heard stories of the plateau, but I didn't imagine it like this. The flat earth, barren of trees and brush, is dotted with snow-covered stones, sparkling like the stars on a clear winter night. The sky above is immense, unlike the hamlet where it's shortened by the tall enclosing mountains. Although exhausted from the climb, the sudden openness gives me a profound sense of freedom, like I can finally take a deep breath.

"That must be Katla," Quibly wheezes, his hands on his knees. A mountain rises in the distant horizon, its top ablaze, pouring earthfire into the canyons beneath it. A billow of gray smoke and ash spirals upwards, as if the fire giant is teasing the humans of the battle to come. We can see this smoke from home, high in the clouds, but to see its source is far more ominous.

"What if the elders are wrong?" Quibly says softly, as if he's afraid Odin's ravens are listening.

"Wrong about what?"

"About everything. Odin and his gods didn't save our warriors. And they didn't save the weak. What if they're punishing us for allowing the monks on our lands? If Odin isn't on our side, we won't get far."

"Odin's on our side," I say. "He won't allow those who kill women and children to live long. He'll help us avenge this enemy. And the monks were in Iceland long before we got here."

Papar once told me the saga of how he came to Iceland. A king rose to power in his land and made laws to hang those who didn't worship the Saxon god. All of the people were ordered to report those who weren't Christians. The monks, however, were peaceful men and refused to do as their king commanded. They believed men and women were free to make their own choice. In fear of punishment, most likely by death, they fled by ship. Lost in the great waters, the winds took them to Iceland, thirty winters before Godi arrived. Papar was the youngest monk on that ship, no older than Grim is now.

I gaze towards the smoldering mountain. The elders say that Katla's destruction will mark the beginning of Ragnarok, and on that day the fire giant will arise from the realm of fire and drag down the sun. Midgard will crack and split the sky into two, and the dwarves will roar within the earth. I imagine myself, sword in hand, racing across the plateau into battle with a thousand warriors. But I'm a Karl—and a girl. The birth of a new world is a sight I'll never see.

We make good time across the rocky plateau. Quibly is markedly quicker on flatter ground. I hope we are going in the right direction, but all I know is the hamlet is south. South is a big place. We break for food and water.

"Why do you think the Danes are going to Westman Island?" Quibly asks, his mouth full of bread.

I've been thinking of this same question for two days but without any real answers, other than the monks. "Westman

Island has a history with the Christians," I remind him. "Ingolf's slaves were monks. Maybe there's a connection there?"

"Who's Ingolf again?" Quibly asks, straining to recall.

"Are you serious?" Quibly has heard the saga of Norseland's explorers many times, but he mostly sleeps or daydreams when the elders tell them. "Ingolf and his brother Leifer were two of the earliest Norsemen to settle in Iceland. Sound familiar?"

"Sort of," he says with a smile. "Please continue."

I sigh loudly. "Leifer brought monk slaves to Iceland on one of his voyages. Not long after arriving in Iceland, the slaves murdered him and fled into the mountains. Ingolf went on a hunt to avenge his brother's death and found them years later hiding on a remote island. He killed them all, and the island where they hid was later named Westman, since the slaves came from west of Norseland."

"But Iceland is farther west than any land ever conquered by the Norsemen," Quibly says. "We should be called the Westmen, and the monks should be called the Eastmen." I think for a moment. He's actually right. I'm not aware of any lands west of Iceland. As far we know, we could be at the very end of Midgard, and the sea serpent could be lurking just off our shores. Now Quibly picks a time to be smart, or at least a smartass.

We finish eating and continue our journey south. By nightfall, our destination finally appears. I don't know who is more relieved, Quibly or me. The valley below us is immense and surrounded by gently sloping hills covered in dark green grass. The farm lands sit in the middle, split by a river meandering south to north. A few dozen structures stand lumped together on the river's far bank.

"The hamlet isn't burned. This is a good start," Quibly says.

"It's much bigger than our hamlet," I say, looking up and down the valley.

"I think most hamlets are bigger than ours."

The hamlet in the valley is the largest settlement in eastern Iceland. The river provides fresh water to feed the farms and livestock, and I've heard the ground is very fertile, for Iceland, that is. The grain grown here is sold and bartered throughout the island. The traders sometimes come to our hamlet at the fiord, but mostly ours come here. It seems odd now that I've never been here, but I've had no reason to trade, and no one to go with me if I wanted to. My focus has been on raising Grim and preparing for our eventual return to Norseland.

By the time we reach the river crossing, Quibly is hobbling and clearly in pain, but he doesn't complain. It's late, but there are still plenty of Norsemen eating and drinking both inside and outside the wooden houses that dot the riverside. Our hamlet would usually be asleep at this time of night, although circumstances at home have now changed forever. I don't know how anyone could ever sleep there again.

"The Danes haven't been here," Quibly says quietly, as we duck into the shadows.

"We don't know that. We have no idea why they're in Iceland."

"You don't think we should warn them?"

"This hamlet is a crossroad for many travelers. Let's be careful until we know more. I say we tell them we're traveling through and looking for work."

"That's a good idea," he says with a smile. "I can be the

warrior and you the cook."

"I'm a terrible cook," I say.

"Yes—you—are."

I punch him in the shoulder, and he pretends to swipe his hand at an imaginary fly.

There's a sign on a large longhouse marking it as the inn and tavern. Laughing and singing echoes through its walls. We enter through the open door. Inside, there are a number of wooden tables scattered across the room, with a dozen or so loud men enjoying their drink. Our presence captures their attention, and the clamor quickly turns to stares and whispers.

Behind a table at the back stands a plump woman with two white braids extending past her shoulders. She wears a blue dress with a yellow apron skirt and matching headscarf. A necklace of glass or amber beads hangs over her neck. On her table rests numerous jars of what are sure to be filled with ale and mead. We approach her.

"Hello, maiden. Can we have two ales please?" Quibly asks.

"It's a tavern, is it not?" she grumbles. "Take a seat and I'll bring them out to you."

We find a small, empty table and sit down. The men have gone back to their drinking but keep us in their sights. I feel very out of place. After a few uneasy moments, the old woman comes to the table with two horns of ale.

Quibly takes the lead. "I'm a warrior and my wife is a cook, the best in Iceland as you can tell," he says, rubbing his belly. "We heard some traders from one of the kingdoms might have passed through here. Have you seen them?"

"Why do you want to know?" she questions.

"We just do," he replies. "Have you seen anyone?"

"You aren't looking for the Danes are you?" she asks, her eyebrows raised.

"Possibly. I don't know which kingdom they're from," Quibly says.

"A Dane ship sailed up the river a week ago. They traded for supplies and stayed for two nights. They were looking for Saxons. The only Saxons I know of live with Godi's clan. Where are you two from?"

"East," I say.

The woman doesn't look convinced. She sits down at our table. "You see the skinny man at the table by the door? His name is Eindride. He was hired by the Danes to show them the passes through the mountains. He's a trapper and lived in the hills most his life. A real loaner, never had a wife whom I know of. They paid him four pieces of silver, and now every bastard wants to be his friend. I would talk to him after he sobers up. He should be able to tell you the Danes' whereabouts."

She leans in, looking around cautiously. "These men are not like us. I wouldn't want to see a young man and his pretty wife get hurt. And son, since you are a mighty warrior, you may wish to dress like one. And get yourself a sword."

The old woman leaves, and I look towards the man by the door, his long matted hair drooping over his sunken face. Quibly is looking himself over as if it's a big revelation that he doesn't look like a warrior for hire. The trapper and his fellow drunks break into a song, with ales in their hands and arms draped over their shoulders.

"We *dreamed a dream last night, of a conquest and raid.
And sailed the seas afar, in search of treasures made.*

With our swords and spears drawn, we built a shield wall.
And victory was ours, and our enemy did fall!"

This clan is not so different than ours. Farmers and craftsmen who left their homeland in search of a better place, and drinking to help forget their sorrows. The plump lady happily agrees to exchange a bog ore pellet for the ales, and we step outside the tavern into the breezy night.

"You see? The monks are responsible for this attack!" Quibly bursts out. "Odin sent the Danes to punish us. I liked the priest—okay, I didn't *dislike* him, but we should have sent them away, back to where they came from."

It seems certain now the Danes were after the Saxons, but I doubt the gods had anything to do with it. If Odin wanted to kill the monks, or us for that matter, he could have sent any of the gods or beasts over the rainbow bridge to do it.

"We'll be judged by the Valkyries in Asgard, not by the Danes," I say. "Let's talk to the trapper and see what we can learn about these men. I can handle Eindride."

"*You* are going to handle the drunk?" he asks.

"Yes, *me!*"

"Okay, he's yours. I'll just be over here—hiding in the dark. Just holler if you need anything."

I shake my head and sit on a stone. It isn't long before the skinny man with the sunken face stumbles out of the tavern. He's alone. I step behind him, placing my hand on his shoulder.

"What do you want?" Eindride crows, spinning around. "Ah, it's you from the tavern. You are very beautiful—and alone. Where's your husband?"

The drunk's foul breath is revolting. "He's not my husband," I whisper in his ear.

65

"Oh, so you want my silver like the other whores." The disgusting man chuckles, glancing down at my chest. "All the whores want my silver, but I guess that's the reason we earn it."

"Or you can help me, and I can help you," I say, holding back my urge to slit his throat with my seax.

"Help you how?" He loses his balance but manages to get his legs under him. I was hoping to see him fall hard on his face. Maybe I'll help him with that in a moment.

"I'm looking for voyage off this island and heard the Danes were here. I wish to find them. Can you tell me where they have sailed?"

"The Danes are gone. I'll pay you in silver," he says, wrapping his dangly arm around me.

I dig my boots into the dirt. "Just tell me where the Danes are sailing."

"You don't want to sail with him. He won't pay you like I will."

"Who's him?"

"Ivar the Boneless."

The Boneless? This is a person? I don't have time for explanations. "Ivar is their leader? You met him?"

"Yes, I met him, and he begged me for his help. He's the son of Ragnar Lothbrok. Ragnar had many wives and many sons, but Ivar was his favorite. His mother must have been a giant—an ugly one."

"Eindride, why is Ivar here?" The trapper seems stunned that I said his name, but he's too drunk to consider it further.

"The little Saxons. The men don't have women, so I don't know why all the effort."

I again resist slicing his flesh open with my knife. "Are

they sailing to Westman Island?"

"How did you know this?" the trapper snarls. "Who are you?"

Quibly steps out from the shadows, his ax in hand. "Just answer the maiden," he demands.

Eindride chuckles. "How about you answer to my new friends?" he threatens. He's looking over my shoulder. I quickly glance behind me. "I guess I was mistaken—not all the Danes are gone."

Five men, four with spears, are upon us. The armed men are thick and tall. They are wearing iron helmets with leather straps tucked under their beards. They look very unhappy. The unarmed man, shorter than the others, steps forward. His eyes are small, and his beard is short. He's wearing a necklace with a large medallion around his neck.

"You asked if the Danes are sailing to Westman," the little man says. "Now why would you ask that?"

I tell him, "We are looking for work."

The trapper interrupts. "This whore was asking a lot of questions about you."

"We apologize, we'll just go on our way," Quibly says, taking my hand in his.

"I'm afraid not," threatens the small man. He has the same accent as our attackers. He whispers something to his men.

"What did you tell them?" Quibly asks the man, pulling me in closer.

"I said, kill the fat boy and take this girl to my room. We'll get to the bottom of this."

Quibly raises his ax above his head, and I pull my seax from its sheath. This time we'll both fight.

CHAPTER 9

The men with the spears move towards us in a battle stance, their weapons aimed forward.

The little man steps away. "You really think this is a good idea?" he laughs. I ignore him and focus on the warriors in front of me.

The long spears give them a reach advantage, and my shield is useless, still strapped to my back. We are outnumbered two to one, and our best chance of inflicting damage is to get close. Our chances of survival aren't good. I have an urge to run, but Quibly isn't going anywhere – not this time.

Without warning, one of them collapses to the ground. He lands in front of me with a blade sticking out of his neck. The other warriors turn in confusion. Now's my chance! I jump forward, directing the nearest spear away with the curved blade of my seax. My feet leave the ground, making direct impact on the warrior's stomach. We fall to the earth together, and I land on his legs. He looks at me in surprise just before an ax impales his chest.

Suddenly, a man crashes into me, knocking the seax from my hand. I'm pinned to the earth. I push with my arms and twist my body, managing to roll him off me. He looks dead.

A girl's voice shouts, "We need to go now!"

I look up. It's Thoren! Where did she come from?

"Now!" she shouts again.

I feel as if I'm floating outside my body, watching myself run along the river. We race across a field until Quibly stops, gasping for air. We fall to our bellies and hide in the tall grass. My body is shaking.

"Are you hurt?" Quibly sputters between breaths.

"No, I'm okay." At least I think I am.

"You are both lucky to be alive," Thoren scolds. "We need to keep moving." She gets to her feet to look over the field.

We run again until we are well beyond the reach of the torch lights that burn in the hamlet. We finally rest under a birch tree at the edge of a farmer's field. The half-moon is peeking through the branches above, reflecting off Thoren's chest. She's wearing a vest made of small iron rings, which hangs from her shoulders down to her belt. A leather sheath, missing its sword, rests across her back. Her long, black hair is back in a braid, exposing purple bruises on her face and neck.

"You made it off the ship!" I exclaim.

"Of course I made it off the ship. Although your headstart almost got me killed." She looks at Quibly. "Our little blacksmith here is quick."

"I just saw that," Quibly pants.

"I didn't think you had it in you," Thoren says. "You are just full of surprises." I wasn't sure I did either but don't say these words out loud.

"What happened on the ship?" Quibly asks.

"After driving a knife through a man's heart, I jumped into the sea. I swam away from Livvy to give her a chance. A warrior jumped in after me but the fool was wearing armor. He sunk to the bottom of the sea like a stone. The men tried to save him, by which time I was gone." She looks at Quibly. "And how is it that you're alive?"

Quibly hesitates but then retells the story of his parents' death and his flee to the mountains. I can't imagine how difficult it was for him to say this to Thoren. I was sick to my stomach listening to it. But this time, Quibly doesn't hang his head. He sounds determined to seek their revenge.

Thoren hasn't said a word. She looks up to the sky before finally speaking. "You both have much to learn. You must always be prepared for battle. Odin teaches to have your weapons ready at all times, even if drinking from a stream. Livvy, your shield tied to your back could have gotten you killed. Lucky for you I was there to save you."

"Yes, you are right," I say. "Thank you. How did you find us?"

"The cliffs on my side of the fiord were impossible to navigate. I traveled a considerable way inland to get around them. By the time I got home, I was told you both had just left for the mountains. My father and uncle are in Valhalla, and there was nothing left for me at the hamlet. I caught up with you in the Linden forest."

"I heard you that night," I recall.

"I don't know why I followed you in the first place. Maybe the gods were telling me you were both going to get yourselves killed. I was going to return to the fiord, and then I heard you outside the tavern. If you know where the Danes are heading, then I'm going with you. Someone needs to live to tell the saga of how you two took on an army with knives and wooden sticks. And this Ivar freak is mine, understood?"

"Did you see him?" I ask. "Ivar—*the Boneless*?"

"Did I see him? Yes, you can say that. And you almost did, too. He whispered in your ear."

The man with the deep voice from the boat. As long as we get Grim back alive, she can have her revenge. If my little brother is dead or hurt in any way, well that's another story.

"We are east of the hamlet," Thoren says. "We can't risk going back. We will sleep here and head south at dawn."

"South is just—south," Quibly says.

"Aren't you the smart one?" Thoren mocks.

"I mean, how are we going to find this island? There are hundreds of islands."

"We'll find a way," I say.

I look up at the stars. In the summer, you only briefly see them at night. In the winter, it's all you see. The sun tells us which direction we are heading, but the great navigators know how to read the stars. At sea, it's a must. Most stars move slowly through the seasons, but the brightest ones wander in the sky every night. I locate Odin's Wagon. There are seven stars in total, four that make up the wheels, and three the long handle. It doesn't look anything like a wagon to me, and if it is one, I think it's broken for it doesn't go anywhere. Like a fool, I search the sky looking for something that will show me how to find Westman. Soon the lights just all blur together.

At morning, we leave and move quickly across the flat lands towards the distant hills and the southern sea. By midday, we reach the end of the tilled earth. The ground here is black and rocky but different than that of the mountain plateau. Here, the stones go on as far as I can see and they're fused together as if poured from a giant's furnace.

"This rock came from Katla's earthfire in another time before humans roamed Midgard," Thoren says. "The fire giant unleashed its power, and the dwarves threw their rocks from Katla's mountaintop."

Wherever it came from, this land looks abandoned by the gods. With every howl of the wind, I look over my shoulder to see if we're being hunted. The small Dane fled last night, as did Eindride. If there are more warriors in the hamlet, they'll want us dead.

The rocks beneath our feet soon become alive with green and pink. The plants have short branches that spread out with dense, flattened lobes. I recognize the stone moss at once. It's edible, but bitter, and is mostly boiled in soup in the winter months. But today we're hungry and eat some uncooked. I think back to the ship and the man with the unnerving name, Ivar the Boneless.

"Did you get a look at Ivar?" I ask Thoren. She stares at me emotionless. "If you're dead, I need to know what he looks like," I say.

"I'll not be dead before you."

We sit in silence, looking over the colored stones towards the rising hills. Thoren is right. Most likely I'll be dead before her. But that changes nothing. I'll try and save Grim no matter the consequence. This is my destiny.

"He's a demon," Thoren says in disgust, breaking the silence. "He's bigger than any warrior I've seen. His fingers are long and bony, and the raven is burned into the flesh of his back.

His hair is red—just like yours. That's enough for you to know."

He sounds like a troll, although I haven't heard of one with hair like mine. Not even my parents have red hair. Trolls are very ugly and an enemy of both gods and humans. Their bodies can contort in ways humans cannot, which makes fighting them incredibly difficult. And the beasts kill without reason, other than hunger. Some of them can apparently cast spells, too. If this troll, or man, is the one who killed Papar, then I need to reconsider my promise to Thoren. My priority is to save Grim, but revenge would also be satisfying.

By late day, we reach the foot of the hills that cross the sky from east to west. I pray to Thor the sea is close on the other side. The journey is taking longer than I had hoped. A sliver of smoke rises from a grassy knoll ahead. We approach slowly, this time with my shield in place. A small structure comes into view, carved into the hillside like a cave. Stacked rocks conceal the opening, and a wooden door, no taller than my shoulders, is closed shut.

"The shaft to a dwarf's mine," Quibly whispers as we crouch behind a boulder.

Dwarves are short with long beards and are fierce fighters. They sleep deep in the ground of the kingdoms and are the greatest metal smiths to have lived. They are capable of crafting magic into their swords, axes, and even rings. They also guard the doorways into the mountains that bridge the realms, much like the rainbow bridge connects Asgard to Midgard. But this cave doesn't look like a secret gateway to another world.

"Maybe the dweller will know the way to Westman," I say. "I think we should go find out."

"Yes, we should," Thoren agrees.

"Why don't we watch for a while," Quibly whispers. "Maybe throw a rock at the door?"

Thoren smirks, "You really think a dwarf lives in there?"

"I don't know, perhaps," he answers sheepishly. "The door is small and it leads into the mountains, does it not?"

"Then we are about to find out," Thoren says, shaking her head as we move towards the cave. A horse is tied to a small tree some twenty feet from the entrance. It looks to be eleven, maybe twelve hands tall, an average size for the horses I've seen. It has a coat with pigments of both red and brown, a black mane, and a tail which reaches the ground. The horses in Norseland are much larger and often used in raids, but only the smallest of breeds could be brought by ship on the long voyage across the open seas. Even then they were brought as foals.

I knock on the small door.

"Enter, my child," echoes a woman's faint voice from within. "And your friends with you."

I open the door, and my nostrils fill with sweet smells. A small woman in a blue robe sits in a chair by the fire. A black hood, with strings of yellow gems, drapes over her white hair, reaching down to her skirt. She has a staff in her hand, which has an iron knob on top that is embedded with colorful gems. She wears white gloves and white shoes made of fur, and a skin bag hangs from her thin belt. Jars are scattered on the ground, and a cauldron on the hearth boils, filling the room with a warm mist.

"My name is Runa," the woman says. "I have been waiting for you."

The woman is surely a seer. A woman of magic has the fate goddess, Freya, as her ally and is entrusted with the highest

74

power, even more so than chieftains. At the hamlet, our seer was not Karl nor Jarl, but when she prophesied, she sat in the chieftain's chair. Women who carry the staff can travel alone wherever they like without fear of being harmed. We duck our heads and enter the dim dwelling.

"Hello, Runa," I say. "We're in search of Westman Island. We wonder if you know how to get there and could provide us directions?"

"Come, come and sit down," the seer says. "I will make you some soup." She picks up on my hesitation. "It is soup, not a spell. Please sit."

As a noble, Thoren has more experience with seers than Quibly or me, and it's evident from her glare that I'm not doing something right. Runa scoops broth from the cauldron into wooden bowls and hands them to us. Quibly finishes his before mine is poured.

"You said you were waiting for us," Thoren says. "The spirits told you?"

"I have been waiting for just one," the seer says, placing three candles on the dirt in front of her. "For a long time now— for a shield maiden. It is prophesied that a shield maiden will unite the gods."

I look to Thoren, and she seems to be in the seer's spell, fully entranced by her presence. Until now, I thought I defeated Thoren in the dunking game at the sea, even if I was lucky. But if the seer is waiting for a shield maiden, then the gods really did let me defeat her. Thoren was meant to visit the halls of Valhalla and must be destined for great things.

"Do you know the way to Westman Island?" I ask again, this time trying to sound more noble. Thoren darts me another scowl.

"I can only share what the gods want me to share," she says. "First, I must ask what you seek at Westman Island?"

"Our clan was attacked by the Danes. They took my brother as a slave, and we believe they may be going there. I'm going to rescue him." I look over at Thoren and Quibly. "We also seek revenge."

"Are you certain it was the Danes?" she asks.

"They speak Norse and fly the banner of the raven," Thoren says. "We are quite sure it was the Danes."

Runa lights the candles with a piece of bark from the fire. "The raven does fly on the Danes' ships," she says. "The Danes worship the same gods as you and me. I can't choose a side but will ask what the gods are willing to share."

The seer reaches into her skin bag while launching into a chant in a strange language. Seers can do many sorts of magic, including casting spells, healing, foretelling the future, and even weaving a warrior's death, provided it's the will of Freya. Quibly looks at me with worry in his eyes, but I'm comforted that Thoren appears calm and focused. She must be familiar with this ritual. The seer dances around the candles on the floor, her chants getting faster. She raises her arms in the air, tossing a powder onto the candles at her feet. At once, a gray smoke, sweet to smell like mead, fills the room. Startled, I jump in my chair, but oddly the smoke doesn't hurt my eyes or lungs.

Runa continues her song, and I become mesmerized by her words. The seer is no longer old but is young and beautiful. She's flying high above the lands, carrying a round shield, both red and blue, and a silver sword. I follow her, sailing through the mountains and then over the sea. There are ships beneath me, more than I can count. I see a battle between men and beasts on the shore of the sea. I'm now somehow holding the seer's sword and shield.

"This is your fate," she whispers. "It is you, Livvy, I have waited for."

The seer vanishes, and I fall towards the earth. Tumbling downwards, I see Grim on the battlefield with a shield in his hand but without a spear or knife. A beast with the red dragon eyes, covered in metal and fur, charges him, swinging the sword of a giant. But instead of defending himself, my brother looks upwards at me and drops his shield to the ground. I scream.

Quibly and Thoren are lying on the earth with their eyes open. They are awake, yet they are asleep. I look around me, and the seer is not in the cave. I stand and rush outside, squinting my eyes almost closed from the sudden brightness. The sun is in the east, and night has come and gone. Runa is strapping leather bags to the horse.

"His name is Varvak," the seer says, briefly looking up towards me. "He's named after the horse in the sky that pulls the chariot of the sun. He, too, can ride for days with very little water, resisting the heat of the fire ball."

"What spell did you cast on us?" I ask, adjusting my eyes to the light.

"You saw and heard what the gods wanted you to see and hear. I provided the bridge, no more. Your fate is yours and yours alone. Do not be concerned, your friends will awaken soon."

She finishes tightening the straps around the horse's belly. "You look to be leaving," I say.

"Yes, it's my time to leave this place and go to another. You, too, need to depart at once and continue your journey. You will find a stream ahead in the hills. Follow it for two days to its source. From there, chase the setting sun for a half day, and there you will find directions to Westman Island."

"How will I find directions in the mountains?" I question.

"That is all I can see," she mumbles, turning back towards the horse.

"One last thing," I say. "Can you tell me anything about the Berserkers?"

She stops and turns to face me. "They were at the hamlet?"

"Yes."

"They are powerful and they fight without fear," she says. "But I think you know that."

"Are they men?"

"Who else would they be? Yes, they are men, but they don't think under their own will, at least not when they fight."

"A witch controls them," I say. The seer only smiles.

"Can you tell me how they can be defeated?" I ask.

"You wish to fight them?"

"Please, anything."

She looks briefly into the forest. "What animal, other than those carrying spears or arrows, can kill a bear?" she asks.

I think for a moment. "A wolf." Although I've never seen a wolf or bear, as there aren't any in Iceland, I've seen their furs on the backs of Norsemen and heard stories of how they hunt.

"Not one wolf, but a pack," Runa says. "A lone wolf will

have no chance, but together they can outsmart the beast, tearing it apart with nothing but a scratch."

The seer pulls a small pouch from her leather bag, tied shut with string. "Come here, Livvy. I have something for you. These are herbs that will help you overcome your worst fear. It is very important you only eat them when you feel your fear at its greatest."

"Thank you," I say, putting the pouch in my skin bag. At this point, I don't fully trust her, and I need to remain cautious. Seers are known to have plants and seeds that they use for their spells. I have even heard of leaves that can change humans into animals, tricking the enemy in battle. The last thing I want is to be turned into some rodent.

I follow Runa into the cave. Thoren and Quibly are still on their backs but stirring. She taps them each on their cheeks with her staff, touches my hair with a white glove, and leaves.

CHAPTER 10

After filling in Thoren and Quibly on the seer's directions into the hills and her sudden departure, we learn we all dreamt of soaring the skies like the ravens. No one volunteers to share the details of their dreams, of which I'm glad, as I don't think Thoren would take well to mine. How will I become a shield maiden? At least shield maidens are girls – that's a start. And what does *uniting the gods* mean? But if this prophecy can help me find Grim, then that's all that matters. I just need to figure out how to fulfill it.

The seer left dried meat on the table, which we devour despite its unfamiliar taste. I'm not sure if it's fox, bird, or something else altogether.

Outside, Quibly spots something through the trees and goes to investigate. Soon he shouts back. "Thoren, I think you want to see this!" We go to him, and there resting on a large mound of stones is Thoren's leather sheath.

"It's a grave," Thoren says. "The man buried here was important."

"Why did the witch put your sheath on a grave?" Quibly asks suspiciously.

"Because of the prophecy," Thoren answers quickly. "Quibly, help me move the stones."

"What are you doing? We can't disturb a grave," he says.

"If a warrior is buried here, it will anger the gods."

"The stones are covered in moss. This warrior finished his journey to Valhalla many seasons ago. There's nothing left but bones. Help me, or I'll do it alone," she says, throwing the first stones aside.

Reluctantly, Quibly joins in, which is no real surprise to me. From the way he looks at her, he's still in a spell, and it's not from Runa. The caw of a raven echoes off the trees. Three black birds circle above us, framing the rising smoke of Katla behind the hills. An uneasiness overcomes me. We are being watched or death is near.

"There's wood in the grave," Quibly announces.

Thoren's right, this man was of great importance. Only mighty Jarls are buried in wooden boats, along with their most prized possessions. Sometimes they are even buried with their Thralls to take with them on their voyage. Something the Thralls were never fond of.

"It's here!" Thoren calls out. She tosses a few more stones to the ground, then raises a sword to the sky. She brings it down for inspection, and both Quibly and I get in close. The blade is red with rust and is quite pitted, but considering how long it's been in the ground, the sword is in remarkably good shape. It has a line of symbols engraved on the blade marked +ULFBERHT+. They're similar to the symbols the monks wrote on their skins but mean nothing to me. I don't know of any Norseman who can understand the meanings of written symbols. A small pouch is wrapped around the pommel, which Thoren opens. She pulls out a sharpening stone and sets it on the ground.

Thoren turns the sword slowly in the sunlight. "I'll cut off

Ivar's head with this very steel," she declares.

"Whoever kills this thing, I still get to hold him down," Quibly blurts out. "But we need to get moving if we're going to find these secret directions in the hills. Oh, and they're from a witch who put us to sleep and fled before we woke. What could possibly go wrong?"

Thoren rolls her eyes, and we go back to the cave. We pack our belongings and continue our journey.

It's two sleeps before we reach the lake that feeds our guiding stream through the hills. Its waters are as blue as the sky and much colder than the sea at home. Speckled birds fly high in circles, taking shallow dives towards the lake. When they do, they neigh loudly like goats, not like the seabirds in the hamlet which squawk or caw. Their beaks are long and narrow as if wielding swords from their mouths. Even the birds have their warriors.

"The seer said we'll find directions a half day east from here," I say.

"But it's late and I need a bath. We'll go in the morning," Thoren insists. She's taking off her mail and pack before I can protest.

"I'll try and spear a fish," Quibly says as he quickly saunters off. I suspect the image of Thoren taking a bath is going to stop him from taking my side. I guess we are leaving in the morning. I take the shield off my back and look for fallen branches in the thin forest that wraps around the water.

Soon the fire is roaring. I go to the shore to gather stones to warm in the flames. I'm tired of being cold at night, and we can put them in our clothes for extra heat while we sleep. Thoren is in the lake bathing, her sword on a rock next to her. I look away.

She has the body which I imagine Freya would have. In addition to being the mother of magic, Freya was the goddess of love, beauty, and fertility. Many giants seek her in hopes of making her their wife. Many in the hamlet felt the same way of Thoren but were too afraid to ask. Her father was the mighty Bryanjar, and she was just as intimidating. Quibly, however, never missed an opportunity. The *fisherman* is also in the lake, but his attention is not on the water. Thoren doesn't seem to notice or just doesn't care.

By some magic, Quibly keeps focused enough to spear a small fish. We cook it over the fire and divide it up. I've never eaten a fish that lives in drinking water, but it's very good, and I wish we had more. Thoren pulls her sword from its sheath and begins to sharpen it with her stone. I watch for a while. She's going to ruin it.

"Do you mind if I help with that?" I ask.

She hesitates before passing her sword to me. I grip the steel between the cross-guard and pommel, pointing it forward and moving it in small circles. The weapon is double-edged and its blade tapers slightly from the cross-guard to its rounded tip. It's remarkably light, much more so than any steel I've touched. The sword is balanced to perfection and almost feels weightless. This is an amazing weapon.

"The blade is dull, but this weapon is superb," I say. "We don't have steel like this in the hamlet, but it's made of steel nonetheless. You will save strength in battle if you sharpen it correctly."

"It will cut through flesh just fine," Thoren dismisses.

"But it will cut through bone, as if it were flesh, if sharper."

Thoren tosses me the sharpening stone. "Go ahead then."

I spit on the stone. "You need to hold the blade at a higher angle—you are too shallow. Slide it in straight lines, not in circles." Thoren watches closely. I take out the copper I have in my pack and scrape it across the steel. "Copper is softer than steel. It will take off the rust without damaging the metal."

I hand the sword, stone, and copper over to her. She looks over the copper as if seeing the metal for the first time. Silver and gold are the more common trading metals for the nobles. I'm reminded of my status in the clan. At least the clan we used to have. She begins to work the sword free of rust.

At morning, we continue east. The clouds have descended, and we can hardly see twenty feet around us. We don't know what we're looking for, and now we won't see it if it's standing on a stone waving a spear. At least we can see our feet. The ground is soaked in purple flowers, which have tall stems and cascading petals. They continue to appear through the mist with every step, and I wonder if we're just wandering in circles. Maybe we should just turn south towards the sea, but now I'm not sure which direction is south. It's been more than a half day walk, and I pray we've not lost time in our search for Grim.

"I was thinking about what the seer said, that a shield maiden will unite the gods," Thoren says as we walk, looking down at our feet. "But the prophecies told by the elders will come to pass. The gods are already united and will battle Loki and the giants at Ragnarok. I can't think of what Runa's words could mean."

"No mortal is needed to unite the gods," Quibly says. "The witch was talking nonsense. Now we are lost."

I feel something fly by me. What was that? A diving bird from the lake? There it is again.

"Get down!" Thoren yells. "Arrows!"

I drop to my belly and quickly remove my shield. Moving to my knees, I crouch behind it, hoping I'm facing the direction of the attack. Thoren and Quibly squeeze in behind me.

"The witch sent us into a trap!" Quibly barks. "Where are they?"

I look around. We are surrounded by clouds. They could be anywhere. "We are going to run," Thoren orders. "There's nowhere to take cover. We'll run back the way we came. Are you ready?" I try to think which direction we came. I don't want to die with an arrow in my back. I take a chance instead.

"Runa sent us!" I holler into the mist, my voice cracking. Thoren gives me a look that could kill. It's too late now.

"What do you want?" a man's voice shouts back, roughly in the direction we are facing. I feel a moment of relief that we got the location of the attackers right. "We are twenty in number and will kill you all if you make any quick movements!"

"A seer sent us this way," I yell back. "We are searching for directions. Nothing else."

"Throw your weapons and your shield to the ground!" he commands.

That's not going to happen. We'll take our chances running before surrendering. Quibly is thinking the same thing. "Never!" he hollers. "Come out and show yourselves, you cowards!"

My shield jolts towards me with the splintering crack of

wood. The iron tip of an arrow is an ax width from my eye. I gasp, having to tell myself to breathe.

"Where are you seeking?" the man in the mist calls out.

"Westman!" I shout back. The hills of purple flowers are silent for thirty breaths or more. A man then emerges from the mist, his face behind an arrow locked in its bow.

"What do you want in Westman?" he yells.

"The Danes!" I almost scream. "They attacked our clan and took my brother as a slave."

The archer slowly drops his arrow and starts walking towards us. "How is the old woman?" he says as he lowers his voice.

I can't find my words, but Quibly steps out from the shield and answers. "The witch put me to sleep and fled before I could ask about her feelings."

The archer is now close and laughs. "Yes, she does that. My name is Wulf. Please excuse the welcome as I don't get many visitors. Come with me, and we can eat."

"Where are your men?" Quibly questions, looking around.

"My men? Oh, right—I have a cat. His name is Charles. I think you'll like him."

CHAPTER 11

The archer approaches, his bow by his side. I grip my seax, my hands still shaking from the impact of the arrow. He is young, older than me, but not by much. His shoulders are wide, but he looks thin. Not scrawny thin, but lean like he's been in battle for weeks. His hair is dark and wavy, and his face without a beard. His jaw is square and not round. He looks different than any Norseman I've seen. His green eyes lock onto mine. I want to look away but I can't.

"I'm going to take my iron tip back if you don't mind," the boy says.

He has an accent like Papar's. I step back and raise my shield. "You're a Saxon!" I exclaim.

The archer laughs. "I'm not from Norseland if that's what you mean, but I have no quarrel with you. I'm going to snap the arrow from your shield now. Don't swing that knife of yours at me. Please." He breaks off the shaft, and I pull the iron tip out from my side and toss it over to him. "Thank you. Now, what are your names?"

Thoren takes the lead. "I'm Thoren, daughter of the Noble Bryanjar of Norseland. This is Quibly and Livvy."

"I'm in the presence of nobility," the Saxon boy says, smiling at Thoren. "I thought so when I saw you."

"I like your name," I say.

Wulf smiles at me, and Quibly gives me a strange look. I don't look at Thoren.

"Let's go. It's not far from here," Wulf says.

We follow the archer through the mist, our weapons still out. Quibly is looking over his shoulder and side-to-side. Thoren seems to be at ease. I don't know what to think. We soon stop at a stone wall that goes straight up into the clouds.

"Watch your footing," Wulf says.

"Up there?" Quibly questions.

"It's not too far." Wulf begins to climb, followed by Thoren and, reluctantly, Quibly. I go last. We climb our way up the cliffside, reaching hand over hand. If the Saxon boy wants us dead, this would be a good way to get rid of us. One loose stone and we would tumble over each other to the earth below. I'm now very nervous that Quibly is above me. I should have gone before him.

We manage to reach the summit safely, with no stones or boys falling from above. Quibly is breathing hard and lies down on his back, his hands on his chest. Before us stands a small house, shrouded in the clouds. The walls are built entirely from flat, black stones and the roof from branches and grass. The door is made of logs, tied together with twine.

"It's not much but it's safe and warm," Wulf says.

Quibly gets up and we enter Wulf's home. Thick branches are stacked against the rock walls, with dense yellow moss woven tightly around them. Three wooden benches, raised on round logs, lie against them. A sheepskin is spread out on the bench against the far wall. A stone hearth is in the center of the room, and three wooden boxes, each big enough to store a small ax, sit on the ground next to it. We are immediately greeted by a small, white creature which lets out a weird shriek.

"This is Charles," Wulf says. "Runa wanted his fur for her boots. She offered me a silver piece for him, but I've grown too attached to the thing."

I've never seen a cat and I'm taken back by its appearance. It's much smaller and not nearly as ugly as I imagined a cat to be. Freya's chariot is drawn by two cats. They were given to her by Thor, and she blesses those who are kind to them and curses those who aren't. I imagine for a moment a chariot strapped to this cat, and I almost laugh. "Where did you get this creature?" I ask.

"That is a long story. First, we eat. I hope bird is fine. And don't be concerned, it's not of the raven variety."

The bird tastes more or less the same as the seabirds at the hamlet. I'm hungry enough that I could eat pretty much anything, and it's much better than the bitter rock moss.

Wulf tosses what's left of the carcass to the cat. "Tell me about the Danes and their raid on your home," he says. He's looking at me. I make eye contact with Quibly, not sure what I want, or don't want, to say.

"How about you first tell us what a Saxon is doing hiding out in the clouds?" Quibly asks, picking his teeth with a small bone.

"That is fair. You have me outnumbered," Wulf says. "I'm from England, from a kingdom called Wessex. Have you heard of it?"

"No," we reply.

"Right. Where should I start? Well first, England is an island of kingdoms, much like Norseland. There are four kingdoms in total. Northumbria in the North, East Anglia in the

East, Mercia in the middle and Wessex in the South. I'm from Wessex, the greatest of the kingdoms in my opinion. The people there are mostly Saxons, and we speak a language of the same name. I was born in a small shire in Wessex. Shires are what you would call hamlets."

"Sounds lovely," Quibly says sarcastically. "Where is this mythical land called England?"

"Where do you think the monks came from?" Thoren questions. "Let him finish." Quibly opens his mouth to say something but closes it with a huff.

"It's a long sail south of here," Wulf says. "So far, in fact, that England's winters are much shorter and warmer than here in Iceland. In the darkest of winter, it's light in the day as much as it's dark. The ground crops grow easily and abundantly. The soil is deep and easy to till, not like the rocky land here."

"Then why would you leave such a land of paradise for long winters and rocky earth?" Quibly asks. I guess he couldn't keep his mouth closed for long. Thoren looks annoyed.

"Yes, that is the right question, but best answered over mead. Let's have a drink."

Wulf starts a fire, and we gather around to fight off the damp air. It feels good being in a home, even though not my own. Wulf fills four horns up with the sweet drink. I wonder for a moment why he has four horns if living alone with an animal.

"How did you make mead?" I ask. "Is there honey in these hills?"

"I wish," Wulf replies. "I haven't found any. I traded for this." He raises his horn to the air. "This jar is the last of my mead, but it's better to drink with kinsmen than alone with a cat. Skal!"

With voices raised, together we shout, "Skal!" Quibly isn't overly enthusiastic but looks pleased enough to have a drink in his hand. We sip the sweet honey wine as Wulf continues his story.

Wulf's eyes look at me like they did on the field in the mist. They look more green now, like the water in the fiord in the cold of winter. "For fifteen years, the Danes and their chieftain, Ragnar, raided the shores of England," he says. "But one day, by the mercy of God, Ragnar was shipwrecked off the coast of Northumbria. He was captured by the Saxons, and the King of Northumbria threw him into a pit of snakes. The snakes bit and poisoned him until he died."

"England has snakes?" Quibly asks.

"*Huge* snakes," Wulf says, raising his eyebrows. Quibly cocks his head as if determining whether Wulf is telling the truth or a tale. Wulf smiles and continues. "In retaliation, Ragnar's sons sent an army to attack us. They brought more than three hundred and fifty ships. They first took Northumbria. In revenge of Ragnar's death, they cut out the king's ribs and pulled his lungs out through his back."

This death is the same way Godi was executed. What horrific thing did Godi do to deserve to be tortured like that? Letting the monks live so they could make wine for the nobles is hardly a hideous crime. All attacks have a reason. Even Fairhair, as mad as he is, didn't attack without a purpose. We just need to find out the Danes' reason.

Wulf pours us the last of the mead. I'm already beginning to feel dizzy, and this horn is more full than the first. "Within a few winters the Danes conquered all of England, except for Wessex, the last of the kingdoms," Wulf says, setting the jar down.

"The Saxon armies must be made of children," Thoren says. "They don't know how to fight."

"The kingdoms of England fought against each other for hundreds of years, and their warriors are skilled in battle," Wulf says. "Don't get me wrong, the Danes are fierce warriors. They battle in ways the Saxons haven't seen before, and their ships are fast and agile. But if the Saxons had united together, I believe they could have beaten them."

"Our warriors are as strong as the Danes," Thoren says as a fact. That may be true, but we will never find out now. Our warriors are dead.

"To my knowledge, Wessex still stands today," Wulf says. "The king has defended the kingdom despite being severely outnumbered. He is a very clever man and will do anything to win."

"What is the name of this Saxon king?" Quibly asks.

"Alfred, son of Athelwulf. In England, kingdoms are passed down from king to prince, that is from father to son. At least that's how it's supposed to work. It's not like Norseland where the chieftains are chosen by the clan."

"But what if these princes aren't warriors?" Thoren questions. "What if they are weak?"

"King Alfred has won many battles without drawing a single drop of blood."

"You can't win a battle without fighting," Thoren says with a smirk.

"We didn't fight today, did we? Now we are together drinking mead. A much better outcome I think."

"Why are you hiding here, anyway?" Quibly questions.

"You have many questions, but if it's that important for you to know, I'm not in Iceland on my own will. The Danes attacked my shire and killed both my parents. My father was a warrior and died in battle. My mother—she died later. I was taken a slave as a young boy."

"They brought you to Iceland," I say.

"The Danes sold me to a Norse chieftain for two pieces of silver—the price of two cats," he says, looking down at Charles. "He was returning to Iceland and was looking to find the best location to build his settlement. When land was in sight, he threw the pillars of his throne into the sea. They were carved in the image of Thor, and he decided the gods wanted him to live wherever they went ashore. We lost sight of them in a storm and searched months for those cursed logs. We finally located them on the west end of the island. I spent the next seven winters there. Sevens winters with the bastard Ingolf."

Ingolf? The Norse hero who went to Westman Island to avenge his brother's murder. Wulf was there. This is why the seer sent us to him. Thoren, too, has put it together and she jumps to her feet with her hands reaching for her sword.

"You are one of the slaves who killed Ingolf's brother," Thoren accuses, her hands now touching the pommel.

Wulf doesn't stand but instead puts another branch onto the fire. "No, I am *the* slave who killed him," he says.

CHAPTER 12

Thoren pulls the sword from its sheath as Quibly stands. "A slave who kills his master must also die," she says.

"Yes, that is the way of your Thing," Wulf says. He takes another sip from his horn. "But where I'm from, the elders don't allow masters to beat their slaves. And beating slaves to the point of near death is a crime of its own. You would have done the same if it were you."

Quibly moves towards him. "But we are not slaves," he says.

"But what if you were taken as one?" Wulf asks.

"I would never be taken as a slave," Quibly snaps.

As soon as he says it, I can see he regrets his words. Thoren was beaten, and worse. And how is Wulf being taken a slave any different than Grim? Thoren reluctantly releases her grip on the sword. The room falls silent, except for the crackling of the fire. Wulf puts another branch into the flames. I realize I haven't breathed in a while, and I take in a deep gulp of air, drawing a glance from everyone. Should I be standing with my seax raised?

Thoren looks over at Wulf. "We are not in Norseland, nor are we in England," she says. "Who is to say what laws apply?"

Quibly hesitates but then sits. "Yes, only a chieftain can pass such a sentence, and there are no chieftains here."

"The Valkyries will cast their judgment when they're ready," Thoren says. "Let's not speak of this again."

Wulf nods. He's a different boy. The boys I know would have attacked if threatened by a sword, even if wielded by a girl. But judging from our encounter with the arrow, Wulf isn't weak. A coward would have ran or hid. He's a warrior, but a clever one. Perhaps like his king in England.

"It's late and I'm tired," Wulf says, gulping down the last of his drink. "Please sleep here. I have skins and a warm fire. Tomorrow we can talk of Westman."

Although I'm anxious to hear everything about Westman, this seems like the right time to stop talking. Wulf offers his bed first to Thoren and then to me, insisting he likes to sleep on the ground. At home, our warriors would offer to *share* their beds but would never give them up. We both decline. I'm getting used to sleeping on the ground. It looks to rain tonight, and I'm just happy to have a dry roof over my head.

Thoren lies down by the door, and Quibly and I find a spot against the wall. I'm very thankful Quibly is here with me and not dead. If he had stayed in battle that night, he would be gone. And for what purpose? To have *maybe* killed one Dane? He's alive because there is a destiny awaiting him. I wrap myself in a skin and rest my head on his belly. Within moments I'm asleep, flying again above the sea and the battlefield.

I suddenly awake, swiping with my hand but missing. Charles was licking my face, maybe trying to eat it. For a moment I want to kill it, but then I remember Freya's cats and decide that's a bad idea. A faint billow of smoke is coming off the blackened wood in the hearth, gasping for its last bit of air. The boys are asleep. I get up and exit the stone house. The suffocating clouds are gone and the sky is back, bluer than I've seen in a long time. I feel a renewed sense of hope.

Stepping out from the stone walls, I take a sudden breath as I look out before me. We are perched on a knoll high above the surrounding lands, and a field of snow and ice stretches below me as far as I can see. It's as if a mighty sorcerer cast a spell, and the waves of the sea were frozen in time. At the distant end of the tundra stands Katla. Fire is pouring down its slopes, like it's waging war with the ice. I can only think this place must be Jotunheim, the realm of the frost giants. I imagine for a moment Thyrm, the king of the frost giants, thundering across the ice to his frozen citadel. Loki himself is a frost giant and will eventually lead the monsters of Jotunheim into the battle of Ragnarok. This is not a place we should be.

"It's dazzling, is it not?" Wulf asks, walking up behind me. I jump at his unexpected presence.

"It's beautiful, but it's also ominous," I answer, trying to sound calm. My heart, though, is beating faster and it's not from being surprised. Wulf makes me nervous. Not nervous like I'm afraid—more an excited nervous. Like how I felt when I had my first fish on a line and didn't know what it was. No, that's not the feeling, but I can't think of a more comparable one.

"That's a good way to describe it," Wulf says.

"Sorry, what's that?" I say, wondering if I said my thoughts out loud.

"Beautiful but ominous," he says with a smile. "The snow

field doesn't melt in the summer and it's constantly moving and changing shape. Many believe this land is alive and doesn't take kindly to visitors. It has swallowed many men, and I have gotten lost more than once crossing it."

"You crossed this realm?" I ask in disbelief.

"It's the quickest way to the southern sea and also to Westman. Going around it will take weeks."

I feel a lump in my throat. We are doomed. How can we cross this frozen kingdom and survive? My thoughts are interrupted by another shriek from the little white creature. Charles is hiding between Wulf's legs, rubbing his head on his ankles. Cats are very strange beasts, and I wonder how they would taste.

"You were going to tell us how you got the cat," I say, distracting myself from the overwhelming obstacle in front of me.

"I guess I was. Ingolf brought Charles for his son, a boy named Torstein, as a gift of sorts for leaving his home and friends in Norseland. But Torstein came to resent the thing and abused it. So when I fled the settlement, I took him with me. As far I was concerned, he was one of us."

"That is when you went to Westman Island?"

"Yes, although it didn't have a name then. We all went there. The monks were all beaten at one point or another, and this was their chance to escape. They trusted me. I saw the island on our search for the pillars. It's very remote and I was certain we would never be found there. But Ingolf was a revengeful man and he searched Iceland until he found us. It's my fault they are all dead."

"The Norsemen see Ingolf as a hero," I say. "Our chieftain

told us stories of Ingolf's first voyage across the open sea. He sailed the seas in search of new realms. Our people believe he was both a brave explorer and warrior."

"I understand, Livvy. I'm sure he was a good explorer, but I got to know the man very well, and he was not a hero to me. He tortured the monks before he killed them. They refused to fight back as that was their way. Their god would deliver them—so they thought. I saw things a little differently. I killed two of Ingolf's men before jumping from a cliff into the sea."

"They thought you died in the sea?" I ask.

"It was a miracle I missed the rocks, but my time to die hadn't come. I found a cave in the water below the cliffs and hid there for three days until they left. I found Charles a few days later at the burned longhouse. I guess we were both meant to survive. We eventually settled here. I can see the enemy coming from far away, and there are plenty of fish in the lakes and birds in the air to eat."

Thoren and Quibly come outside and both curse when they see the snow field in front of them. Wulf points towards the direction of Westman and explains to them that going straight across is the only viable way of getting there.

Thoren scans the horizon. "Then we better get moving." She pulls my copper coin from her pocket. "Wulf, can you spare any food?" How can she be so brave? Nothing seems to intimidate her. Wulf flips the coin between his fingers. The copper isn't Thoren's to barter with, but she's right as we're unlikely to find anything to eat on the ice.

"Yes, you can take everything I have—except Charles," he says with a grin. "I've never gone hungry. But can you first tell me what happened with the Danes and why you think they're at

Westman?"

Thoren reluctantly nods her approval. "How about you tell him, Livvy?"

Why me? Is she testing me somehow? Everyone is staring. I take a deep breath and begin to share what happened the night of the feast, including the Berserkers and Ivar the Boneless. I tell him of Papar and the monks, and that the Danes were looking for them. Finally, I tell him that Grim was taken a slave. I don't cry. I want to but need to be strong – or at least appear that way.

"I'm sorry, Livvy, about your brother," Wulf says. "Your story is not so different than mine. The Danes enslaved me as they enslaved your brother. And if I survived so can he. I'm not a Norseman, but we share a common enemy. May I ask how you survived the attack?"

"We were at sea fishing," Thoren says quickly. Quibly and I remain silent. Thoren hasn't talked about what happened when she was captured. She doesn't need to. I'm sure it's not a day she wants to relive with a boy we just met.

"If the Danes are going to Westman then I'll go with you," Wulf says. "I have my own reasons. And besides, the only way you're getting there quickly is if I show you the route."

Thoren gives her approval. "If we find Ivar the Boneless, he's mine. This is not negotiable."

"I can agree to that," Wulf says.

"Good. We'll go at once."

I hope I can be as brave as Thoren one day. If I'm to *unite the gods*, then I better start working on it. We go back into the house to pack our clothes and weapons. Wulf fills his pack with food and pulls out a full quiver of arrows from beneath his bed.

"Livvy, I wasn't trying to kill you yesterday with the arrow," he says. "I'm a good shot and was just giving myself some options."

Yesterday is now far from my thoughts, but I feel compelled to respond. "You still put a hole in my shield," I say. Wulf laughs as he sorts his arrows. Even his laugh has an accent, but it's nice and makes me smile.

"That's a strange name, Charles," I say, looking down at his creature. "Where did you get this name?"

"One of Ingolf's slaves was captured from a land called Frankia. Frankia was ruled by a king named Charles the Great. The monks joked that I worshipped the cat like he was a king, so they started calling him Charles. I grew to like the name and decided to keep it."

I look at Charles. "He won't wander off if you leave?" I ask, unsure why I would care.

"No, he sticks around. I travel often. His only enemy is the fox, and although he's not as quick as he used to be, he's a great tree climber. As I said, we're survivors."

We are soon packed and follow Wulf down the knoll towards the snow and ice. This side of the mountain isn't nearly as steep, and it's not long before we approach the snow's edge. The sunlight is bouncing off the white earth, and I have to squint my eyes to keep them from burning. There are no birds in the sky, and the only sound is the howl of the wind. I guess even Odin's eyes can't reach into the realm of the frost giants.

"The snow was a very long walk from here three summers ago," Wulf says, making his first step onto the frozen tundra. "If we move quickly and don't have any unexpected encounters, we should cross it in two days."

Livvy

We follow his footsteps, the ground crunching beneath our feet, leaving the forests and the hills behind.

CHAPTER 13

Thor must be sending me a warning for my skin is already burning, and it's only midday. At times our feet sink into the snow up to our knees, but mostly the ground is hard. There are no signs of life, no giants, and no citadels – just endless nothingness. Katla's fire is our guiding marker across the tundra, but it doesn't seem to be getting any closer.

Wulf's been in the front since we left but falls to me behind Thoren and Quibly. I held back a smile when I saw him coming. I've been thinking of Grim all day and can use the distraction. In some ways, Wulf reminds me of Erik. Maybe it's because he, too, has been to lands that I've only dreamed of. He is also easy on the eyes.

"You've been guarding the rear in case one of your giants attacks," Wulf teases.

"Someone has to," I say, pretending to reach for my seax.

"When we get to the sea, we'll need to find a boat," he says. "Westman is way too far to swim, and we don't have time to build one like the monks and I did." I'm aware of this challenge but have ignored it as there's nothing I can do about it from here. I can't carry a boat across Iceland even if I wanted to. "There's a fishing hamlet just beyond the ice—it's our only option," he says.

"That makes it simple then."

"If you say so," he says with a half-grin, half-frown.

I watch our feet step together in rhythm on the snow. It's funny how that happens. Thoren glances over her shoulder. She turns back before I think of something to say to her. She speeds ahead, and we pick up our pace to keep up.

I ask Wulf, "What's Westman Island like?"

"For a while I loved it there. There are many islands in the area, but Westman is the only one that has enough dirt to farm. It's much larger than the others, but you can still walk the entire shoreline in a day."

"You grew things?"

"The monks did more than me. I mostly fed on fish and bird eggs. In the spring, the seabirds lay their eggs on the cliffs. I had to climb to get them, but they kept me full until the cold arrived. In the winter, the sea was stormy but the air was warm—for Iceland, that is. It reminded me of the air in England."

Iceland air is all I have known. I look around at the snow which never seems to end. The more I hear of England, the more fascinating it sounds.

Quibly and Thoren slow up, and we stop to eat. We didn't pack any wood for a fire, but Wulf pulls out some cooked bird.

"So, Wulf, how do you know the witch?" Quibly questions. "You know, the devious one hiding in the cave?"

Wulf laughs. "She's actually a good, old woman. A little crazy with the powders, but I don't think she meant you harm. I frequently trade for goods at the fishing hamlet. I pick up things she wants, and she picks up things I want. I see her once or twice a year, and we trade."

"The witch tricked us with her powders," Quibly argues.

"How do we know that you and her aren't sending us into some sort of trap?"

Thoren jumps in. "The seer is a messenger of the gods," she barks. "We don't question her knowledge or visions. You should pray for forgiveness in case Odin's ravens are listening. The rest is over. Let's go."

Quibly is upset and sulks as he picks up his things. I don't blame him for not trusting Runa. I don't entirely trust her myself. I know he is only looking out for me and trying to do the same for Thoren. But sometimes Quibly doesn't choose his words wisely, and it tends to get him into trouble. I hope he finds his destiny. He's not a warrior, shipbuilder, or seaman. And although strong, he hasn't found a way to put his strength to much use.

I decide to walk with him. We step, mostly in silence, until the sun cools and our legs don't want to go any farther. Wulf leads us to a small drift in the snow about my height by two.

"It can be very windy at night, and we are best to make a cave in the ice," Wulf says. "Quibly, your ax would be helpful."

"Glad to finally be useful," Quibly says, raising the weapon in the air. "Just tell me when to stop swinging." He looks over at Thoren, but she doesn't react to his obvious jab.

It's not long before Quibly has a good-sized hole carved out in the bank. We finish it with the knives and spears. It will be snug but should provide adequate shelter from the wind. It reminds me of the snow caves that Quibly and I made as children, only I doubt this one would hide us from a frost giant. We lay a skin down at the cave's edge and settle in to rest. My legs ache and it feels good to sit down. Thoren takes her sword out from its sheath and continues to polish it with my copper.

Wulf looks curiously over her shoulder.

"Where did you get this sword?" he gasps, coming around to her side.

"From a warrior who no longer had use for it," she replies. "Why do you ask?"

"The letters."

"What are letters?"

"The symbols. They tell where this sword was made." Quibly and I come around to look at the +ULFBERHT+ marking. "This sword was made in a monastery," Wulf says. "One of the monks talked often of these weapons. I didn't think they existed. He said they are made of the hardest steel ever forged—steel that can slice through armor as if it were flesh. Yet the steel is so light that a child could take it to battle. He said a warrior carrying one of these swords will never lose a battle."

"Well *one* may have," Thoren speculates, lifting her sword into a battle position. "Quibly, get your ax and Livvy's shield. We shall fight. Let's see if this weapon is as powerful as Wulf's monk says it is."

"Absolutely, *my maiden*," he replies, jumping to his feet.

"Don't break my shield!" I shout. I wonder if this is Thoren's way of saying sorry. If so, it seems to be working. Wulf and I sit together and watch them fight in the snow. Thoren's sword slices through the air almost effortlessly – more like a light stick than a weapon forged from steel. Quibly is clearly outmatched, but Thoren is careful to keep the fight between the weapons.

Wulf leans in towards me. "I apologize for meddling, but are you and Quibly together?" he whispers.

"What?—Where did that came from?"

"You fell asleep on him last night, and you two look close. He seems nice, although he might be stealing some of your food."

I laugh, briefly drawing a glance from Thoren. "Why are boys always so oblivious?" I whisper. "Quibly and I are very close, but we are like brother and sister. We grew up together. Can't you see he's infatuated with Thoren?"

Wulf looks out at the warriors in the snow. "So you're not with anyone?"

My face is instantly warm, and I turn away, afraid that it's turned red. The last time I remember feeling like this was listening to Erik tell his stories of Norseland. I feel an attraction to this boy, one which I shouldn't have, for he's not loyal to Odin.

"Not really," I say. What does *not really* mean? I want to say something else, but I can't think of what it should be.

"And Thoren, is she with anyone?" he asks.

I should have expected that question. I'm now surprised it didn't come out first. I pull out my seax and get up to join Quibly and Thoren on the snow.

Wulf calls after me, "Where are you going?"

"To fight," I shout back, not turning around.

Thoren lowers her sword. "You want to fight with that curved knife of yours?"

"I'm quite fond of this curved knife."

"Very well then, let's see what you have. Quibly, give her the shield. She's going to need it."

Sooner or later I'll have to fight, and it's unlikely I'll have Thoren hiding in the shadows to save me next time. And right now I'm in the mood for it. I lift my shield and raise my seax in the battle position, just like I've seen the warriors do countless times at practice. I catch Wulf's eye, and he looks concerned. I don't know why. Thoren knows how to practice without slicing me open – at least I hope so. The boys sit together. I try and remember what Olaf taught me and what I learned with Grim in the barley fields. The clang of metal hitting metal echoes over the field of snow.

Our weapons strike a few times, and I think I'm doing pretty well. That is, until I see a slight smirk from the side of Thoren's mouth. The seax flies from my hand, and she strikes my shield with her boot. I fall backward to the ground and look up to see her sword pointed at my throat.

"You're going to have to do better than that," she says, as I get back on my feet. I take a deep breath, and we try it again. Three swings later, I'm back on the ground, this time without *both* my knife and shield.

"You're unaware of your surroundings," Thoren says. "I have you fighting uphill, and the sun's in your eyes. You lost before you started. You're also swinging in a panic, like a child in the bee house. You can't fight with speed and control if you aren't focused. Let's try it again."

When I'm too tired to hold my shield in defense, Thoren calls it quits. I argue to keep going, but she says I'll just get myself killed. What she really means is that she'll end up killing me. We return to the shelter and put our weapons down on the snow. Quibly seizes the moment and tackles Thoren when she's not looking. They both tumble to the ground.

"Let's see how you fight without your steel!" he teases. Thoren hits him in the face hard, and I can't help but wince, imagining how it felt. But Quibly is undeterred and picks her off the ground and tosses her over his shoulder. He spins her around a few times before launching her over his head and into the snow bank. Thoren screams, picks herself off the ground and charges at him. She hits him hard, but Quibly pushes forward, wrapping his arms around her and falling forward to the ground. Thoren hits him three or four times in the chest before he pins her arms to the snow.

"Let me go!" she yells.

"Will you let me keep you warm tonight?" he teases again.

"Let me go now or you'll never father a child!" Quibly jumps off her and runs a few steps away while laughing.

"The infatuation looks mutual," Wulf says in my ear.

"Did you say something, Wulf?" Quibly asks, looking our way.

"Nope," Wulf says.

"Would you like to fight?" Quibly challenges, arching his back in a long stretch.

"I thought you would never ask," Wulf says, jumping to his feet. "With or without weapons?"

"Let's do without." Quibly gives me one of his childish grins.

Thoren sits next to me on the snow. "This should be fun," she says with a big smile.

CHAPTER 14

The boys circle each other in the snow, both making false attacks to see how the other reacts.

It isn't long before Thoren grows impatient. "Should we go to sleep?" she shouts.

Quibly responds to Thoren's taunt and charges his opponent with his arms outstretched. But Wulf ducks under him, grabbing his leg and yanking it into the air. Quibly hops on the other one, trying to keep his balance, until it's kicked out from underneath him. He falls hard to his stomach, and Wulf is quickly on top of him, pushing his head into the snow.

"He's fast," Thoren coos, wrapping her arms around her knees to settle in for her entertainment.

Wulf jumps off, and Quibly rolls over and gets to his feet. "Okay, so *that's* how it's going to be," he barks, marching towards him. He tosses a punch which Wulf sidesteps with ease. Wulf darts quickly behind him, wrapping his arms tightly around his belly. He tries to throw him to the ground, but Quibly isn't budging.

"This is going to hurt," Quibly grunts. He grabs his opponent's hands and falls forward, rolling to his back as he nears the ground. Wulf can't escape and is crushed into the snow under the full weight of Quibly's body.

"Ouch!" Thoren and I cry together.

Quibly bounces his body, driving Wulf farther into the snow. "How do you like that?" he asks.

"It feels—just fine," Wulf replies, groaning in pain.

The boys get up, and to Thoren's disappointment, decide to continue their brawl another day. Quibly looks happy to finish with a victory, and Wulf seems fine to let him have it.

The sun is now low in the sky as if Sol's chariot is racing across the fields of snow and not across the heavens above. The temperature is dropping and the wind strengthening just as Wulf said it would. We squeeze into the snow cave for the night.

I'm nestled between Quibly and Thoren, and Wulf lies at our feet at the edge of the opening. Thoren and Wulf are trading pointers on fighting without weapons. I wonder what it would be like lying next to Wulf. My thoughts are interrupted as Quibly starts to snort like a boar. By now I'm use to his nightly growls and soon wander into my own dreams.

Thoren is tossing about and wakes me up. She soon gets up and leaves the cave. The boys are sound asleep. Quibly is lying on his back with his mouth wide open and seems to be having a hard time catching his breath. I wonder if he's dreaming of drowning. It's moments like these that I worry about him getting a wife.

A small cone of ice is melting above Wulf's head. I watch in amusement as each drop falls away, barely missing his nose. I find myself rooting for the drip to hit its target, wanting to give Wulf a little nudge in its direction. When I concede that the water isn't going to win this battle, I get up to join Thoren. I quietly crawl over the boys and step outside.

Thoren looks over her shoulder as she hears me approaching. "The ground was rumbling again," she says quietly. I didn't feel anything but I haven't been awake long. We *are* getting close to Katla, and I think of the dwarves tossing their giant stones out of the mountain's mouth.

"Do you believe what Runa said about the destiny of the shield maiden?" Thoren asks, more to herself than to me.

I think of my dream and that this destiny is mine and not hers. I guess there's the possibility that Runa was just mad or her powdery potion was spoiled. But this isn't the right time to bring any of this up. I finally say, "I have no reason to not believe her."

"After hearing the tales of my sword, this fate must be mine," she mutters. "But all I feel is hatred. Even against Odin for what he's allowed to happen. What I really seek is revenge. This is the destiny I want."

Now I hear the ground rumble. The snow fields must be on the move or the giants can smell us. The sound wakes the boys, and they poke their heads up. Thoren turns back to the cave, unfazed by the earth's warning.

I'm getting more anxious about Grim. Wulf thinks we can make it off the snow by nightfall, and I tell myself that with each step I'm closer to finding my little brother. Katla's peak is hiding in the clouds, painting the sky shades of red and orange. I don't feel as hopeful as I did yesterday but try and bury my worries deep in my head. I need to stay focused. The easy way out would be to curl up on the ground and pray for death. I'm not going back there.

The sun is now facing south and is high above us. We decide to take a rest. I watch Wulf pull the bow off his back. It's almost as long as I am tall. "You kill the birds with that?" I ask.

"It's a lot easier than throwing rocks at them," he says, laughing. "Here, give it a try." He hands the long bow and an arrow to me. Although I have cast arrow tips at the smithy, I've never shot one. All my practice was with weapons made of iron and steel, for that's the training Grim wanted.

Wulf steps behind me and wraps his arms fully around my waist. I haven't felt a boy's touch before except for Quibly's, which doesn't count. I feel like I'm starting to sweat.

"Lock the arrow into the middle of the string," he says, "and hold the bow in your left hand. Now grasp the string with your fingers, resting the arrow between them. Don't squeeze the arrow. As you pull the string it will rest on your fingers. Hold the bow firm and pull the string back all the way to your cheek."

I follow his instructions but am more distracted by his fingers touching mine than I am listening.

"Find a spot you want to hit and breathe slowly," he says softly in my ear. "Let everything but that single spot become a blur. Now relax your fingers and let the string slip past them."

The arrow releases, and I step back in surprise by the suddenness, falling against Wulf's chest. I quickly steady myself in embarrassment.

"Well done!" he says. "You will be hunting before you know it."

The arrow went right where I wanted it to go, and I'm quite pleased with myself. I shoot a couple more before Quibly approaches with my long spear. "Let me show you a real man's arrow," he boasts. He runs forward and launches the spear into the air. It flies high and far but disappears completely when it hits the ground.

"Where did it go?" he asks himself, walking in the direction where his spear should be. As I look towards the landing spot, the snow appears to be moving. I blink my eyes to see if they're playing a trick on me. No, the earth is falling away!

"Quibly, run!" I yell.

He doesn't need me to tell him, for he's already turning around and racing back. A roar, loud like Thor's thunder, shakes the ground, swallowing the snow and ice. The falling earth accelerates towards me. We all turn and run. I can only think Hell is rising from her realm of ice and cold. I look up for ravens but trip and fall hard to the earth. Wulf grabs my hand and yanks me to my feet, pulling me with him as he runs. Thoren already has her sword in her hand, and I draw my seax. The deafening roar is upon us. I dart a glance behind me. A wall of ice is upon us. Thoren stops and turns with her sword high. I follow her lead to battle whatever monsters rise from the earth. The ice quickly overtakes us, pelting my face like small knives. I'm blind and can't breathe.

The ice cloud settles to the earth and the roar slowly falls silent. I don't see any monsters yet. Through the cloudy haze, there's a large hole. It's so immense that I can't imagine a legion of dwarves or the largest of frost giants making it. It must be a hundred steps wide and three or four hundred steps long.

"I've seen these openings in the snow fields," Wulf says quietly between breaths. "But never one made."

"Where does it go?" Quibly wheezes.

"Down—way down."

We wait in silence before crawling on our bellies towards

the hole, stopping short of the edge. Standing slowly, we peer into the depth. There is nothing but darkness – a vast pit of blackness. Quibly picks up a chunk of ice, and before anyone can protest, hurls it into the void. It vanishes. There's no sound of it hitting the ground.

"You're going to anger Hell!" Thoren scolds, dropping back from the edge.

"You think the hole leads to Niflheim?" Quibly questions nervously.

"Look around us. Where else could it go?"

I also retreat, afraid Thoren may be right. Niflheim is the realm of ice and cold – one of the two realms that has always existed. This icy tundra is undeniably a land of cold that never warms. The other realm is Muspell, the land of fire. The legend is that the ice from Niflheim mixed with the fire from Muspell and created the steam that made the first gods and giants. I look towards Katla's fire and the ice beneath it. I wonder if this could be the place where the beginning happened.

"I don't think the hole leads to Hell," Wulf says as he slowly stands.

"What do you know of Loki's daughter?" Thoren scolds. "You don't serve Odin. You have no right to talk of these things."

"Oh, I didn't know Hell was a person—or a goddess—or is she a monster? The Christians have a Hell, too. It's a realm, similar to Niflheim, I guess. The dead go there, but it's a land of fire, not ice."

"The Christians make up their stories," Thoren dismisses. "There are only nine realms."

"I think I would rather be cold than hot," Quibly ponders.

"In Valhalla, you won't be either," Thoren says.

I can see Quibly took her words to mean he will go to Asgard when he dies, for he has a wide grin across his face. I hope Thoren's right. And I hope I will join him.

"Hell is a place of punishment for those who don't worship their god," Wulf says. "They are sent there to burn in fire for a thousand life times."

"Hold on—your people believe that I'll go there to burn when I die?" Quibly questions.

I can see Wulf is thinking carefully of what to say next. "The Christians believe this," he finally says.

"And are *you* a Christian?" Quibly asks, clearly annoyed.

"I was born one," Wulf says flatly.

This is a conversation I want no part of. I don't know what to think anymore. The boys go back and forth as we retreat farther away from the edge. They let it go as we begin to search the snow for our skin packs and weapons. Quibly was alert enough to grab the ax as he ran by it, but both my father's spears are lost. Our food and sheepskins were also swallowed by the hole. We must get off the snow by nightfall. We circle wide around the void and continue south.

"We'll keep west of the fire mountain when we leave the snow fields," Wulf says from the front. "From there, the sea isn't far. We can sleep at the fishing hamlet. I have some friends there."

"How far from there to Westman?" I ask.

"If we find a boat, it will take us two days to row there. What's the plan when we get to Westman?"

Thoren doesn't hesitate. "To get Livvy's brother, kill Ivar the Boneless, and as many of the other bastards as we can."

"Just like that?" Wulf questions. "It might be nice for us to get out alive. If the Dane army is as big as you say, and they have these Berserkers as their allies, this sounds like a quick way to die."

"Then we'll go to Valhalla, and I'll see my father, uncle, and cousin," Thoren says indifferently. "We'll feast and train for Ragnarok. How is that bad?"

"I think even your gods want their warriors to be victorious and not walk into certain death," he says.

Wulf is right – we need a plan. I'm doing this to save my brother, not to die trying, even if the chances of surviving are slight. "We don't know what we are facing until we see it," I say. "Let's get to Westman and pray the Danes are there and Odin's on our side."

Thoren huffs and says, "And we will get Livvy's brother, kill Ivar, and the other bastards."

I whisper to Wulf as I brush past him. "I would appreciate your god's help, too." I don't see how it can hurt.

The terrain steepens, and we carefully navigate it, often on our hands and knees. Finally, we approach a crest. We peer over it, and the icy earth slopes steeply down. Beyond it, the sea! I feel a profound sense of comfort just to see the waves crashing onto the shore. Houses are clustered together in the far distance, their flickering fires imitating the star pictures in the night sky.

"The sea hamlet," Wulf announces proudly. "We can get there by midnight, but the ice here is steep, so we'll need to slide on our backsides for much of it. I once used a sheepskin like a boat, but that's not an option today." Wulf edges up to me and whispers in my ear, "We do have your shield."

CHAPTER 15

"What do you mean, *we have my shield*?" I question.

"You and I can slide down the steep part of the ice on it," he says excitedly. "Quibly isn't going to fit, and Thoren can keep him company. Come on, it's time you had a little fun, and we'll get to the hamlet faster."

I play along and take off my shield, unsure if Wulf is serious or not. Wulf quickly takes it from me and sets it on the cold ground.

"Now sit on it," he says with a smile. Quibly and Thoren are looking at us strangely.

I sit on it just to amuse him, but before I can get back up, he pushes me over the edge. He jumps on behind and wraps his strong arms and legs around me. I scream as we accelerate down the slope, spinning in circles. We both laugh as we go faster until we hit something, tumbling down the hill out of control.

When we finally stop rolling, I'm still laughing and lying on top of him, my eyes looking into his. I want to kiss him. I close my eyes as his hands press firmly against my back. But I stop myself, rolling off him and wiping the snow off my clothes. Grim is gone, and it's not fair for me to feel this way. Looking up the slope, Quibly and Thoren are slowly making their way towards us and don't look impressed.

"Is everything all right?" Wulf asks.

I answer with, "Not really." I pick my shield off the ice. I can tell he is confused, but this is an area I have no comfort or experience talking about. "Let's talk later, if that's all right with you?"

"As you wish, my maiden," he says, wiping the snow off his face.

Quibly and Thoren catch up, and after some scolding that we could have destroyed our only shield, we carefully make our way down the ice.

The sea hamlet is much smaller than ours, with no more than twenty houses, and is nestled on a peninsula jutting out into the sea. We follow Wulf between the darkened homes before stopping at an old door not far from the shore. Wulf knocks.

The door eventually opens, and a tall woman with curly brown hair appears.

"What a nice surprise!" she exclaims, giving Wulf a long hug.

"I'm sorry to wake you. Hilda, these are my friends, Thoren, Quibly, and Livvy. Everyone, this is my good friend, Hilda."

"To health and happiness," we each say. Hilda looks to be the same age my father would be. I imagine she was very attractive in her youth, but as with most Karls, the long days working in the wind and cold wrinkles the skin and darkens the eyes. We enter her home. It's too dark to see anything but shadows, and the air is muggy and smells like fish. Hilda lights some candles, and the room slowly comes to life.

A table is in the center, with a bench on the left and another on the right. The walls are made of wooden logs, stacked flat and mortared together with dried mud. Cluttered shelves line the walls, and strings of drying fish hang from the ceiling.

"Jóra, Wulf is here," Hilda announces, looking across the room. A girl with brown hair tied in a long braid is sitting up on a bench against the far wall. A sheepskin lays over her legs. She looks to be about my age. She springs out of her bed, races over, and jumps into Wulf's arms. She gives him a kiss on his cheek before Wulf sets her down. I feel embarrassed and look behind me at Quibly, but he just shrugs.

"This is my daughter, Jóra," Hilda says proudly. The girl is pretty and looks very much like her mother. Her lips are full and her nose is small. She's wearing a long, white shirt, which hangs down to her knees, and has wool socks on her feet.

"You all must be hungry and tired," Hilda says. "I'll get you some bread to eat and some skins to sleep on. Wulf, are you here to trade? How long will you stay?"

"We're looking for a boat. We're heading to Westman in the morning."

The daughter looks disappointed. She's looking at Wulf like the girls at the hamlet did with Erik. We put our things on the ground and sit on the benches next to the table.

Hilda takes the bread and butter off a thin shelf. "Why would you go back to Westman?" she questions.

"I'm just a guide, and their business is private," Wulf says. He changes the subject. "We saw a hole formed in the snow fields today. Right in front of our eyes."

"It goes to Niflheim," Thoren states as a fact. "Hell was trying to take us to her underworld, but the gods saved us. They have work for us to do." Hilda passes out the bread, and we each thank her.

"Can you explain to me what realms the gods and giants

live in?" Wulf asks. "You have many worlds, and I easily forget." There are so many stories of the realms that I often get confused myself, but Thoren begins before I think of where to start.

"There are nine realms," she says. "The greatest is Asgard, home of Odin and the gods, and also of Valhalla, where the fallen warriors rest. We live in Midgard, of course, and we're connected to Asgard by the rainbow bridge. Niflheim is the home of Hell and the dead, and Muspelheim is the home of the fire giants and the demons. The rest of the giants live in Jotunheim, the light elves in Alfheim, and the dark elves in Svartalheim. Last is Nidavellir, the home of the dwarves."

"Is it possible to visit these realms, while alive?" Wulf asks curiously.

"Midgard is in the middle, below Asgard," Thoren answers. "We are surrounded by the vast waters, which are impossible to cross. The great serpent encircles the entire sea and will not let any human pass, but there are hidden doorways to the other realms. Some are guarded by dwarves—isn't that right, Quibly?"

"C'mon on!" Quibly groans. "It's better to be safe than have a dwarf's ax split your head open!"

"And you call yourself a man?" Thoren laughs.

"Do you want to wrestle again?"

"My sword against your ax, anytime!"

Wulf looks over at Jóra. "They love each other." I kick him under the table.

"You have a sword?" Jóra asks, almost in the way a child would.

"Thoren is a shield maiden," Quibly says. "She has fought

in many battles and killed many Shockheads."

"Really? Can I see it?"

Thoren pulls her weapon from the leather sheath. "This sword is made from the same metal that killed Fafnir the dragon," she says in a whisper. "I'm going to kill a demon with it one day."

"A demon?" Jóra questions uneasily.

"Or just a few more Shockheads," Thoren says with a smile.

Images of the Shockheads pop into my head, with their long hair and inked faces. When I get back to Norseland, they'll still be there. We don't have an army left to defeat them. But I refuse to stay on this island. I think of my dream of sailing the dragon ship with Grim in search of the rainbow bridge. If only I lived in a dream.

Wulf asks Hilda, "Do you know where we could trade for a small boat?"

"The fishermen leave for the sea at first dawn. You can ask them in the morning."

Wulf turns to us. "There aren't any hamlets between here and Westman," he says. "We need to find a boat here."

If we don't, I'm not sure what I will do. The trip is already taking much longer than I thought it would. What if Ivar and the Danes have already left Westman? I say a quick prayer to Thor, asking again for his help.

The morning will come soon, and we settle in for the night. I have a difficult time falling asleep. I miss Grim so much my stomach hurts. By now he must feel certain he'll never see me again. But I won't fail him.

CHAPTER 16

I hear whispers and giggles from the far side of the damp room. It's Wulf and Jóra, and they soon get up and go outside. I don't know when they returned, but they were both asleep when I awoke. Wulf isn't so different after all, but it's for the best. I'll have no trouble keeping all my focus on finding my brother and thinking up a plan for how to get us to Norseland.

Hilda is also awake and is quietly preparing the fire. I get up and help her with the wood. Her fingers are swollen and covered in sores. "Have you always lived here by the sea?" I ask quietly.

"Yes," she answers. "We came from Norseland ten years ago. My husband was a fisherman, and the Shockheads took half of everything we caught. He thought it would be easier if we started a new life here, but the sea took him five springs ago."

"I'm sorry to hear that."

"The people here are good to us, and we survive. There's nothing else one can do."

"I guess there isn't," I say. I imagine my mother wasn't so different from Hilda. Every day she got up early to start the fire. I remember waking up with her on this one cold morning. She kissed me on my forehead and sat me on her lap. Her belly was growing, and she laughed as I kept falling off. She showed me that morning how to use the flint. We laughed as I spent what seemed like forever getting the fire started. When the spark finally turned into a flame, it was one of the happiest moments I can remember feeling.

Hilda prepares hot water with birch and moss, and the others are soon up. We sit and have our drink before making our way to the shore.

A dozen or so boats are anchored to some floating logs about twenty feet from the rocky shore. Long wooden planks bridge the logs to the beach. The fishermen are already busily preparing their lines and bait. We talk to some of them, most of whom Wulf knows, before finally finding a man who has an old, wooden rowing boat he's willing to part with. Wulf takes him aside to negotiate. It isn't long before he returns.

"He wants two pieces of silver for the boat," Wulf says, shaking his head. "He has the only spare one in the hamlet and knows he can command a high price."

Thoren is quick to tell him, "For that thing? Then I'll just kill him and take his boat."

"We don't need to kill him," Wulf says. "I'm sure we can trade some of our weapons. They have very little here other than fish."

"My sword is not for trade," Thoren barks.

Quibly joins in. "We lost the spears. We need the weapons we have."

"Wait," I say, reaching for my belt. "I have enough." I remove my pouch and toss it to Wulf.

"See!" Thoren says. "The gods had a plan. They wanted you to win the dunking game so you would have the silver for this boat."

I thought I won so she could visit the Valkyries in Asgard and see the great hall. And if she won, she would have the silver anyway.

"But where did you get the rest?" Quibly questions with a puzzled look.

"I was saving for a goat," I say with a smirk.

I was lucky with the silver, but the copper and ore is everything I saved for Grim and me to start our new lives in Norseland. My years of sweating in the smithy, and my dreams, traded for an old wooden boat. When I rescue Grim, we'll be starting over with nothing. But we'll have each other, and we'll get to Norseland, somehow. There's nothing left for us on this rock of ice and fire.

Wulf returns with a big smile. "We have a deal." He tosses me the empty pouch.

I manage to muster a smile in return. "We have a boat and Westman is within reach," I say. " Let's go find my brother."

Hilda is kind enough to give us bread, dried fish, and sheepskins for our journey. We promise to return the skins when we return – *if we return*. Jóra isn't at the house, of which I'm happy enough, and although Wulf asks for her whereabouts, he doesn't go looking for her. We go back to the dock and prepare to leave.

Our row boat has two oars and sits low in the water. In rough seas, it would easily sink, but we plan to stay close to the shore until we near Westman. From there, we'll have no choice but to row into the open sea. The boat is small, but we manage to all fit in. Thoren and Quibly take the oars. Wulf and I squeeze next to each other at the bow, resting our backs against my shield. We wave goodbye to Hilda and leave the hamlet.

Quibly is in his realm and in a much better mood. He's much happier rowing than walking. Thoren keeps pace with him, and we seem to be making good time. We pass numerous streams, each dumping their waters into the sea, as well as endless cliffs which reach up to the ice fields now high above us. Seabirds are flying to and from their nests fastened precariously to the stone walls. If not for being so anxious, I think I would enjoy the beauty of this place. However, I don't plan on coming back. I'll either be dead or sailing to Norseland before the winter comes. Wulf starts up a few conversations, but I'm too irritated with him, or maybe myself, to continue them for long. How could I have had feelings for this boy?

"Ahead!" Wulf shouts. "Floating ice!" In the far horizon, dozens of white and blue peaks jut out of the sea. "The ice breaks off from the fields above. They float out of a river ahead."

The ice shards get larger as we near them. I've seen many in our fiord, but these are much bigger and much bluer. Some are taller than three or four masts put together. As Wulf said, they are slowly floating out from a river's mouth, lined up in turn like a legion of ants going to battle.

"The giants are angry and tossing the ice out to sea," Thoren declares.

Wulf is quick to question, "Why would they do that?"

"How am I to know?" she snaps back. "Perhaps they're sending a message to the sea serpent to come and kill us."

I look at Quibly, rolling my eyes. I don't know why the ice moves or why it would crumble into the sea, but I doubt the giants have anything to do with it. I have seen many wondrous and ominous things, much in the last few days, but no giants or trolls – at least not yet.

Wulf and I take our turns with the oars while Quibly and Thoren lie down. It's not long before the waves send them both into the dream world. Ahead, Katla is dumping its fire into the sea, creating a blanket of steam which rises up to the clouds. We are too close to the cliffs to see the top of the mountain, but we'll soon be right below it.

"Thank you, Wulf, for all your help," I say quietly, as to not wake my friends. The wind is loud and helps to drown out my voice. I need his help and might as well be friendly. "We would be lost without you."

"I have my own answers to seek, but I'm also happy to help you find your brother," he says. "You are brave, strong—and beautiful."

"Jóra and Thoren are very pretty," I say quickly.

"I want to talk to you about last night."

"There's nothing to talk about. We are from different kingdoms and with different dreams. We have the Danes to fight, and I have my brother to save. Can we leave it at that?"

"Jóra and Hilda have done a lot for me, and I care for them," Wulf says. "There was a time when I don't know if I would have survived without them. Jóra and I were together, only briefly, two years ago."

"Wulf—"

"We aren't together now, although she would like us to be. It's long over. Last night I told her I'm interested in someone else."

"I wish you hadn't done that," I say.

"She's also a little bit crazy," he adds, grinning.

I don't want to risk any distraction from finding Grim. But maybe a distraction is what I need. I'm curious how Jóra reacted and can't resist. I ask him, "What did she say when you told her?"

"She was upset. She wanted to kill Thoren," he says with a laugh.

Of course, she thought Wulf was interested in Thoren. All the boys want her. I look over at Thoren sleeping. Even on a boat asleep, far from shore, she has her hand on her sword. I smile to myself, thinking that she keeps it close in case Quibly tries something. Wulf is quiet and is looking up at the sky. I can't help but think how attractive he is.

"I need to save Grim," I say.

He stops rowing and reaches over, taking my hand in his. I look over at Quibly and Thoren. They're both still asleep. My heart is beating faster. "Yes, and I'll help you," he says. "We'll do this together."

I smile, and he squeezes my hand. I squeeze his back. His hand is both strong and gentle at the same time. It's much bigger than mine. "You asked if Thoren was with someone," I say with a hint of concern.

He grins. "I was thinking of Quibly's chances."

Thoren stirs, and we return to our rowing. I don't think she's going to like this.

CHAPTER 17

The sea cliffs here are high, and the sun is now behind them. We are very close to the river of fire flowing into the sea. A thick cloud of steam rises into the sky ahead, and it smells horrible, like bird eggs that have gone bad.

"Look there," Wulf says, pointing out to the open sea. "We are close to Westman. Those shadows are the closest islands. If we sleep here for the night, we can make it there tomorrow, as long as a storm doesn't come in."

We are getting close. I pray to Thor that Grim is there. The god may not listen, but I see no harm in asking him for his help. We turn and row towards the shore. The beach ahead is covered in black sand, and behind it stands a large cave. The cave isn't deep but is wide and encased in columns of gray stones which plunge from the ceiling into the ground. Its walls are how I imagined those of Valhalla to look – stone pillars, like the trunks of trees, stacked side by side and strong enough to keep out the giants.

We row our boat until the bottom of the hull scrapes against the black pebbles. Thoren jumps out first to pull us in. "The water's warm," she says, surprised.

I reach over and dip my hand into the sea. It's very warm, like the water in a cauldron preparing to boil. We pull the boat onto the sand and put our things down inside the cave. I gather some driftwood and start a fire. We eat half the bread and fish, and save the rest. If it was up to Quibly, the food would all be gone, and then we would spend all tomorrow listening to him complain. We decide to make the fire large so it will burn through the night.

I've been thinking about my fighting lesson with Thoren, and I want to practice again. If I'm to save my brother, I need to become a better fighter – much better. I pick up my shield and draw my seax. "Thoren, will you train me some more?"

"Not with those," she says. "Get a couple hard sticks."

I search the beach and find two pieces of driftwood close to the length of a sword. We each take one and go closer to the sea where the sand is harder. The boys sit down to watch. This time I don't face the sun.

"Remember what we practiced last time. Stay calm. Accuracy is more important than power." I raise my weapon in the air just as Thoren strikes my hand with hers. I drop the stick in pain.

"*Never* let go of your weapon again," she scolds. "If this were a battle, you are dead." I pick my stick up and raise it again. I grip it hard. "Most fights are won by cutting the hands, arms, or legs. Your enemy will bleed out and weaken, and then you can go for the kill. Don't try to hit the weapon. Aim for the body."

I swing for her leg and miss. She charges, hitting me in the shoulder with hers and knocking me to the ground. Thoren is being much more aggressive than the last time we trained. She sighs, looking over me as if I'm a child, not an opponent. "Most fights are won within moments of them starting. Be sure of your first attack. If you miss, there's a good chance you're dead. And remember, every part of your sword is your weapon, as is your body."

We practice on the sand until the sky is dark. And I'm thankful for the night to arrive as I'm too sore to have continued much longer. I don't think I hit her once. I already see parts of my body bruising, but better that than losing an arm or leg in battle. As I sit down by the fire, Wulf grimaces as if telling me that he can feel my pain. I deserve every bit of it. I didn't do anything right out there.

Quibly pats me on the back as he plops down next to me. "What weapon does Ivar the Boneless carry?" he asks.

"A sword," Thoren answers.

Quibly turns to her. "Why do they call him *the Boneless*? Surely, he has bones."

"It's how he fights," Thoren answers coldly. "He swings his sword with the speed of Sleipnir—like there are no bones holding him back. I saw him kill my father. After he drove the sword through his chest, he just kept swinging. Over and over again. He's a demon."

Sleipnir is Odin's eight-legged horse and is also the son of Loki. It is the fastest creature in the heavens and has carried many gods across the rainbow bridge to Asgard. I didn't know Ivar killed Thoren's father, and that she saw it happen is horrific. I am now certain that Thoren will go to any length to have her revenge. But I'm afraid revenge may be no match for this monster.

"No one can swing a sword faster than I can shoot an arrow," Wulf says.

"Your arrow didn't go through Livvy's shield," Quibly argues. "It has no chance going through armor."

"I had my string pulled halfway back. It will go through a shield. I can promise you that."

"Enough!" Thoren snaps. She gets up and storms down the beach into the darkness.

"I'll talk to her," Quibly says, as he gets up to follow her.

Wulf and I listen to the fire crackle and to the waves rolling onto the beach. The sea is calm and is pushing a light, cool breeze into our cave.

"She's a strong girl," Wulf says.

"Yes, she is."

"You fought well against her. Most men would have quit much earlier."

"In a real battle, I would have been killed many times over. Only this isn't Valhalla where you can die each day and be resurrected in time for dinner."

"Let's go for a swim," he says, getting to his feet.

"A swim?"

"When will you ever be able to swim in water as warm as this? Even your nobles don't bathe in water this warm. And it will help with the pain." He takes my hand and pulls me up. We walk to the shore, my fingers locked in his. I've never had a warm bath before.

Wulf begins to take off his shirt. I turn away and take off my boots and belt. He's in the water before I finish. I run in quickly, relieved the clouds are making the sky darker than usual. The water feels amazing. I submerge my body and rub the warmth into my face and through my hair. I can hear whales singing songs to each other as if the gentle giants are right next to me. If I could breathe underwater, I would sleep here. I stand up, pushing my toes into the sand, and wipe the water from my eyes. Wulf is right in front of me, but this time I'm not startled. He presses up against me. Then he leans down and kisses me. His lips are soft but very salty.

We swim together until Thoren and Quibly return. They join us in the water, but not before Thoren places her sword on a rock close by. My seax is on my belt, back on the beach. When will I ever learn?

There is no seaweed in the cave, so we are fairly certain the sea won't trap us in while we sleep. We put our skins down on the black sand, and I lie next to Wulf. I don't look at Quibly for I'm a little embarrassed. Although he won't be jealous, he doesn't seem to care for Wulf, or at least doesn't trust him completely. I guess this is understandable. Wulf isn't Norse. But he will help us get Grim back, and then Quibly will like him. Thoren ignores us completely, putting her sheepskin down out of the cave. Perhaps she wants a better view of the sea in case an enemy approaches. I fall asleep with my hand on Wulf's chest.

I hardly slept at all. It had nothing to do with Wulf but rather my fear and anxiety about today. What sleep I did have, I dreamt of Ivar the Boneless swinging his sword over and over against my shield as I lie helplessly on the ground. I don't know if I'm more scared now that we will find the Danes or we won't. We still don't have a plan if we do.

We prepare our little boat. The sea isn't as calm as last night, but the waves shouldn't sink us – as long as they don't get much bigger. I need something to keep my mind off the day so I insist on rowing. Thoren joins me. I have a difficult time keeping up with her, and the boat keeps turning left, wanting to go back in the direction we came. Eventually, Thoren slows down and rows at my pace.

The boys are talking about the islands, and Wulf gives Quibly a detailed description of Westman. As we leave the shadows of the cliffs, Katla shows us its ominous peak again. I row a little harder, happy to distance myself from it.

It isn't long before the black beach and cave fade away completely. Twice, I thought I saw the sea serpent lurking in the dark waters beneath me. Maybe it was just the large fish with the teeth, but that doesn't make me feel much safer. I need to just keep rowing.

We take turns with the oars. By midday, we look to be halfway there. I can now count at least five islands, but one is much bigger than the rest – Westman! I squint my eyes, looking for any masts on the horizon. "Do you see any ships?" I ask the others.

Wulf answers first, "Nothing yet."

The reality is hitting me that finding Grim on this island is a remote possibility. Did Ivar the Boneless even say Westman? If my brother isn't here—I can't think about it. I row harder, and Thoren matches me stroke for stroke and then some. She eases off when we start to stray off course once again.

Westman is now close. Steep cliffs rise from the sea as tall as small mountains, and above them, fields of green continue up slopes almost as vertical. Birds, thousands of them, circle the cliffs while squawking and cawing. If I lived here, I don't think I could handle listening to this noise day after day. The cliffs are brown and gray, and I think they would be impossible to climb.

If this is where Wulf says he jumped into the sea, then a god somewhere is on his side, for I can't imagine a boy surviving a fall that far.

"There's a small fiord on the eastern side which tucks in behind the cliffs," Wulf says. "It's the only place where ships can be beached safely. If the Danes are here, that's where we'll find them."

"So we row east," Thoren says.

"We won't get up the fiord unseen, and if they have archers on the cliffs, we won't stand a chance. The fiord is narrow. I know another way. Let's stay south."

A fat bird with a red beak and orange feet lands on the stern of the boat. Its back and head are black but its cheeks and belly are white. It tilts its head as if trying to understand what these strange beasts are doing at its island.

"I lived off these birds," Wulf says, slowing pulling an arrow from his quiver. "I either ate them or their eggs. I missed them a hundred times with my arrows and realized I was going to starve if I didn't improve my aim. And I got tired of making arrows. I eventually figured it out."

Wulf slowly gets to his feet, bringing the arrow behind his shoulder. I think he's going to throw it at the bird like a spear. But before he does, Quibly jumps at the bird. He misses and tumbles into the bottom of the boat. We rock violently back and forth and almost end up in the water before the boat settles down.

"Watch it, Quibly!" Thoren shouts. "Do you want us all to drown?"

"Sorry, Thoren, I thought I could get it."

Wulf puts his arrow back into his quiver. "Do you mind if I

row from here, Livvy, since I know the way? Quibly, why don't you join me? We could use some of your power to keep us away from the rocks." Quibly pouts but takes the oar, and Wulf gives me a wink as he joins him.

The boys row us in closer. There are seals everywhere, popping their heads up within a spear's throw from the boat. A single one could feed us for a week. We have plenty of seals in the fiord but nothing close to these numbers. I wonder if I could live here, feasting nightly off these creatures.

Wulf directs Quibly along the cliffs and rock outcroppings before stopping in front of a small cove. "There," he points. An opening into the cliffs is straight ahead, and the sea is rolling into and out of its mouth. It's easily big enough for our boat, and maybe large enough to fit a small dragon ship. "This is where I hid for three days from Ingolf," Wulf says. "We can row in but we need to be careful. The sea will try and push us into the walls."

The boys row slowly into the cave. The walls are smooth and layered in stripes of purple and yellow. The ceiling is green and moist, and at places water slowly drips down in a steady rhythm. The stone hollow darkens as we row in farther. The air is damp and cool, and I wrap my arms around my chest in a pointless attempt to fight it off. My eyes begin to adjust to the blackness, just as we stop at a stone shelf near the back of the cave. It is flat with plenty of room to fit us and our weapons. Wulf gets out of the boat first and ties it to a large stone. We each follow in turn.

"I didn't think I missed this place," Wulf says. "And I was right. I almost died from the cold. I lost my flint when I jumped in, but even if I hadn't, there isn't any dry wood in here. It took me three days to discover there was a way out other than swimming."

I subtly check that I still have my flint in my pouch. There is some floating driftwood slapping against the ledge, but it would be impossible to set on fire. I look around the cave and don't see any other exits.

"Follow me," Wulf says. "Let me show you. Livvy, you'll have to leave your shield here. It isn't going to fit."

We follow Wulf up a short wall and then crawl on our bellies through a dark tunnel in the rock. Quibly cried out he was stuck at one point but managed to fit through it, although barely. After navigating over some slippery ledges, we arrive at the bottom of a tall cavern. The walls quickly narrow as they rise up. The sun's light is entering from the top, casting a flickering light onto the wet walls.

"It's easier than it looks," Wulf says, as he spreads his legs across the walls. "There's plenty of small ridges and ledges to step on."

"Why do we keep climbing up stuff?" Quibly complains.

"I'm going next," Thoren says. "I'm not risking you falling on me."

"I'm right after you," I say.

"Look, I'm just saying Wulf likes climbing things," Quibly continues. "It's from hanging out with that cat. It's not right."

"I'm right here," Wulf chimes in, looking down from above.

We slowly edge our way up the cavity in single file. The narrow walls make the climbing quite easy, but it doesn't stop Quibly from cursing the entire way up. I pull myself up the final rock and out through the opening. I look over the cliff, and the entrance to the sea cave is below me. Above me, the rocks climb higher.

"At the top of this bluff, we'll be able to see the fiord," Wulf says. "It's not too far, but the rock is wet so watch your footing."

My heart begins to race, but not from fear of slipping and falling down the face. I'm moments away from knowing if there's hope of seeing my brother alive. I'm light-headed and want to get sick. I take a slow, deep breath and follow Wulf up the bluff. Wulf reaches the top first. I'm right behind him. I step onto my final hold and peer over the edge to the fiord below.

CHAPTER 18

My heart is racing, and I tell myself to breathe. The gods heard my prayers. I should have never doubted them. I whisper, "Thank you," hoping they can somehow hear my voice. I also say one to Wulf's god, just in case.

There are at least two dozen dragon ships anchored in a wide harbor at the end of the narrow fiord. More are pulled up onto a beach. Dozens of tents are pitched on the white sand, and more than two hundred men are moving around busily. I'm too far away to see who they are or what they're doing, but this isn't a permanent settlement.

"They're here!" Quibly gasps as he pulls himself up with a groan. "Livvy, I knew you were right."

I doubt Quibly, or any of the others, actually thought the Danes would be here. Yet they believed enough in me to join me on this journey. I owe them a lifetime of thanks which I can never pay back. I grab Quibly's hand and squeeze it tight.

Below, the dragon ship sails are down, lying flat over the hulls, most likely to stop the birds from pecking at the food. The warriors won't be staying here for long.

"We don't know for sure if Grim's here," Thoren says, as she pulls up next to me.

Maybe not all my friends believed in me. I resist the urge to kick her feet off the ledge. "He's here," I say.

"This is a big army," Quibly says. "Much bigger than what attacked us. What are they doing here?"

"I don't know, but it doesn't change the plan," Thoren says.

"Great! I missed it," Wulf says. "What's the plan?"

"To kill Ivar the Boneless."

"You mean to save Grim!" I blurt out.

"You didn't let me finish."

I get that Thoren wants to see their leader dead. I do as well. But looking below, I don't see how that's possible without dying. We need a plan to find and rescue my brother without being seen. And I need to ensure Thoren sees it the same way. After Grim is safe, Thoren can do whatever she needs to do.

I can see the entire island from here. Perched on a ring of cliffs, it is almost round, like the top of a mushroom. The fiord is the only passage in, extending almost halfway inland. At the fiord's end, tents are pitched up on a flat beach where the army scuttles about. Above the sand, the land gently rises up to a green plain, which covers most of the interior. In the sea, I count thirteen smaller islands, and there are that many rock crags or more strewn between them.

"Now what?" Quibly mutters.

"We get closer and see who's here," Thoren says.

"I agree with Thoren," Wulf says. "But they'll see us if we do it now. We should go at dark."

Thoren doesn't argue, nor do I. It won't be a long wait, and it's better to be prepared than to die foolishly. We scramble down the bluff, picking up fallen branches from the thin birch trees along the way. We also find hardened sap on a few trees and scrape it off.

At the hamlet, we harvested the sap in the spring when it

ran like water from the trees. It's sweet and makes a very tasty drink, but it also makes a great fire starter, especially when the wood is wet. We reach the opening and throw the branches down the narrow shoot to the stone floor below.

"Hold on, I'll be right back," Wulf says. He climbs over the edge of the sea cliff and is out of sight before I can ask where he's going. Quibly and Thoren don't seem worried and they lie down to warm in the sun. I look at Iceland's mountain peaks across the sea. From here, they look small, like I could climb them in the morning before breakfast. I imagine I'm looking at Norseland.

Grim and I sail our dragon ship into a nestled cove at the edge of a thick oak forest. We wander through the trees until we reach a clearing. In the center stands a stone castle so grand that you could get lost for a day in its halls and chambers. A small wall surrounds it and the grass fields, keeping in the stock of horses and cows. The Thralls are busy making buttermilk and fetching honey from the hives.

"We are in luck!" My dream is interrupted.

I look down to see Wulf pop his head up over the cliff. His shirt is off and it's bundled in his hand like a skin bag. "Eggs!" he announces. "There are nests just below here."

He puts his shirt on the ground and carefully unfolds it. He has four eggs, each the color of goat's milk. They are larger than I would have expected given the size of the birds I've seen. I don't have an appetite but I'll need the energy, so I gulp mine down.

We descend the cavern and crawl back to the cave, starting a small fire with the branches we gathered. I lay my sheepskins on the flat rock, close to the flames, and Wulf sits next to me.

He wraps his skin over our backs.

"You two are getting close," Quibly prods.

"And you just noticed this now?" Thoren scoffs.

"We should focus on tonight," Wulf says. "I think Livvy has enough on her mind."

I knew this discussion would happen sooner or later. And although I don't need Wulf defending me, I'm happy he did it this *one* time. We need all our focus on rescuing Grim.

Wulf describes the route from the bluff down to the fiord. His settlement has long since burned and was located where the tents are now pitched. Wulf says there are plenty of trees and rocks to hide behind, and we should be able to get in close. And the sky is cloudy, so the darkness should conceal us well. We can't think of any reason for them to have guards watching the forest.

I didn't sleep at all, and I'm not sure anyone did. Wulf kept shifting, and I didn't hear Quibly's usual growls. I saw Thoren pacing at one point with her sword in her hand.

We gather our things and fumble our way in the dark to the top of the bluff. Below us, the fires are flickering throughout the camp. Even from here, we can hear the echoes of drunken men, singing and fighting.

"So this is what it feels like to be on the other side," Thoren says. "This time they are the ones eating and drinking, and we're the ones preparing the ambush."

"Let's not do anything we'll regret," Wulf suggests. "Tonight, we are only scouting."

"You aren't in charge here," Thoren says with contempt. "We didn't ask you to make this journey."

I can't risk Grim's life with a quarrel and cut in before it escalates further. "We all want the same thing. If it wasn't for Wulf, it would have taken us much longer to get here—if we got here at all. He will show us the way to the camp, and we'll scout it as we all agreed. Agree?"

"Agree," Quibly answers. He always has my back. Thoren, however, ignores me. It's as close to a yes as I'm going to get.

We cautiously follow Wulf down the rocky slope towards the tents. We eventually reach the water's edge without anyone tumbling down and breaking something. We move along the shores, staying in the shadows of the trees and stones, and soon reach the edge of the camp. We're within hearing distance of the first tents. At least ten men are drinking and laughing around a fire.

"Now what?" Quibly whispers.

"We move around the perimeter and look for Ivar," Thoren answers. She turns and looks at me. "If we find Ivar, we'll find Grim."

That's not necessarily true, but she's right in that the slaves are most likely with the nobles. I nod my approval, although I doubt she was asking for it. We circle the tents, keeping a safe distance away so that a snapped twig won't alert the enemy. We are less than halfway around when I spot a large tent near the center of the camp. It's about the size of the smithy in the fiord, maybe a little bigger. A white, woolen sail from a dragon ship hangs over its wooden frame. The black raven droops from the top over the sides.

"That looks like it," Thoren whispers as we crouch behind a rock. "We need to get in closer." A group of men are talking around a fire. They are too far away for me to see their faces. Three tents stand between us and the large one. "I'll go in alone," Thoren says.

"I'm going with you," I demand. "It's my brother we're here to rescue."

"No, you're not a warrior—"

"I'm going," I say, louder than I should.

She huffs and looks me over, as if she's assessing my skills for the first time. "Fine—but you're staying behind me." She catches Wulf and Quibly's attention. "If we get caught, I don't suggest you try and be heroes. We can all die today, but I don't see the point."

"We should stay together," Wulf insists.

"This isn't negotiable."

Wulf sees that he's not going to win this battle. "I'll keep my bow locked. If you get into trouble, I'm releasing it. *That* is not negotiable!"

Thoren draws her sword. "Let's go, warrior."

I pull out my seax and crouch low, following her onto the sand and behind the first tent. My heart is racing, but I'm not scared. This exact moment is why I'm here. This is my destiny. We stay low and quickly move forward behind the next tent. The men at the fire are closer. I slow down my breathing to listen.

Thoren holds up her hand as if to silence me. These men must be Ivar's. They have to be. Thoren grabs my arm and yanks me to the ground. She motions to an old log lying flat on the sand, dangerously close to the center tent. She crawls on her belly towards it. I follow her, without time to consider if it's foolish or not. We reach the fallen tree and lie tightly against it, shielded from the view from the tent but not from anyone who might walk by on this side of it. I hear their voices clearly now.

One sounds familiar – too familiar. I slowly raise my head, high enough that I can see over the log. I freeze.

I don't know how long I looked, but Thoren yanks me by the hair, pulling my head into the sand. We are too close for me to risk a whisper. Judging from the look on her face, she saw it all, too.

A hulking man, wearing a fur coat with a bear's head, stood towering over the others. His beard was red and braided down to the middle of his chest. A long sword was in a black sheath tied across his back. He was speaking in Norse. It's him. It's Ivar the Boneless.

Thoren motions back to the tree line. I want to lie still to grasp what I just saw, but I'm too exposed to stay here. We crawl back to the nearest tent with my thoughts in a clutter.

We're about to make a dash for the safety of the shadows when something catches my eye. Not far from the large tent stands a tree, with someone hunched at its base. At first, I think it's a man asleep, but this figure is small, like a child, and hanging forward unnaturally. Something isn't right. I can now see the rope tied around the head.

I feel sick and unsettled. Thoren tugs on my shoulder to go, but I push her hand away. *I must see who's tied to the tree.* I move in a little closer, ignoring the risk of being seen. I strain my eyes in the dark. A flare-up of the fire briefly casts a light on the tree, and the figure comes into focus. It can't be!

CHAPTER 19

Papar is alive, if only barely, and tied to the tree like an animal waiting to be slaughtered. He looks unconscious, his body held upright only by the rope around his neck. His chest is bare, and his ribs are poking through his skin. I want to run to him and cut him loose. I never thought I would wish him dead, but I do now. He must be praying to his god for it.

Thoren grabs my arm, and I let her pull me blindly to the trees. Wulf has his bow in hand with an arrow drawn, aiming it at the men laughing around the fire.

"Ivar is here," Thoren whispers to the boys. Wulf lowers his bow, and we retreat farther into the trees.

"Any sign of Grim?" Quibly asks.

"No, but Papar is here," Thoren answers.

"The priest? He's alive?"

"Somewhat."

"We should get back to the cave," Wulf urges. "It's going to get light soon."

I'm not ready to leave. If Papar is here, then so is Grim. I have to find him. I must see inside that tent. And we need to free Papar before he dies.

"I'm going to find Grim," I protest.

"We're going back," Thoren demands. "If they see you, we're all dead. I have a plan. Trust me."

I want to believe her, but Thoren's hunt for revenge may put my brother's life at risk. I doubt she even knows what Grim looks like. We are so close I can feel him. Wulf takes my hand. "We need to go, Livvy. We'll get him tomorrow."

I try and think of options, but my thoughts are all over the place. I give in but won't wait again. "Tomorrow—even if I have to do it alone," I demand.

Wulf squeezes my hand and assures me, "You won't be alone."

At the cave, we start another fire with the last of the branches and twigs. They won't burn for long, and we agree to get some sleep before the warmth fades. I'm both anxious and uneasy to hear Thoren's plan, but she's already shut her eyes. I lay my head on Wulf's chest, and he wraps his arm across mine. I try to sleep, but each time I close my eyes, all I see is Papar at the tree. I lightly nudge Wulf.

"I can't sleep," I whisper. He awakes and rolls over. "I can't stop thinking about Papar."

"He is like a father to you?" he asks with a yawn.

I think about it for a moment. "Yes, I guess he is. I never told anyone that."

He moves over closer. "What happened to your parents?"

This is another talk I've never had – at least not truthfully. But I feel safe with Wulf. "My mother died giving birth to Grim," I say. "My father took his life three years later. He wasn't able to live without her."

"He must have loved her a tremendous amount."

"Much more than Grim or me. I saw him do it. I can still remember that day as if it happened yesterday."

Wulf brushes his fingers through my hair. "Tell me."

I recall lying in my bed in the darkness. Grim was asleep next to me. "It was cold," I say. "More cold than usual. I felt the wind's chill as he opened the door to leave. When he didn't return, I got up and went outside. I didn't put on a fur coat as I wasn't planning to go far. I remember stopping to look up at the dancing pictures in the sky. I remember thinking they were more beautiful than usual. The gods were happy, I thought.

I saw fresh tracks in the snow and followed them. They took me to the top of the sea cliffs, a place I often played. My favorite game was to throw sticks into the water below and see how far I could count before they vanished. I would imagine that a large fish or the sea serpent swallowed them up.

I saw my father standing silently at the edge of the cliff. I thought he must have heard a sound and was looking for enemy ships. I almost shouted to him but feared he would scold me for disturbing him. So I decided to stay quiet and wait. Then he fell forward, without a sound. I screamed for Thor's help, but no gods came to his rescue. If only I hadn't stood there in silence."

I lie on my back, and Wulf continues to run his fingers through my hair. I try and make out the ceiling above me but all I see is blackness. Eventually, I'm just too tired to stay awake, and I fall asleep, only to relive that night one more time.

I sit up quickly and look around me. The boys are stirring, but she's gone. I jump to my feet and look about. "Where's Thoren?"

"I don't know," Quibly says, yawning. "She was gone when I woke up."

"I knew it. She's gone after Ivar. I'll kill her!"

I hear the scrape of boots against loose pebbles. "You can try, but you'll be the one dead." Thoren tosses a bundle of branches onto the rock ledge and climbs down the small wall.

"Sorry, I thought—"

"Yes, I heard you."

"I'm starving," Quibly says. "Wulf, can you show me where those nests are?"

"Sure. Livvy—"

"Go." I've been on my own a long time, and other than Papar, I haven't relied on a boy or man for anything since that cold, winter night.

The boys leave, and Thoren starts preparing a fire. I'm a little embarrassed she heard me, but I still don't trust she'll put Grim before her revenge. She takes out the stone to sharpen her sword.

"I shouldn't have assumed," I say.

"I wanted to kill him last night," she mumbles. "I wanted to attack while he stood by the fire laughing and gloating. We will find your brother. But I swear on Thor's hammer that I'll have my revenge. If this sword is as powerful as Wulf says it is, then I have nothing to fear."

"It's a special weapon. It may be made by men, but I think it came from the gods."

"Well, we are about to find out. We'll strike tonight," Thoren says.

"Thank you, Thoren. I can't wait another day to find Grim, and Papar may not live another."

"Rescuing the priest is not part of the plan."

I let her words sink in. I know her well enough now that she wasn't leaving room to negotiate anything different. But to her, Papar is nothing more than an annoyance. To me, he is family. "We thought he was dead until last night," I plead. "He helped Grim and me more than you'll ever know."

"The priest is old and weak. We won't get off this island if we take him, and that means your brother dies, too. And I won't risk angering Odin."

I need to find a way to save *both* Grim and Papar. I'll have to think of something on my own. "What's your plan?" I ask.

We are interrupted by the clatter of the boys returning. Why are boys so noisy? They walk loudly, eat and drink loudly, and even sleep loudly. Quibly is very pleased with himself and brought an entire nest, which he's crammed full of eggs. And he didn't complain this time about the climbing.

They finally settle down, and Thoren lays her sword across her legs. "Here's what we're going to do," she begins. "We need to draw the warriors away from their tents."

"How are we going to do that?" Quibly asks, cracking an egg into his mouth. "There are over two hundred men."

"By attacking."

"What?" Quibly questions, as he slurps the liquid down.

"By making them believe they're under attack." Thoren collects some twigs and creates a likeness of the island and the fiord on the stone ground. "We burn their ships." She places small stones where the ships are anchored. "The sails are down, draped over the hulls. Wulf, you can hide here, on the cliffs above the ships. You will light your arrows with fire and shoot them into the sails."

"How do we light an arrow on fire?" Quibly asks.

"With sap," Wulf answers. "It will make the arrows difficult to aim, but the sails are large targets. The sap should burn long enough to ignite the wool. If I get close enough, it should work."

"Good," Thoren says. "We'll go after midnight when the sky is at its darkest. We'll wait in the trees near the camp while Wulf goes to the cliff. When the Danes rush to the boats, we'll sneak into Ivar's tent and those around it. After we have Grim, I'm going after the demon. Oh, and Livvy agrees we leave the priest alone. We'll meet back here."

Quibly gives me a puzzled look. I know he's questioning why I would leave Papar tied to a tree. I'm not willing to do so, but I haven't thought of a plan yet.

Thoren and I go to collect sap from the birch trees, while the boys take the boat out to hunt for birds. Wulf is probably enjoying the companionship of another boy, having been alone for so long. For Quibly, I'm not sure, but perhaps he appreciates having an ally who's both a warrior and an equal. This wasn't the case at the hamlet. The Jarls and Karls were never equals. Regardless of the reasons, I'm happy to see them getting along.

Thoren and I go up the bluff for one last view of the camp. Men are loading the ships. The tents are still up, but the army is leaving soon. If it wasn't for Wulf's help getting here, I'm sure we would have missed them.

"Look!" Thoren grabs my arm and points up the fiord. More ships are coming. I count at least ten. There is no panic from the army on the shore. They were expecting these ships.

"Are they Danes?" I ask.

"I don't know, but the army is getting bigger. They aren't here looking for monks. They're preparing for battle."

"What do we do?"

"We stick to the plan. We kill Ivar, rescue Grim, and get out of here."

"You mean we rescue Grim, *then* kill Ivar."

"That's what I said. Now, let's get the birch sap. We have work to do." I take a breath and focus on the task at hand.

The boys beat us back to the cave and are plucking the feathers off one of the fat birds with the red beaks and the orange feet.

Quibly is quick to brag. "Wulf killed it on his first shot. I'm going to make one of these bows when we get back to the hamlet. Livvy, you can make me the arrow tips."

"Sure, Quibly," I say, but I don't mean it. There's nothing left at the hamlet for me. I'm never going back. After we get Grim, I'll talk to both Quibly and Thoren about going to Norseland. We need to get away from this island, even if we must battle the Shockheads. There must be kingdoms in Norseland that are still fighting Fairhair. When we get there, we'll find and join them.

I watch Wulf prepare the bird for the fire. I should learn how to cook these things, but I'll save that for another time. I smile, thinking Wulf is a better cook than me. Although, it wouldn't take much. I wonder if he'll join me in Norseland. I sure hope so.

After eating, Thoren offers to help Wulf prepare the arrows. I can use some time with Quibly. I haven't talked to him in days. I ask him to join me, and we go sit down in the row boat. It's much warmer today than yesterday, but I brought a sheepskin with me anyhow. I drape it over our legs.

"Grim will be there," Quibly assures me, wrapping his arm around me and pulling me in close.

"I know, but I'm still scared."

"Me, too."

"We must free Papar," I mutter. "We can't let him die like

this."

"I knew you wouldn't want him left like that. I'll go for him after we find Grim. He'll be too weak to run, but I can carry him."

"Thank you, Quibly. Thank you for everything."

"So what's with you and the Saxon boy?" he asks with a laugh.

I laugh with him. "I don't know. I really like him though."

"He told me he likes you, too. He asked me if you would consider leaving Iceland when this is all over."

"Yes, I would! Do you think he would go with me to Norseland? Would *you* go with us to Norseland?"

"He was thinking somewhere else."

"Where?"

"England."

CHAPTER 20

It's time. We coated the arrow tips with the tree sap. Wulf wrapped a hot ember in a piece of sheepskin. It will be much quicker for him to start a small fire with it than from a flint. We sharpened all of our weapons. Thoren has her sword secured in the sheath across her back. I hope its engraved letters are more than a fool's legend. Thoren seems sure of it. I'm bringing my seax and a small knife. Wulf has the other knife and his bow, and Quibly has the ax. My shield is too big to fit up the cavern, so I have to leave it. It's probably for the best. I hope to get in and out without engaging in a battle, and it would slow me down considerably.

Thoren gathers us around the fire. "Let us say our battle prayer to Odin." Thoren gets down on one knee, as do Quibly and I. It takes Wulf a moment to do the same.

"Hail, All-Father," she begins. "Wise warrior, one-eyed wanderer, come sit at our fire. You who chooses the slain, look on our deeds, and when our time comes to run the sky with you, let our end be worthy of song. But today, let us feel fury and joy. Let us understand sacrifice. Think long, remember well, and journey far, Odin. Witness this which we do as your servants."

"Let's do this!" Quibly shouts, jumping to his feet.

I lean over and whisper in Wulf's ear, "Say a quick prayer

to your god."

"I already did," he says.

We crawl up the wall, through the tunnel, and out the cavern to the air above. The stars are peeking through the holes in the clouds, but the moon is not out tonight. I don't remember if this is a good or bad omen for battle, but I decide not to ask Thoren in case I won't like the answer. We reach the top of the bluff and peer down to the fiord below. Although late, the camp is very much awake. There are more fires today than yesterday, and the clamor echoing off the cliffs is louder than before.

"This is where we part ways," Wulf says. "I'll give you plenty of time to reach the camp. May your gods be with you." He turns to leave, but I grab his arm. I reach up and kiss him on the lips. This time they aren't salty at all. "Good luck, Livvy," he smiles. "I'm looking forward to meeting Grim."

"You will like him," I say. "And may your god be with you." Wulf disappears into the darkness.

We climb down the slope and into the trees. We make our way around the camp towards Ivar's tent. I hear voices and motion the others to stop.

"It's Norse," I whisper. "It doesn't sound Dane."

"Yes, I hear it," Thoren says. I move in closer to the fires, and the others follow. I watch my feet, being careful not to step on a branch or kick a rock. I hope Quibly is doing the same.

I stop and crouch low, looking through the last of the branches between us and the camp. Men are laughing loudly around a fire. The hair on their heads is long, at least halfway down their backs. They are wearing fur skins with the heads still attached. Their faces are covered in ink. Most have iron necklaces dangling over their necks and wrapped around their arms.

"Shockheads," Thoren whispers.

The Shockheads are here? I watch the men as I slow down my thoughts. Maybe the Shockheads ran out of kingdoms in Norseland to plunder and now want Iceland. Something big is happening — something much greater than ridding Iceland of a few monks. Papar would have heard or seen something. It's another reason we need to save him.

"It was the Shockheads' ships that rowed in today," Thoren says. "We need to keep moving."

She's right. Wulf will soon be above the boats and there's no turning back. We continue through the trees and reach the spot by the center tent where we hid last night. The old log from yesterday is gone. There's a small fire burning, but the area is quiet. I squint my eyes and look for Papar.

"He's not here," I whisper.

Quibly looks towards the tree. "It doesn't mean he's dead," he says. "They didn't bring him all the way here just to watch him die. They have him for a reason." I hope he's right, but after seeing the old man yesterday, I'm not so sure.

The trees are blocking our view of the sea and the boats. Our signal will be if the Danes, and now the Shockheads, rush to the ships. All we can do is wait. My stomach feels sick, thinking Papar may be with his god. Quibly is breathing hard. I notice I am as well. Thoren appears calm and focused. She's been in battles before, but this is my first — unless you count the ambush at the hamlet a battle. I think of the things Thoren taught me. Be calm and focused. Make your first strike count.

Voices are approaching. Through the branches, I see the red hair. Ivar the Boneless is back. His arms are wrapped around two girls, one on each side. He's wearing his fur, but this time the animal head is on top of his own. I imagine the mighty bear standing on its back legs would not look much different. Ivar's sword is tucked in his belt. A warrior is always prepared with his weapon. He goes into the tent with the girls. Thoren has a tight grip on her sword. I suddenly realize my seax is still in its sheath! I slowly pull it out.

"Good for you to finally join the fight," Thoren whispers, glancing over her shoulder. I'm angry at myself but have no excuses. I vow not to let this happen next time – that is, if there is one.

We continue to wait. There are no sounds from the tent, and no more men, or girls, come or go. The camp is beginning to quiet down. The sky is dark but it won't stay this way for long. It must be well past midnight. Why hasn't Wulf shot the arrows? Something's happened to him. I can't just sit here.

"We are running out of time," I whisper.

"Just wait," Quibly pleads. "Wulf will come through."

"Livvy's right," Thoren says. "It's time to go."

"Ivar's still in there," Quibly argues. Thoren gets up and crouches below the branches, ignoring his concern. She motions for us to join her.

"I was just saying he's in there, like it's a good thing," Quibly says with a forced grin.

"I'm glad you see it my way," Thoren says, focused on the tent in front of us. "Follow me."

Thoren takes a step towards the tent just as a voice hollers in the distance. She quickly retreats. Another voice shouts, and then another. Within moments the camp is awake. Men and women dash out of their tents and run towards the shore, all with weapons in hand. Wulf did it! Now it's time to get Grim. I keep my eyes on the wool door.

Ivar the Boneless steps cautiously out of the tent. His shirt is off, and he's holding a sword. His weapon appears as long as I am tall. The Danes' leader looks much larger today than yesterday. His arms and chest are massive.

Ivar slowly spins around, checking his surroundings. He pauses when he looks in our direction, and I stand motionless, afraid to blink or breathe. I'm staring into his eyes. His face is wide and long, and his red beard is tied in a braid, hanging down over his chest. His eyes dart away as he turns around. On his back is the raven, just as Thoren said. It's not painted, but rather cut or burned into his flesh. It appears to be swelling out of his skin.

If Wulf were here, he would have a clean shot with an arrow. Thoren wouldn't be pleased if he made it, she was clear on this, but I wish he were here to do it nonetheless.

Ivar takes off towards the sea in long, quick strides. Thoren races towards the tent. I lunge out to grab her, but she's out of reach. I run after her. Quibly is right behind me.

Thoren stops at the closest tent. She watches Ivar disappear into the swarm of warriors. I look in the same direction. I can now see the ships on fire, and the men are already working to extinguish them. Black steam is billowing into the air. I turn back to Ivar's tent. It is less than ten paces away. Men and women are rushing through the camp, but they're focused on the fires. Our path to the tent looks clear.

This is my destiny, not Thoren's. "He's my brother, I'm going in first," I say.

I can see on Quibly's face that he doesn't like it, but he also knows what I have to do. "We'll be right behind you," he assures me.

I still don't know what the seer meant about a shield maiden uniting the gods. I could be a fool, and Quibly would think so if I told him my dream, but I can't change my destiny, whatever it is.

"I'm ready. Let's go," I say. I take one last deep breath and run to the tent. A white, wool sheet covers the entrance. Quibly and Thoren crouch on either side. I don't hesitate. I push it open with my seax and step into the dim room.

Numerous lit candles are on the floor, casting a flickering of light against the tent walls. A bed covered with skins is in the middle of the room, and next to it are clay jars and bowls of food. Armor and steel weapons are strewn about.

"Grim," I whisper. "Grim," I say louder. I feel Quibly and Thoren now behind me. It takes me a brief moment to adjust to the change in darkness. The girls are huddled at the back of the tent with skins tucked up to their chins. They are younger than me. One looks briefly into the far corner, and I quickly follow her eyes, tightening the grip on my seax. Papar lies slumped on the floor.

The rest of the tent is empty. I rush over to my old friend. His small hands are tied together and his eyes are closed. I kneel in front of him and put my hands on his face. "Papar," I say. "Papar, it's me, Livvy."

He lifts his head and slowly opens his eyes. "Is that you?" he says. His voice is weak and frail. "How?"

"Yes, it's me. Quibly and Thoren are here, too. We're going to get you out of here, but you need to tell me where Grim is."

Quibly helps Papar sit up, and Thoren watches both the girls and the wool door. I cut the ropes loose with my knife, while Quibly gives him a drink from one of the jars.

"We have to go, Livvy. Now!" Thoren barks.

"Papar, where's Grim? We don't have time. Where is he?"

"The children," Papar wheezes. He swallows and clears his throat. "The children are tied up in the boats."

It takes a moment for his words to sink in. No—No! What have we done? I can't catch my breath. I imagine the boats burning in my head, and hear Grim screaming, unable to escape the flames and smoke. I turn to rush out of the tent, but Thoren jumps in my way.

"Move!" I shout.

"Keep your voice down," Thoren orders.

I try and sidestep her, but she matches my move and grabs my shoulders. "I need to get to the boats!"

"Running down there will do nothing but get us killed," she says calmly. "The rescue is over—for now. They are looking for us. You and Quibly need to get out of here."

"Quibly and I?"

"I'm going to kill Ivar. This was the deal."

"The deal was to rescue my brother first. I'm going after Grim!"

"No, you aren't."

"Get out of my way!" I shout, pushing my way past her. Thoren grabs onto my wrist. I think of using my seax but hold back the urge to swing it at her.

Quibly pushes his way between us. "Take her with you, Thoren," he says. "I'll take Papar to the cave."

"Fine," Thoren snaps. She lets go of my wrist and steps

past me towards the wool door. She opens it slowly and peeks outside.

I look at the engraving on Thoren's sword. If there is any chance the blade has magic in it, then I must have it. If I can get her to set it down, I can take it and run. Runa was waiting for me, not her, so why isn't the weapon mine?

I remember now what the seer gave me. I take the leather pouch off my belt and open it. The black herbs inside are the size of barley seeds. *Take them when your fear is at its greatest.* I remove a small handful and toss them into my mouth. They taste bitter and disgusting, far worse than any rock moss I've eaten. I swallow them down and spit the loose bits out. I feel nothing except the urge to vomit.

"There are too many men outside," Thoren says, closing the wool door shut. "This is a bad idea."

"I'll go out the back," Quibly says. He doesn't wait for approval. "Papar, I hope this doesn't hurt too much." Quibly effortlessly lifts him up by the waist and flops him over his shoulder like a bag of grain. Papar grunts in pain. Quibly holds onto his legs with one arm and picks up his ax with the other.

"I'll be back after I get Papar to the cave," he says. Thoren and I lift up the sail at the back of the tent, and Quibly ducks under it.

"I'll see you soon," I say.

"Just find Grim." He and Papar disappear into the trees.

Quibly will get Papar safely to the cave. I know he will. And I must get to the boats. The girls still haven't moved, and it's clear they don't understand anything we're saying. It occurs to me they'll give us away the moment we leave.

"What do we do with them?" I ask quickly.

"We could kill them," Thoren says, smirking.

I don't think she is serious, but I don't know anymore. "No, we aren't going to kill them."

Both girls are crying, likely knowing we are deciding their fate. Thoren motions them to be quiet and slides her finger across her throat. I doubt the threat will keep them quiet for long, but I don't have time to think of a better idea.

Thoren hurries to the entrance and slowly pushes the cloth aside. Immediately, she jumps and moves swiftly back, pushing me behind her as she goes. I step hard onto one of the girl's legs, and she lets out a scream. It doesn't matter if she made a noise or not, for the wool door flings open. At first, I see the dark silhouette, and then the blade. Ivar the Boneless ducks his head and steps into the tent.

CHAPTER 21

I suddenly feel the blood shooting through my veins. My arms and eyes begin to burn with pain, almost as if catching on fire. Ivar looks at us, then at the girls, and then at the empty corner where Papar was tied. He's a giant. The top of my head is no taller than his chest, and his arms are as big as my legs.

His eyes look confused, but it doesn't last for long. He lowers his sword to his side and begins to laugh. At first, it's only a snicker, but now it's loud and bellowing. My hands and legs are shaking but not from fear. I don't feel sick or weak. I feel fearless – stronger than I've felt in my entire life. I want to push Thoren aside and fight this troll myself. My arms are burning hotter as if they're blistering. I quickly look down to see if they're on fire.

Ivar's laugh weakens to a chuckle. The sound of that awful voice brings me back to his ship. He takes a deep breath from behind his red, braided beard. "I'm a fool," he says slowly. "I thought I was under attack. But then I was confused because there's no one left to attack me. Now, I see it was my own slaves. You must have been very motivated, or very stupid, to come here. But now that you're here, I have a decision to make. Do I kill you, or do I give you to my men?"

Ivar looks again to the corner of the tent. "But first, where's the priest? The Saxon is very important to me."

My hands are shaking worse, and I grip my seax as tight as I can. I want to fight! "We don't know who you're talking about," I say, stepping out from behind Thoren. I raise my seax into my battle position.

Ivar laughs loudly again as if daring me to fight. "I'm happy you're awake," he chuckles. "That's it! I've made my first decision."

"I'll trade you the priest for one of the slave boys," I shout out.

"Is that what this is about?" Ivar laughs. His voice is now loud and angry. "You came all this way to die for a little boy? How about I burn them one by one until you tell me where the Saxon is!"

My urge to attack is overwhelming. It's now in control of me, and I can no longer hold myself back. I lunge forward with my seax, aiming for his neck. He strikes my hand with his arm, jolting the weapon from my fingers. His other arm immediately hits my side, knocking me off my feet. My back hits the ground, and then my head bounces hard off the earth. I try to get my legs underneath me, but I fall back down. Everything is blurry. Something is wrong with me! Helplessly, I look up.

Thoren swings her sword, but Ivar steps back, easily evading the blade. He raises his own sword and strikes back. The clash of metal on metal echoes through the tent. The frightened girls are screaming. Thoren has both hands on her weapon and is barely defending his onslaught, retreating backward with each blow. I try again but still can't get to my feet.

Ivar rears back and swings hard. Thoren's sword flies from her hand, and she falls backward to the earth. She scrambles to get up, but Ivar's already standing over her. He doesn't hesitate. Ivar heaves his sword up with two hands and thrusts it down.

Thoren screams. The sound pulls the air from my lungs. This can't be happening! Thoren is writhing on the ground, reaching hopelessly for her sword. Ivar calmly picks it up. He holds her weapon out and studies it as he turns the blade over.

"I thought so," he snarls. "Today is just full of surprises." He turns and steps towards me, with one sword in each hand. "Now what do I do with you?" He picks up my seax and tosses it from the tent as if it were a small stick.

"I hope you die in a snake pit, just like your father!" I shout. Ivar squats down and grabs my cheeks and chin with his huge hand. He squeezes hard and looks straight into my eyes, almost bewildered. The bones in my faces are going to be crushed into tiny pieces.

"Well, isn't this interesting," he growls. "What witch have you befriended?" He releases his grip.

"I'll see you in Niflheim," I say, spitting at his face. "Odin will have no place for you in Valhalla."

"Odin is going to be very pleased with what I'm about to do," he grins. He wipes the spit off his face.

Ivar turns around as the wool curtain flings open. Two men rush in. They stop suddenly and half-turn back to the entrance as if apologizing for interrupting their leader. They're carrying spears and breathing hard.

Ivar calls one over, and the man speaks in his ear. Ivar hollers at the girls, and they scurry from the tent with their sheepskins covering their chests. He gives Thoren's sword to one of his men.

"You didn't come alone," Ivar smirks. "My priest is being

carried up a cliff. We'll get him and his donkey friend, and then we'll have some more—how do you say—excitement?" He storms out of the tent.

One warrior points his spear at my neck. The other has the sword aimed at Thoren's chest. I feel my ribs and cringe. At least one is broken. My eyes hurt badly, but my sight seems to be improving. I need to get out of here. I turn to see if Thoren is alive. This is all my fault. I don't know what overcame me.

"Thoren," I call out. "Can you hear me?" A warrior shouts for me to shut up, but he's not going to kill me unless he has to. He won't risk the inevitable punishment if he spoils his master's game.

"Yes," Thoren groans. She is still alive.

"How bad is it?" I ask, worried to hear the answer.

"Through the shoulder." She grunts as she turns from her side to her back. The man above her yells, "Quiet!"

"If you are going to use it, then use it!" Thoren screams. The warrior doesn't know what to do.

"Ivar had the same one," Thoren groans.

"Same what?"

"The sword—the same symbols." The wool door flings open again. There's no one there. Our guards shout towards the opening. They argue before one hurries to the entrance and peers outside.

The warrior crumbles to the ground. An arrow is stuck deep into his neck. Thoren's sword falls from his hand. The other warrior yanks me up. My legs are now feeling stronger, at least enough to hold my weight. He pulls a knife from his belt and presses the blade against my throat.

Wulf steps in front of the tent's opening, an arrow locked in his long bow and resting against his cheek. The warrior yells, pulling his knife tighter against my throat. The sharp blade is cutting through my skin. I stand on my toes and hold my breath to keep it from digging in deeper.

Wulf steps slowly into the tent. The warrior yells at him and retreats, pulling me with him. Wulf is adjusting his aim, but the arrow looks to be pointed straight at my head. I think I trust him, but that doesn't mean he can make the perfect shot. The Dane is hidden well behind me, and a sudden flinch could put the arrow through my eye and not his.

I think of what I can do, but I'm too paralyzed with the knife against my throat. Suddenly, I'm jolted forward, and the warrior drops his knife. He collapses, grabbing at my clothes as he falls to the ground. Wulf's arrow is still locked in his bow. I quickly turn around to see Thoren standing behind me. She winces in agony and drops to her knees.

Wulf lowers his bow and rushes in. "We need to go!" he shouts, looking hurriedly at Thoren's wound.

"The children were in the boats," I say in a panic.

"I kept clear of them," Wulf says. "They're okay."

I rush to him and wrap my arms around his neck, wincing in pain as my ribs press against his. "Thank you," I say.

Wulf leans back with a look of confusion before turning to Thoren. "Let's go!"

Thoren slowly gets to her feet and retrieves her sword. She hands it to me. We sneak out the entrance and run as fast as we can to the trees. My legs almost buckle, but I keep them beneath me. I forget to pick up my seax, but there's no going back. I try and take short quick breaths to lessen the jabbing pain in my side.

"Quibly is taking Papar to the cave," I say quickly between breaths. "The Danes went after them."

"We have to go another way," Wulf says. "Pray to your gods that they make it." We have to live to fight another day. Going to the boats now will be certain death. As long as Grim is still alive, we can regroup.

We follow Wulf through the forest and wind up the cliffs. Once above the tree line, I turn to look for the boats. The camp is moving like ants on a hill, and fires are coming to life. Half a dozen dragon ships are smoldering, and the air above them is blackened with smoke. Wulf made a useful distraction, but that's all it was. The ships don't look damaged beyond repair, and there are dozens more untouched. I strain to look for the children, but it's dark, and I'm too far away to distinguish a man from a child. We need a new plan to get Grim, and we need to come up with it quickly.

Wulf takes his shirt off and wraps it tightly around Thoren's shoulder to slow the bleeding. Within moments it's completely saturated in blood. He leads us along the cliffs, and we reach the cavern entrance. I'm feeling more in control of my thoughts. The hit to my head on the ground must have rattled my skull.

Thoren is covered with sweat, and her body is the color of the dead. She's not going to make it much farther. There are no signs of Quibly or Papar. I don't know what I'll do if Quibly is captured. I can't imagine what Ivar will do to him, and it will be entirely my fault.

We quickly descend into the darkness. Thoren loses her footing a few times, but we reach the bottom without a fall. As long as the Danes don't hear us, they won't look for us down here. Wulf helps Thoren over the ledges and through the tunnel.

It's not like her to accept help, but today she's not turning it away.

As we near the sea cave, I shout out Quibly's name. The only voice I hear back is my own, bouncing off the rock walls. "Quibly!" I shout again.

"Livvy!" echoes a faint, hollow voice in return. I scamper down the last ledges and the short wall. Quibly is standing at the bottom, and Papar is lying on a sheepskin near the boat. "I was just about to—" Quibly stops short when he sees the blood-soaked shirt around Thoren's shoulder. "What happened?" he exclaims.

I quickly tell the events in the tent.

"I should have stayed and killed the bastard," Quibly fumes. "Thank you, Wulf for saving my girls—Liv, you look hurt."

"I broke a rib or two. I'll live."

"What about your eyes?" he asks.

"What do you mean?"

"They're red, like the eyes of a dragon."

I rub them with both hands. That's why everyone's been looking at me strangely. They still hurt, but the watering has all but stopped. "I think I reacted from the herbs," I say.

"The herbs?" Quibly questions.

"Something Runa gave me."

"What?" he roars. "You ate something the witch gave you? Are you mad? Not to alarm you, but the Berserkers' eyes looked just like yours."

"It's just a reaction," I dismiss. I don't want to talk about it anymore. We need a new plan to get Grim.

Quibly puts a sheepskin next to Papar for Thoren to lie on and sits next to her. He looks her wound over. Papar doesn't look well and is going into and out of consciousness.

"You told Ivar you were looking for a child," Thoren groans. "Good luck now."

She's right. What was I thinking? I wasn't. The herbs did something to me. I couldn't think straight. I just wanted to kill. Quibly may have been right about Runa all along. Maybe everything she said was trickery. Loki is a shape-shifter. Perhaps Loki was disguised as the seer.

"We'll think of something," Wulf says. "But we need to stay hidden for a little while. You can't save him if you're dead. Someone very smart told me that once."

Taking those seeds wasn't smart at all. Our only advantage was the Danes didn't know we were here. We lost our opportunity, possibly the only one we'll have. I should have scouted the camp better. I'm sick to my stomach.

"Livvy, I need this wound closed," Thoren says. "Quibly, start a fire."

"What do you want me to do?" I ask. I'm nervous as I already know the answer.

"Heat the sword and seal the wound with it."

"Thoren, I can't do this."

"Yes, you will," she says. "I'll die if you don't, and you're the best one here with metal and fire."

"I've never done something like this. You need a healer."

"Do you see a healer anywhere? I can't do it myself. Heat the sword and press it against the wound until I stop bleeding. Simple."

Papar reaches out to me, and I take his small hand in mine. "You can do this, Livvy," he says. His words are quiet and barely reach me. I forgot how much I needed him. I'm so thankful that he's alive.

"Okay, Thoren. I'll try my best," I say.

Quibly is already gathering the last of the branches to start the fire. He's acting more nervous than I feel. Although we're on the other side of the cliffs that face the camp, Wulf is concerned about the smoke giving away our position. It's still dark, but his worry is a real one. He decides to row the boat out of the cave to see where the smoke moves. Papar is sitting up now, resting against the cave wall. I'll ask him later about the Danes and the Shockheads. He's too feeble to talk and needs rest.

"The sword looks ready," Quibly says.

Thoren got hurt helping me. She never betrayed me, and I feel shameful that I thought she might have. I need to do this for her. I unwrap Wulf's shirt from her shoulder to see what I'm dealing with. The wound is between her shoulder and chest, and gurgles blood when she moves. From the strength which Ivar came down with his sword, the cut must be deep. I ask Quibly to press the shirt on it while I check the sword.

I've seen many wounds, and the blood doesn't bother me, but I'm not a healer. The hamlet healers were all women, but that doesn't give me any advantage over the boys here. I've seen healers bind minor wounds, but these were mostly from training or from games that went too far. The significant injuries, including those needing fire, such as the loss of limbs, were treated in a closed house – a house which I've never entered. Godi paid both the healers and the injured a bone-payment in compensation. The greater the injury, the more they were paid. Thoren and I would both be paid well for this one.

Wulf is back and gives Thoren a thick branch to bite down

on. The sword is a dark gray and is plenty hot to burn flesh.

"Let's get this over with," Thoren winces.

I kneel down and carefully position the sword over the wound. Quibly removes the shirt and grabs both Thoren's hands in his. I try and find a place where I won't burn too much of the living flesh. Thoren bites down on the branch and squeezes Quibly's hands. I don't know who's worried more, Thoren or me. Here I go.

CHAPTER 22

Thoren has been resting since yesterday, although I doubt she slept much. I thought she might have died when I burned her the second time. When she woke, she cursed that the cave wasn't Valhalla. Quibly then covered one eye with his hand, pretending he was Odin, and asked for her mortal hand in marriage. He said he saw a slight smile, but I suspect he was in a spell again.

A tear fell down Quibly's cheek when Thoren screamed. He cares for her a lot, and it's much more than a boy's infatuation with beauty and nobility. Quibly has always cared for others more than himself. He's been sitting quietly with her all morning, attempting to carve arrows with the last of the branches, despite not having any spare iron tips to attach them to.

Papar is looking worse. His hacking cough sounds like that of the old ones who died from the sickness the winter before last. All of the seer's herbs and magic couldn't save them. And the black seeds from Runa aren't going to help Papar. The last thing Papar needs is an overpowering urge to fight.

I tuck the skin tightly around my old friend's frail body and sit quietly with him. Wulf went out on the boat last night and killed another bird. He's amazing with his bow. No archers in the hamlet could do what he does. We cooked the bird in the last of the embers and haven't started a fire since. The Danes may still be searching the waters, and we can't take any risks of being discovered. We tried giving Papar some of the meat to eat, but he was unable to keep it down.

Wulf sits next to me. It's time. Papar slept most of the day, but we need to find out what he knows.

"Papar, are you well enough to talk?" I ask. He attempts a smile and nods. "We saw both the Danes and Shockheads. Do you know why they're here or where they're going?"

"England," Papar wheezes. He breathes in deep, capturing just enough air to get his next words out. "Godi wouldn't join them."

The last kingdom standing in England – the Danes and Shockheads must be joining armies to attack it. Ragnar Lothbrok and his sons conquered the other ones. Godi hated Fairhair and the Shockheads. He would never join them. Our chieftain wasn't motivated by the promise of treasures or land. And he died a horrible death as a result.

"Wulf is a good friend and he's helping us," I say. "He's from England. The Danes conquered most of England except his kingdom."

"Wessex," Papar wheezes again. Wulf leans in close to Papar and speaks to him in his Saxon language. This is the first time I've heard Wulf speak Saxon, and it sounds much nicer than I thought it would.

"I told Papar that Wessex was home and I was taken as a slave," Wulf says.

I hold Papar's hand. It's as cold as the stone I'm sitting on. "Why did the Danes take you?" I ask.

"I speak Saxon," he says, unable to stop a painful bout of

coughing. I help him lie down, and we sit in silence until he falls asleep. My old friend, my guardian, reminds me of home but mostly of Grim. I can't help but cry. I want to return the kindness he gave me, but I don't know how to help him.

Wulf and I decide we'll scout the camp tomorrow at first dawn before the army awakes. This time, they'll have guards at the perimeter and most likely on the cliffs. Quibly agrees to stay back to watch Papar and Thoren. Hopefully, Ivar's army has given up its search. I haven't thought of a new plan to rescue Grim, but I hope seeing the camp will help. If they leave for England, I'll never see Grim again. That can't happen.

I didn't sleep any better last night than the night before, but I can hardly complain. A broken rib is a slight annoyance compared to what Thoren and Papar are going through. I reach over to wake Wulf, but he's not there. I sit up and look around. He and Thoren are talking quietly in the row boat. I slowly get up and go to them. They stop talking as I approach, like I've interrupted something. Now that I think of it, this isn't the first time.

"It's good to see you up, Thoren," I say. "How do you feel?" Wulf's shirt is wrapped in a sling around Thoren's shoulder, supporting her arm. He must have made it for her this morning.

"I'm still alive," she answers. "Thank you for yesterday. You did well." She gets out of the boat and walks slowly back to her sheepskin. She picks up the sword with her good arm. "You should take your sword with you today," she says.

"*My* sword?"

"It was meant for you."

"Your sheath was on the grave, and you found it," I say.

"Runa wanted you to have it."

"No, she didn't want me to have it, not that I haven't wished she did. Runa talked to me in my dream that night. I was flying high in the heavens as if I could reach out and touch Asgard. She told me *you* were the one she was waiting for. You are her shield maiden. I wanted to believe that it was just a dream, but Freya speaks through the seers, and the seers don't lie."

"You've seen me train—and fight," I say. "I can't fight like you."

"It's not up to you and me to decide our destinies. We don't know what would have happened if the sword was in your hand and not mine. You're fast and you're fearless, although a bit reckless at times," she says, with a grin. "Runa asked me to help you. This is me helping you. If you die, I'll take the sword back. I promise you that." She hands the weapon to me, and I hesitantly accept it.

"Thank you," I say. "It's yours as soon as you want it back."

"But that means you're dead, so let's not be in such a hurry. Take the leather sheath as well. It won't fit into that tiny thing on your belt."

I sling the sheath over my shoulder and move the sword through the air. For a moment, I'm slaying Sigurd's dragon. But I'll need to rescue Grim first, and that means getting through Ivar the Boneless. It didn't work out so well for Thoren.

The sun is rising quickly. Wulf and I leave, and we ascend the cavern and the rocky bluff above it. We don't speak much, and when we do we whisper, for there could be scouts anywhere. We reach the ridge and peer over once again. I gasp as I desperately look up and down the fiord.

"They can't be gone," I say in denial. But the ships are nowhere in sight, and except for the fire pits and burned debris, the beach is empty.

"I'm sorry, Livvy," Wulf says.

There's no more need to whisper. I feel the tears dripping down my face but am too exhausted to sob. Grim is gone and I failed him. I'm overwhelmed with anger – at Ivar, at the gods, but mostly at myself.

I don't remember how we got back to the cave, but Quibly is waiting for us, his eyes swollen and red with tears. At first, I'm confused how he knows, but then his words hit me like a stone. "He's with his god."

I rush to Papar, hoping Quibly was wrong or I misunderstood. The old man is lying on his sheepskin, his eyes closed as if asleep. I whisper for him to wake up, and then again louder, but he's no longer in this realm. Wherever he is, I want to join him. If the gods are not on my side, maybe his will be.

My friends sit down with me. We don't talk. Papar was my guardian light. It would have been easier for both of us if he had died in his bed the night of the feast. Instead, he suffered in pain at the hands of Ivar the Boneless. I wish more than anything that I had a moment to say goodbye and tell him thank you.

My journey to save Grim from a life as a slave is finished. I can pray that my little brother will somehow escape, but the gods don't listen to me. I'm lost for where to go and how to live without him. I don't want to stay in Iceland, but without Grim, there's nothing for me in Norseland either. The castles, and the feasts of honey and buttermilk, are nothing but a dream. They aren't real. The Shockheads rule that land now. And they'll rule this one, too, if they don't already.

Wulf takes my hand. I don't know if this thing between us is real and what it means. I pull my hand away and wipe the tears from my eyes. I look over at Quibly. Our friendship will never be broken, but he wants to return to the hamlet, and I can never go back there.

I don't know how long we sat in silence, but it's time. "We need to bury him," I say. "He would want to be in the dirt, not under stones. That's how they buried their own. Where can we do this? I don't want to take him to the beach."

"There's a small island a short row away," Wulf says. "It's a perfect spot for him."

"Okay. Let's take him there," I say. I assume the sooner we get him to his god the better. We wrap Papar in the sheepskin and lay him in the bottom of the boat.

I sit at the bow, and Thoren sits at the stern. She hasn't said a word since we returned from the bluffs. Her family, too, is gone, as is her opportunity for revenge. Where will she go? If her shoulder doesn't heal well, she won't be able to look after herself. It will be near impossible to fish, build a shelter, and protect herself with one arm. As a noble, she would have the Thralls do this for her, but her nobility means nothing now. Perhaps it is Quibly's destiny to look after her. He would do it if she would let him.

We leave the cave. The clouds have lifted, and the warm sun is high above us. The sea doesn't worry about battles and death. The seals are still hunting for their fish, and the birds are still squawking and cawing.

The island isn't far and it's small as Wulf said. Like Westman, it's perched on cliffs, but they aren't nearly as high. The land above them is shaped like a bent bow, with the low dirt in the middle and the steep dirt on the outer edges. Green grass covers the ground, and a few scraggly birch trees grow near the edges.

We tie the boat to a tree at the base of a short cliff. Quibly and I carry Papar up to the grass above. He's as light as a small child. Wulf offers to help, but this is something that I need to do. I find a spot where the dirt looks thick, and we set Papar down. With Quibly's ax and the edge of my shield, we dig a grave. Thoren and Wulf gather wood for a fire.

We'll return to the sea hamlet tomorrow. I need to get as far away from Westman as possible. From there, we'll each decide where to go. The seer's prophecy of the shield maiden was a lie. My destiny is to have all those near me die. Wulf can return to his knoll, and maybe to Jóra. It's best we go our separate ways. Thoren and Quibly can return to our hamlet. I don't know where I'll go.

I look up towards Iceland and at the fire flowing down from Katla. There are no demons in the fire mountain. And there are no giants hiding in the snow fields that surround it. Around us, there isn't a sea serpent lurking to stop us from visiting the other realms. If our gods live, they are far from here. We live in a place where men do as they please. They take and kill as they see fit. The gods do nothing.

Wulf and Thoren return and help us put Papar in the hole. "I want Papar to have a Christian farewell," I say. This is the one thing I can do for him. "Wulf, do you know what custom we should follow?"

"A priest will usually repeat a few words from his god. They are written in a book."

"Do you know any of these words?" I ask.

178

"I know a few, yes."

"Will you say them?"

"I'm not a priest and I'm hardly qualified to say the last words to a dead man."

"Please. What harm can come of it?" My eyes begin to swell with tears.

"Very well," he says. "I'll do it for you, but I may not get all the words right."

"How do we begin?" I ask.

"First, we hold hands together and then we close our eyes." We all do as he says.

"God shall wipe away every tear from Papar's eyes," he says quietly. "And death shall be no more. Neither shall there be mourning, nor crying, nor pain anymore, for the former things have passed away. Amen."

Wulf falls silent.

"Is that it, Wulf?" Quibly asks. I open my eyes, and everyone else has already done the same.

"Yes, that's it, Quibly."

"The Christian farewells are much shorter than ours," Quibly says. "If it wasn't for the lack of a feast, I think I would like them better."

"Thank you, Wulf," I say. I feel less anxious. We all die eventually. Although, people close to me seem to die quicker than most. Maybe I've been praying to the wrong god. I wonder if Papar's would take Grim and me.

Quibly and I put the dirt back in the hole. Wulf makes a wooden cross, a smaller replica of what hung from the back of the monastery, and sticks it in the ground at the top of the grave.

"He's with God now," Wulf says with a sound of

completeness. Yes, I believe he is.

The next morning, Iceland is hidden completely behind a veil of dark clouds. Above us, the birds are out to play, flying motionless in the gusting wind. The sea is being pushed in all directions, with each wave crashing upon itself in a tantrum of white and black. We decide we have no choice but to leave. Thoren's wound looks vile and smells just as bad. Wulf says there's a healer at the sea hamlet who can help her, and it's best we get her there soon. I don't know how a sword wound burned with steel normally looks, but it can't look worse than hers. Thoren isn't sweating with sickness, but if it starts, death will quickly follow. If she dies, it will be my fault.

The boys row, and I sit on the bow facing towards Westman. As soon as we're separated from the small island, the waves toss us about at their will. I grip the splintering wood on the side of the hull to keep from slamming into it. Our little boat is squeaking and crackling, like young wood on a fire, and I'm afraid it may disintegrate into the sea. I look into the choppy water for a big fish, wondering if they're waiting patiently below for their breakfast. For a moment, I want to turn back to Westman, but then I think of Grim. A few unpleasant moments sinking into the cold water is an easier path to the next life than what he must endure.

Although I see it emerging from behind Westman, it takes me a moment to realize what I'm looking at. At first, I say "a ship" almost under my breath, and then I yell it. The boys look up, and Thoren spins around. A dragon ship, with its white sail flapping hard in the wind, is heading towards us.

"Can they see us?" I ask, locating my sword.

"It looks that way," Wulf answers. The boys row harder but

their efforts are pointless. The ship is gaining on us quickly, and we are too far from Iceland to get there before they catch us. We could try and turn back to the small island, but even if we made it, there's nowhere to hide. The boys toss the oars into the bottom of the boat.

"This is it," Thoren announces. "We won't be taken captive. Is that understood?" There isn't a sound of fear or concern in her voice.

"Yes," I say loudly, over the roar of the rising sea.

"Absolutely, my maiden!" Quibly shouts.

"I'd be honored to fight with you," Wulf says.

"You are all warriors," Thoren proclaims. "I am honored to fight to the death with each of you. May our gods and Wulf's be on our side. Let's see how many of these bastards we can take to the bottom of the sea with us."

"Thoren, please take your sword," I urge, pulling it out from the sheath.

"No, it's yours to die with," she says. "I am certain of this."

I don't argue with her. We are going to die either way, and there's something about this weapon that makes me want to fight. I will take it to the bottom of the sea with me. It's too special to leave in the hands of the enemy.

Wulf prepares his bow and squeezes the last of his arrows between his knees. "I'm really lucky I got to meet you, Livvy," he says, his green eyes piercing into mine. "I was hoping to take you to England one day."

"Quibly told me," I say.

"Promise me you will let me die first. I don't think I could bare it being the other way."

I'm not afraid of dying today, but I don't want to see any

more death. I smile but make no promises.

The ship is closing in. I grip the steel tightly in my hand. I'm ready.

CHAPTER 23

Our boat is rising and falling with the swells. Quibly almost loses his ax in the white-tipped waves, and I don't see how Wulf can possibly aim. Thoren has her back pressed against the stern and is being pummeled by the salty water with each crest and trough. I can hardly keep my feet on the slippery planks, and standing to fight will only send me into the black sea.

The ship is approaching fast and its sail is close enough to block the sun. If it hits us head on, we'll be crushed beneath it. The warriors will spear us in the water as they glide by as if we're seals surfacing for air, helpless against the enemy above us. We can only hope they want to take us alive, for then we can die fighting. Wulf's arrow is locked in his bow, and I raise my sword and shield.

The dragon ship is now upon us. It is slowing down and has veered off its direct path of impact. Its warriors are standing, but the tumult of the sea is too much for me to see what weapons they have aimed. Wulf lets an arrow fly. It goes high, slicing through the white sail. He quickly reloads. I tighten the grip on my sword.

Their ship's bow is crossing our stern and it's no more than a spear's throw away. Quibly yells, standing with one hand clutching the edge of the rocking hull, the other gripping his ax.

The dragon ship drifts forward and its warriors yell back, their voices carrying over the sea's roaring waves. The dragon neck is towering above us, and then I see it – *a red dragon is painted on the sail, snapping sharply in the wind.*

I think I hear Thoren's name cut through the howling wind, and then I definitely hear mine. And now I see a boy in a blond, scruffy beard, bobbing up and down with the sea. Is it really him this time? Wulf lets his arrow go before I get my words out.

The arrow pierces the wooden mast, just missing the boy's head. Wulf already has another arrow in place, aiming it once again.

"Stop!" I scream.

Both Thoren and Quibly yell out Erik's name. He is thinner and looks more like a Karl than a Jarl, but it's him.

I shout to Wulf, "Erik is our chieftain's son!" It's the first I can remember smiling in days.

Wulf hesitantly lowers his bow as a warrior on the ship tosses us a thick rope. Quibly catches it and pulls us in. The waves beat our little row boat into the ship, and it creaks and groans as if succumbing to the sea's final word.

Erik reaches down and pulls his cousin onto the ship. He's wearing leather armor over his chest, and his blond hair and beard have already grown longer. They hold each other tight. Watching them embrace gives me hope, but I can't help but feel envious. I lost my chance to unite with Grim, and I'm starving for the feeling they have right now.

Quibly and I board, and are greeted by the crew with shouts of "Health and happiness!" It seems an odd time for these words, but it's our customary greeting, and we don't have a more appropriate one that I'm aware of. I count twelve warriors on the ship, the minimum needed to move the vessel against the sea's current without a wind. I recognize most of them. These men are Erik's most trusted fighters, hardened by battle, but today they look worn and tired.

The crew stays guarded as Wulf boards. Although he greets them in Norse, they know he's not one of us, just as I did in the misty meadow when we first met. Erik is focused on Thoren's wound. As he tends to it, Thoren begins to tell him the events over the last couple of weeks.

In front of me, the warriors are staring Wulf down, most with their arms crossed. This isn't good. The tallest of the group is Bjorn. He's at least a hand taller than the others, has an oversized nose, and a thick, wiry beard that reminds me of a clump of rusted iron shavings. Bjorn doesn't talk. The only sound he makes is a thundering bawl when he fights in battle. The big man was well respected by Godi and the elders. He was often honored at public assemblies, although he rarely showed pleasure to receive them. After Bryanjar, Bjorn has killed more Shockheads than any of our warriors.

Standing in front of Bjorn is Gunner. In stark difference, Gunner is the shortest of them all. Although not brothers, Bjorn and Gunner might as well be. It's rare to see one without the other close by. Gunner is loud and is all the voice that Bjorn needs. The stocky man is known to be particularly fond of his hair and obsesses over it more than any girl I've known. Gunner claims it was a gift from Thor himself, and I will admit that it looks like it was. Unlike the other warriors who wear chainmail or leather armor, Gunner is wearing a fur coat that's tucked neatly under his short beard. He took it off a Shockhead noble whom he killed in a battle last summer, and I don't think he ever removes it.

I better say something. I step next to Wulf and look up at the men. "This is Wulf," I say. "We found him in the mountains."

"The mountains?" Gunner echoes back. "You *found him* in the mountains?"

"Well, he found us really. It was foggy—"

"He's like a mouse," one of the men in the back chuckles. "Lost in the forest without his mother mouse." The men are now all laughing. Expect for Bjorn that is, but he has a big smile planted across his face. That didn't go as I thought it would in my head.

I think of what to say next, trying to choose my words carefully, when Tore steps forward. Tore means Thor's fighter, and I don't know if that's his real name, but I can see why he's called it. The giant is the strongest of them all, with a massive chest matched only by the size of his arms and legs. He has a scar running from his left ear to his chin. He's still searching for the Shockhead that gave it to him.

"Are you a monk?" Tore bellows, looking down at Wulf.

"Do I look like a monk?" Wulf asks.

Tore inspects him from top to bottom and looks confused by the question. They say Tore got hit a few too many times to his skull and isn't that clever. I doubt he was clever to begin with, but I hope Wulf doesn't upset him. I can't see this ending well if it does. The brainless ones are usually the first to swing the ax.

"I don't know," Tore answers. "What does a monk look like?"

"Exactly," Wulf says.

"Huh," Tore grunts.

Erik and Thoren approach, and Tore steps back. I'm relieved the confrontation is over, at least for now. Thoren's shoulder is wrapped tightly with a clean piece of wool. Erik looks determined. I hadn't thought of him much in the last two weeks. For the most part, this was a deliberate decision on my part. I would have lost my sanity, like the old who forget their names, if I dwelled on the others who were killed – especially him. But now, I strangely crave his voice. It reminds me of my dreams of Norseland, a place far away from here.

I also forgot how tall he was. Erik gazes down at me with his blue eyes. "Red, this is a wonderful surprise. I've been thinking of you. I learned both you and Thoren went into the mountains. I was hoping you found each other."

"It is good to see you, Erik," I say, clearing my throat. "Thoren saved me."

"And you saved her. Thank you."

"You know Quibly," I say, stepping back next to my childhood friend.

"We have met once or twice," Erik answers. "I heard you buried my father."

"I did, Earl. I'm sorry I didn't have a boat to put him in."

"Please, call me Erik. You built a strong boat with the stones. He is safely in Valhalla, and I thank you dearly for what you did. I am indebted to you as long as I live on Midgard."

"You are most welcome, Earl—I mean, Erik."

Erik now turns to Wulf. "And *you* I haven't met."

"No, we have not. My name is Wulf. I'm thankful the sea bounced the arrow from my bow."

"And here I thought you were just a bad shot," Erik says

with a grin. "Wulf, that's not a name I've heard before."

"We both know it's Saxon," Wulf says.

"Well, I haven't heard it, but I'll take your word for it. All the Saxons I know are dead. Except you now, of course."

Thoren steps over and puts her good arm around her cousin's waist. "Wulf took us to Westman and helped us escape from the Danes. I owe him my life."

"Well, then for that, I am eternally thankful. Wulf, we have some urgent Norse business we need to discuss if you don't mind?"

"Why would I?"

"Good." Erik and Thoren walk towards the ship's bow, navigating the hull's roll. The dragon ship is far more stable in the sea than our old wooden row boat, but it's not entirely immune from its fury. Erik stops and turns. "Livvy and Quibly, are you coming? You're Norse, aren't you?"

Quibly gleefully follows Erik, patting Wulf on the back as he staggers past him. This is Erik's ship, but it doesn't feel right leaving Wulf out of any major decisions. He may be a Saxon, but we wouldn't be here without him. And like Thoren, I also owe him my life – what's left of it, that is. "I'm going to stay here with Wulf," I say to Erik. "Just tell me you aren't planning to join the Danes."

Erik hesitates, before turning around. "You trust this man?" he asks.

"I do."

"Very well. Wulf, please join us. It seems you've made quite an impression on the girls."

"Why thank you, *Earl*," Wulf says with a forced smile. Quibly gives us both an edgy look as we sit down on the rowing benches.

I sit in anticipation, hoping Erik is going to share a plan to return to Norseland. Maybe revenge on the Shockheads will give me a reason to keep fighting.

"We're going to England," Erik announces.

England? At first mention of the place, I'm confused. But now I'm overwhelmed with excitement and relief. Erik can help me find Grim! I squeeze Wulf's hand. "I can still save my brother," I say. I'm beaming both inside and out.

He squeezes mine back. "I never doubted you wouldn't," he says. I listen with anticipation as Erik starts from the beginning.

Ivar the Boneless and some of his warriors came to our hamlet, before the attack at the feast. They were guided by Eindride, the trapper, over the mountain, and met with Godi and the elders in secret. Ivar had formed an alliance with Fairhair and the Shockheads and was seeking Godi's help to finish off the last Saxon stronghold in England. Wulf says "Wessex" under his breath. I can see the anger in his eyes. This is a feeling we share together. The Danes took everything from *both* of us.

Godi's ships were the largest and fastest in Norseland, and our warriors some of the fiercest. Ivar promised Godi as much land in England as he could farm. He said the soil would yield better crops, and with less effort, than in Iceland. And there was the promise of Saxon women.

Godi declined Ivar's offer. Our clan would return to

Norseland to take back our kingdom. If the Shockheads weren't there to defend it, then all the better. The lands belonged to us.

Ivar warned Godi that the Saxons worshiped a phony god and were an enemy of Odin. As Norse, it was our duty to conquer them. If Godi changed his mind, and he would be wise to, the Danes were meeting the Shockheads at Westman Island and would soon sail to England.

A week later, ships were spotted by our fishermen. Not trusting Ivar, Godi sent Erik to investigate. And as we thought, Erik and his men were ambushed by the Danes. But Erik's ship was fast, and they were able to outrun the enemy. They returned to the hamlet as soon as they could, only to discover everyone they loved was lost. They left for Westman to seek revenge. The Danes were gone when they arrived, but luckily they saw our fire burning on the small island and chased our row boat down.

"Now, we will go to England," Erik commands. "I will find Ivar the Boneless and avenge my father's death. We will go at once. Livvy and Quibly, if you don't wish to come, we can take you to shore."

"He has Grim," I say immediately. "Ivar the Boneless has Grim. I'm coming."

"Everyone promised me I could hold Ivar down while he's killed," Quibly says. "As long as the offer still stands, then count me in."

"Very well," Erik says. "Wulf, we'll take you to shore. No words you heard on this vessel must ever be spoken."

"I also must go," Wulf demands. "The Danes killed my family and took me away from my people." He pauses for a moment before continuing. "England is much bigger than

Iceland. If you are to find Ivar, you will need to speak the
language. Take me with you, and I'll find him. I'll be under
your command until I do. I give you my word."

"We need him," Thoren urges.

Erik places his hands on Wulf's shoulders and looks straight
into his eyes. "If you betray us, you will die." He then pats him
on the back with a big smile before turning back to the rest of us.
"Let's sail south, to England!" he shouts.

"To England!" we all shout together.

CHAPTER 24

Sven says it will take at least seven days to reach England. But I also heard him say three and fourteen. Sven's family were the hamlet's master shipbuilders as well as the navigators. They designed and oversaw the construction of the nobles' dragon ships. After Godi's, they were the next wealthiest family in the hamlet. As far as I know, Sven is the only shipwright who survived. He and Erik are at the ship's bow now, checking our heading.

Sven is acting very spirited, as he normally does, waving his arms all about as he speaks to Erik. He looks like he could be Quibly's older brother. He's a round man, with an even rounder face, with pink cheeks, and arms that look too short for his body.

Gunner is on the steerboard, and the rest of the men are rowing, including Quibly and Wulf. Thoren fell asleep shortly after we set sail and hasn't woken yet. I don't know what herbs they gave her, but they seem to be working. I checked on her twice to see that she was still breathing.

I feel useless sitting on this wooden bench and doing nothing. I should be rowing. Erik says he needs to keep the oarsmen balanced on both sides, but I'm sure he doesn't see it as a girl's task. I'm also sure the ship doesn't care who's behind the oars.

The white sail above me is fluttering, and at times, banging.

The dragon painted on the canvas looks like she's flying. Maybe they painted it to be a boy, but I always thought of dragons as girls. I peek over the hull at the sea rushing past us. We are moving much faster than I could run at full speed. The waves are still spilling over each other, but Erik's ship is cutting through them effortlessly. Our row boat is most likely at the bottom of the sea. Both the winds and the sea move from the west. They always do as far as I know. The elders said the sea serpent blows her breath as a warning for us to stay away. Nonetheless, Sven and the shipbuilders found a way to make our ships sail into the wind.

Sven motions me over. I hold onto the hull for balance and make my way to the front of the ship. "Erik says you are looking for something to do," he says, his arms almost hitting me in the head. I go back half a step to keep out of their reach.

"I'm going to row when one of the men needs a break," I say.

"I'm afraid they don't quit until I tell them to," Erik says. He winks his eye at me.

"The wind is doing all the work now," Sven says. He looks up and down the row benches. "Half the men's oars are barely hitting the water. Where I need help is keeping us going in the right direction. Are you up for it?"

Since I know nothing of navigation, how can I possibly help? But I need to keep busy and will do anything at this point. "Why not?" I say.

Sven looks in the direction of the ship's heading. "It's midday and the sun is directly south. So we are going the right way," he says.

"England is directly south of here?" I ask.

"I have no idea," Sven answers, shrugging his shoulders. "But I can tell you with complete certainty that we are going south right at this very moment." Both Sven and Erik crack a smile.

"How then do you know it will take us seven days to get there?" I ask, anticipating a vague answer at best.

"The men need to hear something – much longer, and we will run out of food."

That's not very encouraging. Norsemen have been lost at sea, never to be found, and that's when following routes our people have taken a hundred times. We are sailing into the unknown, with only the word of our new enemy as to where we are going. Yet, I'm more excited than nervous. I've always wanted to sail Midgard's seas, and although there won't be a rainbow bridge on our voyage, we are explorers nonetheless. And I'm with Erik, on his magnificent ship, just as I always dreamed.

Sven catches my eye, and I snap back to the present. "When we travel to Norseland, we have markers that we follow," he says. "We read the color of the sea and the way the wind blows. We know where the whales hunt and which birds fly close to shore and which fly far from land. But where we are heading, we know nothing. So it's rather simple—we sail south."

"Gunner is on the steerboard," Erik says. "If he veers us too far east or west, you need to get him back heading south."

"And how do I know where south is?" I ask. "The sun doesn't stand still. I'm not a navigator. Or is the sea making you crazy?"

"I have always been crazy," Sven says. "But aren't we all

at some point or another? Anyhow, at midnight, the sun points north. So if you think the sun's halfway between midday and midnight, it's directly west. Likewise, if it's halfway between midnight and midday, it's directly east. But you don't need to be crazy to figure this out."

At the hamlet, we had markers that told us the position of the sun. At midday, the sun was always above mount midday. Similarly, at mid-morning, it was above mid-morning mountain. The names kept it simple for everyone, including the young children, to keep track of the day. But there are no markers in the middle of the sea.

"How will I know if the day is halfway over?" I ask. "There are no markers to follow."

"Your guess is as good as mine," he grins. "Off you go now."

I look into Erik's eyes, hoping for some help, but instead he says, "Gunner doesn't like being told what to do, so be gentle with him."

I go back to my bench, thinking of how I can keep track of the sun's movement. Perhaps I can use the mast's shadow somehow. I look at Gunner sitting at the back of the ship, his hand on the large plank hanging down over the hull. He's still wearing his fur coat and looks very serious and focused.

I'm becoming convinced that Erik assigned this navigation job to me to keep me busy or perhaps distracted. Or maybe they're both trying to get a reaction from Gunner. Truth is, I could use a distraction. The more I think of Grim, the less I remember what he looks like. How is this possible? I've seen my brother every day for seven years, and in less than three weeks he's vanishing from my memories. I fear this is a sign that Grim is no longer on Midgard, but there's something deep in my stomach that knows he's alive. He has to be.

The tapping of water on my cheeks wakes me up. I didn't dream of anything, but I don't think I was asleep long. I'm beginning to miss the snowfields, where at least we had Katla to guide us. I look back at Iceland in the far distance. The island looks tiny from here. The sun is low and behind it, just out of sight. We are going south or at least close enough to it. It doesn't really matter. Gunner is still on the steerboard and doesn't look the least bit tired.

I'm suddenly thrown to my stomach and hit the planks hard. A thunderous boom, a sound louder than anything I've heard, overtakes the ship. Are we falling off Midgard? I grab the edge of the ship and yank myself to my knees. Katla is crumbling away. An immense billow of gray smoke is erupting from its top, and the entire side of the mountain is falling to the earth. Red fire is spewing out of the mountain in all directions.

Men are shouting. The smoke continues to surge out of the ground and fill up Iceland's sky. Bjorn and Erik are leaning over the stern of the ship. They heave Gunner into the vessel.

"Is everyone else still on-board?" Erik shouts as he looks around the ship. Quibly is lifting himself off the floor. Wulf is staggering towards me, countering the lurching and rocking with each step.

"Are you okay?" Wulf asks. We both sit down on a row bench. "Your lip is bleeding."

"I'm fine."

Quibly stumbles over. "What in Thor's name happened?" he exclaims.

"Katla finally had enough," Wulf says. He seems sure of his words as if surprised it hadn't happened earlier. "If this isn't a sign to leave, I don't know what is."

The smoke and ash are filling up the sky in every direction. It won't be long before it reaches us. The earthfire continues to gush out of the massive hole in the side of the mountain.

"Do you see the fire giant?" Quibly asks, his eyes fixed on what's left of Katla.

"Some mountains just die," Wulf answers. "I don't think you'll see your fire giant or your dwarves."

Quibly doesn't take his eyes off the fire as if hoping to prove Wulf wrong. But the sun is still in the sky, fighting to shine through the clouds and ash. The fire giant hasn't dragged Sol's chariot into its lair. And although Katla is mostly gone, Midgard hasn't split in half. The elders were right that Katla would be destroyed. But it was burning within for years, and its looming death hardly takes a seer to foretell.

Erik and Thoren approach, while the others raise the sail. "Looks like we got out of there just in time," Erik says.

"Is this the start of Ragnarok?" Quibly asks, half under his breath.

"Ragnarok?" Erik questions. "The end of the realms?" He grins and pats Quibly on the back. "Not yet, my friend. But we need to get moving before the smoke catches us. It won't be pleasant to breathe. Livvy, can you take the steerboard? Gunner is in no mood. After all these years, no one knew he couldn't swim."

I would still prefer to row, but it's better than sitting and doing nothing. I leave the others and make my way to the stern of the ship. I pass Gunner, and he's cursing away with Bjorn standing above him nodding. I sit on the small bench at the very back of the ship and take hold of the large plank. It's much heavier than I expected it to be. Maybe I'll get some work in after all.

Soon the white, square sail is up, and the wind grabs it, jerking us forward. I heave the steerboard, and the ship veers sharply to the right. I straighten it out, and we begin to accelerate away from the burning island. The men take to rowing and break into a song, their words timed to the oars cutting through the choppy sea.

"I come to Valhalla,
From a battle at sea,
To ask the mighty gods,
A drink and feast for me.
We will fight and train 'til dark,
For ten thousand more days,
Then we'll kill all the giants,
And in Asgard we'll stay."

Now I really want to row. I keep the boat heading south, singing quietly along with the men.

CHAPTER 25

It's been three days at sea. To my surprise, I haven't been sick, but Quibly can't say the same. I had to run to the far side of the boat and cover my ears to keep my own food from coming up. We managed to outrun most of the smoke and ash, although I could smell it in the air for two days. Now, I just smell it in my clothes, but that's no worse than the stench coming from my body. I need to go for a quick swim.

I push the oar through the water, then swing it out and forward. I figured out how to get the most power, using my legs and back more so than my arms. We aren't getting much help from the wind today, and I'm sweating from the heat.

We stop for a drink, and Tore throws his fishing lines into the water. It looks funny for a giant man to hold out his little line and bob it up and down. But he's very good at it and catches something almost every time. He and Quibly have become chummy, and they are together now. I hear Quibly telling him how he took out one of the Berserkers with a stone to the head. In this version of the story, the beast doesn't get back up.

I stand up and stretch my legs and back. Wulf and Thoren are sitting together and talking at the stern. They stop talking as I approach. It has been different between Wulf and me since we boarded this ship. I feel like I'm starting to go mad. Right now, the most important thing is we find land. Maybe then, I can make sense of these thoughts and feelings.

Erik approaches and motions with his hand for me to sit down. He notices me glancing at his cousin and Wulf, and he looks their way. He sits next to me on a rowing bench. "Livvy, I've been wanting to talk to you about something," he says. Suddenly I feel nervous. "Wulf is not like us. I know how close you and Papar were. Perhaps he reminds you of the priest. But the Saxons are not friends of the Norsemen. You may trust him now, but you know very little of this man."

"We share a common enemy, don't we?"

"Yes, for now, we do. But sharing an enemy doesn't make you allies. Our gods are not on the same side. There is no friendship that can overcome that. I'm sure he means well, but we are your family now."

I look back at Wulf. He and Thoren are still hushed in conversation. Wulf has helped me get this far in finding my brother, and it shouldn't matter what clan he was born into. I don't have to trust the Saxons. I just have to trust him. I feel like I can trust him. But are these feelings real?

"I've been wanting to get a closer look at your sword," Erik says as he stands. "Thoren says there's magic in the blade."

"I don't know about magic, but it's a wonderful weapon. And it's more Thoren's sword than mine." I pick it up and hand it to him. He moves the sword about and eventually studies the symbols on the blade.

"This is the finest steel I have ever seen," he says. "Do you know how to use it?"

"I'm learning. I had a seax before but lost it on Westman."

"Well, I think you will fare much better with this. Let me

see what you can do with it."

"Here? Now?"

"I have fought many battles at sea. This a good place to train."

"Very well," I say with a smile. I never thought I would be so excited to fight Erik. I loosen my clothes and stretch my arms.

Erik retrieves his sword and kicks an area clear near the mast. Wulf and Thoren come over to see what we're doing. They both have their arms crossed, with surprised looks that we are about to fight.

Check my surroundings, relax, strike first—

I immediately strike Erik's gut with my foot, hitting him much harder than I thought I could. He stumbles backward, trips, and falls to the floor. I jump on him with my knees straddling his chest. I point my sword down at his neck.

"What was that?" Erik exclaims. His arms are over his head and he shrugs as he looks over at his cousin.

"That was me living, and you dying."

"I wasn't ready!"

"So your enemy waits for you to get ready?" I jump off and grin.

"Okay, you have a point," he says, getting up on his feet. "You are fast."

"Yes, she is!" Thoren shouts.

The men are now gathering around us. It doesn't bother me. I raise my sword up and charge towards him. I fake swinging it at his blade, and then change direction, swiping it low towards his leg. Erik counters but it's too late. The blade strikes his thigh. I was expecting his leather armor to stop it, but the sword slices right through it.

"I'm sorry!" I scream.

"Why?" he grimaces, jumping on his other leg.

"You're bleeding."

"I am?" he says, laughing.

Sven comes over and looks at his leg. "I'll get some cloth," he says, shaking his head.

"I think there's magic in your arm, not your sword," Erik winces.

"I told you," Thoren says.

"I appreciate the lesson," Erik says. "Let's call this one done for the day."

I sit with him and watch Sven wrap his wound. The shipwright's cheeks are extra rosy, and I hope it's not because he's upset with what I did. Sven did say the cut is shallow and doesn't think it did much damage.

Wulf sits down with us. "Thoren has been training her well," he says.

Erik smiles and looks at me. "That's good to know. Next time I won't take her skills for granted. Tell me, Wulf, do you fight with a sword?"

"My bow mostly."

"Yes, the Saxons like to keep their distance. Probably for the best." Sven is done wrapping the leg. "To the oars!" Erik shouts as he stands.

Wulf looks irritated. I need the boys to get along. Not just to make this voyage more bearable, but so that nothing unexpected will interfere with me finding Grim. I can't let that happen. Erik's men grumble but make their way to the benches. I take a seat at one near the back. I can see Erik wants to say something, but he stops himself short and turns towards the bow. *Yes, Erik, I'm going to row.*

Quibly is fitting in, and Tore is his latest best friend. It seems there are no distinctions between Jarls and Karls at sea. They are talking about the Shockheads and the different ways they are going to kill them. They sit across from each other on the row benches, directly in front of me.

"The Shockheads are responsible for all of this," Tore says. "I will strangle the next one I see with his own hair." He hits himself in the side of his head with his own fist. This may explain a few things.

Thoren takes the steerboard. She still can't move the one arm, but the wound looks like it's improving. She's lucky as there aren't any healers on the ship. I push my oar into the sea and heave it back. I start singing the rowing song, and the men join me. Although stuck on a ship with nothing but water in all directions, I feel at home. If only Grim were here. We continue our journey south.

It's now day six at sea, with no sight of land or even a bird. We were running from a storm since daybreak, but it finally caught us. The rain drops started slow, but that didn't last long. Now, the water is pouring from the sky. I think it's early evening, but it's hard to tell as the sky is as black as the sea. We pull the sail and batten it down over the hull. It doesn't help much. The salty water is bursting over the prow with the onslaught of each incoming wave.

Quibly is heaving his lunch over the side of the ship, and I'm afraid I could be right behind him. It suddenly occurs to me that Grim's ship might not actually make it to England. Until now, that was always a given in my head. But after this, it's far from a sure thing. I try and think of something else.

The ship's prow is rising higher with each swell and falling steeper with each trough. Everything not tied down is being thrown about into the splintering wood. I'm now very worried we could capsize.

Wulf and Quibly stumble towards me. "Hold on!" Wulf yells.

Quibly is gripping the hull's edge with both hands. "We aren't going to make it!" he shouts.

"We'll make it!" I yell. No sooner than the words leave my mouth, a rope snaps. The back of the sail whips into the air, flapping hard in the wind as it flies over our heads. Sheets of rain pelt us from all directions.

"Get the sail!" Erik shouts.

I scramble to my feet. Most of the sail is now in the water. If the other ropes fail, and we lose it, we'll starve before we row ourselves to England. I crawl towards the stern.

A shadow draws my eyes upwards. A mountainous wave is hovering high above the ship. It looks suspended in time, and for a moment I'm frozen with it. But then the wave opens its mouth and dives towards the ship. I wrap my arms tightly around a bench just as the sea swallows us whole.

It's day eight. Erik is standing on the prow, holding onto the dragon's neck. We all are sitting in silence, awaiting his words. The sea took two of our warriors.

Erik clears his throat. "When the gods want us in Valhalla, that is when we will go," he begins. "No sooner and no later. We will show the gods that Sven built a ship that can survive any peril the sea throws at us."

The men near Sven pat him on the back. The round man stands proudly and attempts to shake the tall, wooden mast with his hand. The warriors laugh with him.

"We have lost many men fighting the Shockheads," Erik continues. "We will lose more fighting the Danes. But this is our destiny. Be brave and be strong, but above all things, do not fear death!"

The men cheer.

Gunner steps forward and silences the men with his hands. "We all lost our families to the Danes," the short man says. "I lost mine and you lost yours. We are the last of our kingdom that can right the wrong. But every kingdom, no matter the size or the riches, must have a chieftain. I propose we cast a lot for ours. I will go first. My lot goes to Erik."

"As does mine!" Thoren shouts.

"And mine," Tore calls out.

Each warrior, one by one, repeats the same words, except for Bjorn who just nods. When it's my turn, I proudly say them, too. No one objects that I am a Karl. I will fight for our kingdom, and for these warriors, to the death.

Wulf, however, remains silent. His lot wouldn't count if he cast it. No matter how much I care for him, or what he's done for us, he will never be part of this clan. It shouldn't matter whether you are born Norse or Saxon. I remember Papar said those words to me once. But right at this moment, it does seem to matter. These warriors are Norse, as am I. It may be unrealistic to think Wulf and I could ever be something together. My head is spinning.

Erik steps forward. "Thank you, men, and my two maidens. I humbly accept. I can't promise we will all live to marry and raise children, but I can tell you that I will give my life for each of you without hesitation. And I believe we have a little ale left. I suggest we drink it."

"Skal!" we all shout.

The men are very happy with their drink, including Wulf and Quibly. I want to keep my mind clear, so I drink water and sharpen my sword instead. Bjorn sits with me for a while, and I tell him a few stories of Grim. His eyes seemed to light up when I shared the time that Grim tried to wrestle an elder. He was only four winters old at the time and had never met the man before. Grim grabbed the man's leg and wouldn't let go, despite the man asking and then kicking. Eventually, the elder laid down and took a nap.

Wulf and Thoren are having another one of their discussions at the stern. What are they talking about? I try and ignore it and go to talk with Quibly. He complains there isn't enough ale to go around. There isn't much food left either. Eventually, the two of us fall asleep.

I hear a caw and open my eyes. A shadow darts over the ship. A large, white bird with black-tipped wings circles the vessel. I haven't seen a bird in days.

"Land!" someone shouts.

CHAPTER 26

Erik picks me up and spins me around. He stops and my feet are still dangling. My arms are wrapped loosely around his neck. His blue eyes look into mine before he slowly sets me back on the wooden planks. "We did it," he says with a big smile.

"*You* did it," I say. My eyes are still locked on his. I can't look away.

"No, we did it together."

Erik takes a small step back. "When we return to Iceland, we should get to know each other better."

"I would like that," I say. I'm not sure what he means exactly, but my heart is pounding.

Tore comes thumping over, and Erik gives the giant a long embrace. I look around for Wulf, but Thoren steps in front of me. She looks more serious than she should. "We lived long enough to find England," she says.

"Grim is here, somewhere. We will—"

"Look, I need to tell you something," she says, cutting me off. "It's about Wulf."

"What about him?"

"Your boyfriend has a secret."

"What do you mean, he has a secret?"

Wulf suddenly appears and we both jump. "I am finally

home," he says with a wide grin.

"Yes, I suppose you are," Thoren says, stepping aside. "I'm going to take the steerboard." She makes her way to the back of the ship, but not before giving him a noticeable scowl.

I wrap my arms around Wulf, but he holds me much tighter than I hold him. I resist the urge to ask him what Thoren is talking about. This is not the time. Besides, I can't see how Thoren would know something about him that I wouldn't. But do I know him? Do I really know her?

"So, Erik is your chieftain now," Wulf says.

"He's the best person to lead our fight against the Danes," I answer. "We also need your help."

"We, or you?" he says.

"We—me—does it matter?"

"It doesn't." Wulf removes the quiver of arrows from his back. "You are going to like England. I can't wait to show it to you. I'm going to help row us in. Join me?"

"You heard my thoughts." Well, he heard some of them.

I find Quibly, and we share our excitement before taking a seat on the rowing benches. I don't think anyone on this vessel is looking forward to land as much as he is. His belly is much smaller than it was a week ago, and I'm getting tired of listening to how hungry he is.

The land slowly appears through a cloak of fog. It's beautiful. Rolling hills, like carefully placed giant shells, stretch out as far as I can see. They aren't as big as the mountains at home, but they are much more alive. The earth is covered in green grass, and thick clumps of colorful trees dot the hilltops like castles made of tall, wooden pillars. I don't see any signs of settlements or ships, just black waves ending their journey against the sand and rock. I picture Grim and I planting our crops on a farm overlooking the sea. If he's on this island, I'll find him.

Wulf is across from me, and I shout over to him above the growling sea. "What do you call this kingdom again?"

"It should be Northumbria," he answers. "East Anglia is in the East, Mercia in the middle, and Wessex is in the south."

The Saxon words are so strange, and they're hard for me to remember. I have a difficult time saying them out loud. If I'm going to be in England for a while, I should probably learn their language. I'll ask Wulf later if he'll teach me.

As we approach land, the men take the sail down. They prepare their weapons and pull their shields from the outside of the hull. I unfasten my shield and set it at my feet. I take one last look at the dark shadows in the water, wondering if the sea serpent is letting us get just a little closer before swallowing us whole.

I decide to sharpen my sword. I've done it every day we've been at sea. There's something about doing it that makes me feel stronger. Erik stands at the mast and waves to get our attention.

"My warriors," he calls out. "My friends, my family." He might as well be on the commanding black stone at the hamlet. He is the chieftain now.

"If we're attacked by the Danes, or the Saxons for that matter, we will defend with the shield wall. Follow my commands. If I'm killed, Thoren will give them. May the gods be with us."

Gunner and Bjorn have proud smiles on their faces. These men don't just fight for their honor and revenge, they enjoy it. If they die in battle, they will go to Valhalla – if they die of old age, they won't. I've heard of warriors, who are old or sick with disease, leading the charge into battle, sacrificing their lives for the others. Dying in your bed is only for the weak.

I have plenty of nightmares, like losing Grim, but death isn't one of them. I've thought more about what Papar said, why girls should be allowed in Valhalla. Freya is a goddess and she takes half the warriors when they get to Asgard. Odin takes the other half. Why wouldn't Freya want me? I'll find out soon enough, I suppose.

The land is getting closer, and I can probably swim from here if I had to. The warriors are eerily quiet. Voices travel far on the water, and they've been trained well. Even the oars pushing the ship through the sea are almost silent.

Erik is standing up, holding onto the mast. "There," he says in a hushed voice, pointing far down the beach.

At first, I see nothing, but then I find it. On a distant perch stands a rocky structure. It's a castle! It's too far away for me to see much, but from here it's exactly how I imagined one to look. A wall surrounds the fortress, and numerous towers reach high above it. I imagine all of our clan could have lived inside it. Instead, some of us lived on the frozen ground in kots made of dirt.

Erik directs us to the beach, and we row ourselves in. The warriors don't need their new chieftain to tell them what to do. Almost in unison, they jump over the hull the moment the keel scrapes against the sea floor. Their shields are up and their weapons drawn. The men pull the ship until it wedges into the sand, and then immediately form a shield wall.

"Livvy, behind the wall," Thoren commands, as she jumps

off the ship.

I've never been in a shield wall, and have only seen the men practice. At first my legs are wobbly, and I have a difficult time keeping my balance. I was warned the sea will do this. Wulf is crouched at the prow with his bow drawn and an arrow locked in the string. He's carefully studying the tall grasses at the edge of the rolling hills.

The men have their round shields up, overlapping them to form a solid wall, two rows high. There's not a single gap for an arrow to find its way through. If arrows come in from above, the warriors at the back will put their shields up over the heads. Our army has won many battles with this defense. On command, the warriors can move the shields just enough to thrust their swords or spears through, and either injure or kill their enemy. They then close it as fast as it opened. I take my spot next to Quibly, putting my own shield into place.

"You look like a shield maiden," he says with a big smile.

If only he knew. I remember back to when the seer said the shield maiden would unite the gods. It still doesn't make any sense to me, but this is where I belong. I've never felt surer of anything.

Erik gives the command to move forward, and we march in step towards the tall grass. I grip my sword tight in my hand. I almost wish we would encounter the Danes right now. I shift my shield and thrust my sword through it. It takes Quibly by surprise, but he takes his turn by doing the same with his ax.

I hear Erik whisper to Tore, "Watch the Saxon. Our backs are exposed."

"Yes, Chieftain," the huge warrior answers.

There is no way Wulf would betray us. He wants the Danes

dead as much as we do. He risked his life for us. But I need to find out what this secret is about. I'm sure it's nothing important. I hope not.

We reach the grass, and Erik tells us to stand down. The beach is quiet. There are no footprints in the sand other than our own. Wulf approaches.

"Is this England?" Erik asks.

"I can't say for sure, but it feels like it."

"It *feels* like it?"

"There is also Ireland, which is close by. We could be there."

"You don't recognize the castle?"

"I was just a boy, and England is a very big place. I've never been to the North, and there are many castles."

Erik turns to Thoren. "We need to scout this castle. Wulf isn't being much help." Wulf throws his hands in the air in frustration and puts his arrow away.

"I'll do it," she says.

"No," Erik objects, shaking his head.

"I don't need two arms to scout the enemy. I need to do something useful. I'll take Bjorn and Gunner with me."

"Like I said—"

Gunner interrupts. "Bjorn has something urgent to say." We all look at the towering warrior. He points. I follow the direction of his finger. Horses are galloping our way. Whether I like it or not, my wish may have come true. There must be ten horses, and it won't be long before they get here.

"We have them outnumbered," Gunner says.

"Only if this is all of them," Erik says. "More could be coming over the hills. Shield wall on my command. I'll greet them."

"I should go with you," Wulf says. "In case they're Saxon. I can interrupt their words for you."

"If this is England, the Saxon armies are destroyed. But come with me anyway. Maybe we can trade you as a slave." Erik smiles and hits Wulf on the back. It's much harder than a pat, but Wulf doesn't flinch. The two walk together on the sand towards the approaching horses.

The riders have long hair and inked faces. I've seen them before. "Shockheads," Gunner mumbles under his breath. Tore clenches his teeth and grunts loudly. He pulls the end of his spear out of the sand. Unlike him, I'm happy to see the enemy. We are at the right place.

The riders slow their horses to a trot and finally a walk. The animals are gigantic. I expected them to be larger than the ones in Iceland, but they're much bigger than I imagined. Riding these horses into battle would give one a tremendous advantage. We may have them outnumbered, but now I'm not sure we could beat them.

The Shockheads hold up a hundred or so paces away. Two of their warriors get off their horses and approach on foot. The Shockheads are in full armor. Tore hits himself again in the head with his fist. There isn't much holding him back.

"You'll get your chance," Quibly assures him. Tore grunts.

The men meet in the middle. I don't like that Wulf is out there. He's a strong warrior, but he doesn't know the Shockheads. They don't fight for honor – they fight for greed. And I've seen how greed turns men into monsters.

The men talk for what feels like a season. I slowly exhale as Erik and Wulf return. "Ivar and the Danes made it here," Erik says as he approaches. "They landed a day south of here, in a place called—what's it called, Wulf?"

"Lindisfarne. It's a monastery. Or at least was one."

"Let's go then!" I exclaim.

"We'll go soon enough but need to rest and eat. We'll stay here tonight. The Shockheads invited us to the castle."

"You want us to sleep with these savages?" Tore questions.

"Not in the same bed," Erik says. The men laugh. I'm not sure Tore knows why. "We need them to think we're allies," Erik says. "We'll deal with the Shockheads later. We first find Ivar the Boneless. Understood?" The men nod in agreement. We need our strength to fight, so I can wait one day – as long as it's *one* day.

"We have one little problem," Erik says. "Our Saxon friend here is not invited."

"What?" I ask.

"They don't trust him."

"Their instincts are right," Wulf says. "I'll stay with the ship."

"Done," Erik says.

"Wulf may not be Norse, but he's one of us," I say. "I thought you were indebted to him for life?"

"It's not our house to command the rules," Erik says. "We are at war and must choose our battles carefully. This is not a battle to fight. Not now."

"Then I'm staying here, too."

Erik sighs. "This conversation seems all too familiar, Livvy. It's not a good idea you stay here."

"Why not?"

"It's not safe."

"But it's safe enough for Wulf. Why not me then? I can fight. Oh, and I can push a stupid oar through the water."

Erik sighs again, but louder and longer. "If you want to stay with the Saxon, then you should stay."

"Fine, I'll stay."

Erik storms off.

Quibly saunters over. "Well, that was interesting," he says. "I don't like this, Liv."

Thoren is right behind him. "They have some things to talk about," she says, giving Wulf a familiar scowl. "Let's go, Quibly."

"You should go, Livvy," Wulf says.

"I'm staying," I say, loud enough that most of the men turn and look.

"Okay, you're staying."

It isn't long before they all leave and follow the Shockheads towards the castle. I'm too angry with Erik to say goodbye. Although I know I'll regret it tomorrow. I'm starting to regret it now.

We start a fire on the beach. It gets darker much earlier in England, just as Wulf said it would. He puts another branch on the fire and sits next to me. My sword and shield are at my feet, and Wulf's bow and arrows are at his.

"How have you been doing?" he asks.

"We haven't been more than fifty feet from each other in over a week!"

"Too many warriors in a cramped space," he says.

"Can I ask you something?"

"Sure, anything."

"Thoren said you're hiding something from me. I know

she's probably mistaken, but I thought I would ask."

"My full name isn't Wulf. It's Athelwulf."

I can't help but start laughing. "That's it? Your name is *Athel-wulf?* I can see why you kept it a secret. For what it's worth, I happen to like Wulf better—*much* better. Are there any other dark secrets you're hiding from me?"

"There's one more little thing. It's not a big deal."

"Okay?"

"My father's name was Athelred." Wulf is suddenly serious. "I've spent many years hiding his name."

"What is it about your father you don't want people to know?"

"My father was King of Wessex. He was killed in battle against the Danes. His younger brother, Alfred, became the king after him. It was supposed to be me."

CHAPTER 27

"Not a big deal?" I exclaim. "This is a *huge* deal!"

"Thoren said she wanted me to tell you first, but she's probably told Erik by now. I slipped up while drinking yesterday. She suspected something from the beginning and has been asking a lot of questions. She's very persistent."

My head is spinning. Wulf is a noble? He was almost king of the Saxons?

"There's one more thing," he says.

"There's *more*?"

"My Uncle Alfred—he traded me to the Danes."

"He what?"

"My brothers were very young—"

"You have brothers, too?" I look at him like I'm seeing this man for the first time.

Wulf takes a deep, slow breath. "My brothers were too young to become king," he says. "Maybe I was as well, but this wasn't a risk my uncle was willing to take. Alfred gave the Danes land and silver in exchange for peace." Wulf pauses again. "Although that didn't last long. Alfred threw me into the deal. Two birds with one stone."

"Two birds with what?"

"Sorry, it's a Saxon expression. He bought himself time with the Danes and got rid of me at the same time. It cleared the way for him to become king."

What does that have to do with throwing rocks at birds? But if Wulf can hide a secret this big, what else is he hiding? What if everything he has said and done was just to get back here?

"What else isn't true?" I question.

"Everything I've told you is the truth," he answers quickly.

"Except that you're a noble."

"I'm the man you know. This is me."

I don't know what to say or feel. I need time to think about this—about him. I say the first thing that comes into my thoughts. "So tell me about your brothers."

"Their names are Athelwold and Athelhelm."

"What's with your family and *Athels*?" I ask.

"It's a nobility title thing."

"Ah, now that your secret's out, you aren't holding back," I say with a grin.

Wulf seems suddenly distracted and serious. "Don't look," he whispers.

"Don't look at what?"

"There's someone in the grass, a hundred feet away."

I resist the urge to spin around. "Shockheads?" I whisper.

"You shouldn't be here. I knew better."

"Well, I'm here. We need to get to the boat. If they have arrows—"

"Agree, let's go," Wulf says. We stand and pick up our weapons and begin to walk quickly towards the ship. I carefully listen for any sounds the enemy is approaching. If they shoot arrows, we won't hear them until after they hit our backs.

Looking briefly towards the grass, I lift myself over the hull and into the ship. I don't see anything moving, so I quickly look away. We crouch down behind the protection of the dragon's long, wooden neck.

"They're waiting for us to fall asleep," I say. "Let's give them what they want." We lie in silence, resting against the planks such that we can peer over the hull unseen. The tall grass is swaying in the wind, playing tricks with my eyes. Twice, I thought I saw someone, only to see dark shadows of a log or rock.

Our silence is interrupted by a familiar bellow. I hear my name echoing over the water. Quibly is approaching on a horse. I dart a look towards the grass and tighten the grip on my sword. Why is he here? The animal is moving slowly, and my friend is swaying back and forth. How is he staying on? Wulf quickly locks an arrow in place on his bow's string. Quibly shouts my name again. He's drunk. I poke my head over the hull of the ship.

"There you are!" Quibly shouts as he spots me. His words are slurred. "I brought food. I also had mead, but drank it 'er on the way over. Sorry, Wulf! They let me take Hester here. He's a plow horse. They're gonna cook 'em tomorrow."

I can see why. The horse is much older than me. His hair is the color of charcoal, but his forehead and chest are as white as an old man's beard. Quibly practically falls off *Hester* and stumbles over to the ship.

"You didn't think I'd leave you alone, did ya?" Quibly stammers as he heaves himself into the ship. "Wulf, you better be good to my girl here. She's a terrible cook, ya know— horrible."

Before I can tell him we're being watched, he trips over a

rowing bench and falls flat on his back. By the time I get over to check on him, he's snoring.

We decide it's best to let him sleep. In his condition, he'll be more burden than help. In the worst case, he'll get us all killed. Wulf and I again wait. Only this time, we have to listen to Quibly's snorting while we do it.

I am hoping what Wulf saw in the trees was an English animal of some sort. Maybe a bear or a wolf. I've always wanted to see a wild creature. I want to know if these beasts are real or just the stories of drunken men. But today will not be that day. Two shadows emerge from the grass with their swords drawn. They creep silently toward us. Wulf slowly pulls the string on his bow back.

"I can get them both," Wulf whispers, his eyes locked on the approaching shadows. He crouches, raising his bow and resting the arrow against his cheek. They break into a sprint towards the ship. They see us. Wulf stands. They are less than fifty feet away when he lets the arrow go.

Wulf is already reaching for another when the closest warrior crumbles to the ground. A sharp twang explodes through the silence. The bow's string snaps, and the arrow ricochets off the dragon's neck, falling into the bottom of the ship. Wulf curses as he tosses the bow and scrambles for his knife.

There isn't time. I leap onto the prow of the ship, balancing my feet on the narrow edge. The warrior is almost beneath me, but it's too dark to see a thing. I jump forward into the blackness, gripping my sword with both hands and thrusting down. My blade hits something before my feet touch the ground. I hit the sand hard, letting go of my weapon and rolling to my feet.

Wulf is standing on the edge of the ship. "Okay, we *each* got one," he gasps.

I look at the man lying motionless on the sand. I feel instant regret. I pull the sword free and clean it in the salty water. How can this be my fate? I tell myself that I have to do whatever is necessary to rescue Grim. And despite what the sagas say, I can't believe these men are on their way to the golden hall, feasting on meat and drinking ale and mead. What god would reward them for what they've done?

It occurs to me, we are now in a very bad place. It is unlikely the two Shockheads acted without orders. Even if we hide the bodies, they'll know we killed them. Not only will their Thing sentence us to death, but all of Erik's men will be in danger. We only have one option.

"Wulf, we need to go," I say.

"Go where?"

"The Shockheads will come after us. We have to leave now. These men won't be reasoned with."

"They wanted to kill *me*," Wulf says.

"Me—you—perhaps all of us. Maybe they brought horses with them. We can't all ride on that old thing." Hester is lying on the sand, seemingly oblivious to anything that just happened. I wonder if he's blind.

Wulf jumps down onto the sand and checks if the men are dead. I know for certain the man I pulled my sword from is. We could try and get to Erik and Thoren, but they could be anywhere behind the castle walls. The likelihood of finding them unseen is almost zero.

Wulf returns and lies down on the earth. I sit next to him,

crossing my legs. My hair is full of sand, and I rub my hands through it to shake it loose.

"Ivar is at that monastery south of here," I say, furthering my argument that we should leave.

"Lindisfarne," Wulf says.

"Lindis—yes, that place." I will never get used to these Saxon words. "Erik will go there next. If not tomorrow, then the day after. We'll meet him there."

Wulf sighs and gets to his feet. "You are right, like most of the time. It's a little annoying."

"Most of the time? You mean *all* of the time."

"Let's see if we can find those horses. And I'm sure we will." He rolls his eyes. I'm liking this boy more.

It's not long before we find two horses over a nearby hill. They are tied to a fat tree and pull back on the ropes as we approach. The animals may not be as big as Varvak, the sun horse which pulls the ball of fire through the heavens, but they are the largest creatures I've ever seen.

The tallest one is black, and the slightly smaller one is white. Their manes and tails aren't as full as the horses in Iceland, but they are majestic creatures.

"Now *these* are real horses," Wulf says proudly. "It's been a long time since I've ridden a beauty like this."

"They look like they could eat us."

"They're no different than the ones in Iceland, just a little bigger."

At home, I could jump onto the horses from the ground. Not on these ones. "How do we get on them?" I ask.

"Just put your foot in the stirrup, grab the saddle, and pull yourself up." Wulf takes the black horse by the reigns and rubs the animal's head. The horse pulls against the ropes, kicking his front feet off the ground. Wulf unties him from the tree and pulls hard on the reigns. He quickly climbs on top as the horse backs up and twists. The animal spins in a full circle, arching its back and kicking its legs. Wulf holds on. "See, nothing to it," he stammers as the horse settles down.

"Yeah, nothing to it." I've fitted many horses with iron shoes, but I haven't ridden many. And which ones I did ride, they were tiny compared to these. I rub my hand against the thick, coarse hair on the white horse's belly. I slowly move towards her head. She is a lovely creature. The horse snorts as I touch her cheek, and I jolt back. I don't want her to eat my fingers. I place my hand against her face again and talk to her softly. "I need your help, girl. I need to find my brother. His name is Grim. Can you help me with that?"

The horse puffs out the air in her mouth and gently pushes her nose against my hand. I wrap my arm around her head and rest mine against hers. She leans in and I close my eyes. Her heart is beating loudly. It's much slower than mine. I untie her from the tree and reach up for the saddle. I step into the stirrup and lift myself up. She doesn't move.

"I gave you the better horse," Wulf says.

I smile. "Of course you did. I'm going to call her Sassa. It was my mother's name."

"It's a beautiful name."

"Yes, it is." I squeeze my legs, and Sassa takes off in a trot towards the sea. It's like she already knows where we're going. I almost forget to wake Quibly.

CHAPTER 28

At daybreak, we stop at a small river to rest the horses. Sassa behaved like she was always mine, listening to my commands almost before I made them. I might think her temperament was that of all English horses if it wasn't for watching Wulf ride his. The black horse hasn't tried to buck him off, but I wouldn't be surprised if he's just waiting for the right time. Perhaps he knows we killed his master. As for Quibly and Hester, they both look like they're in pain.

A farm is nestled in the hills ahead, and we're careful to stay hidden in the trees. We have to assume it belongs to the Danes now. A long wall of stacked stones, up to my waist high, meanders along the far side of a stream. I cross over the water, balancing on a fallen tree, and climb up a small bank to the wall. On the other side, a handful of sheep are grazing on the tall, green and yellow grass that grows out on the rolling hills.

Quibly is drinking from the stream, and Wulf comes up the bank next to me. He hops onto the wall and sits down. "This farm was likely handed down from father to son for two hundred years," he says. "Even this stone fence took generations to build. If the family who owned it was allowed to live, they're slaves now, sleeping with the animals in the barn."

My father's farm was taken from me, but not from the enemy. I was too young to fight for it, and I didn't have any other family to help. But this is the way of the clans. The land and crops were far too valuable to be left in the hands of a little girl. It was less than a week after burying my father that the elders stuck Grim and me with the Thralls. I had to sneak back onto the farm to get my father's weapons. It took me three trips to carry them to a hiding spot in the sea cliffs.

I stand between Wulf's legs and rest the back of my head against his chest. Closing my eyes, I see the warrior with the raven carved into his back – the one responsible for starting all of this. For the last week, I've seen him every day in my dreams. And my dreams are getting longer every night. How many Saxon children have seen their fathers killed or their mothers taken? I can't be the only one who wants to fight. This army must be destroyed. Perhaps there is a way. The last kingdom of England is still standing. They want to destroy the Danes as much as we do.

I open my eyes. "Do you want to kill Alfred?" I ask.

"What kind of question is that?"

"A simple one."

"Are you sure you want to hear the answer?"

"I wouldn't have asked it otherwise."

"If he traded my brothers into slavery, then yes, I will kill him. If not, then maybe. I haven't decided. I don't know if I would have been a better king. I may have gotten everyone killed."

"You would have been a great king," I say, turning around and wrapping my arms around his waist. "The Danes must be stopped. Not just kept out of your uncle's kingdom, but vanquished from this land completely."

"Then we need to summon your gods in Asgard for help.

Maybe with the help of Thor's hammer."

Quibly is now up at the wall, and his pants are soaked with water. I don't bother asking what happened and hold back the urge to laugh. "I have a suggestion," Quibly announces.

"And what is this suggestion of yours?" Wulf asks.

"If the farm was stolen by the Danes, we take it back."

"We can't just take it back," Wulf says.

"Why not?"

"Because they will just take it back again."

"Let them. By then, we'll have taken another."

Quibly may be onto something. Perhaps he should fall into the cold water more often. "It's time to get Ivar the Boneless chasing *us*," I ponder out loud.

Wulf laughs. "What happened to the girl too afraid to ride down a hill on a shield?"

"Who said I was afraid? What about *you*? I saw the look of fear in your eyes when you got on that horse."

"I picked the mean one. I did it for you." Wulf smiles as he takes my hand, and we slide down the bank. Quibly wades through the stream as Wulf and I edge over the fallen tree.

Wulf gets Quibly's attention. "Let's say the Danes have this farm, and we take it from them. They aren't going to just leave, so we'll have to kill them. And then what? The army will come and kill all the work hands. More of my people will just die."

"It was going to be too much work anyway," Quibly says, content to forget he asked the question.

Wulf unties the horses from the tree and hands Sassa's reigns to me. The horse pokes me gently in the chest with her head as if pressing me to say something. If only I knew what. I need to think about this some more.

We mount our horses, and Sassa leads us along the beach. We approach the longhouse at the farm. We are shielded by a clump of thin, gray trees. We hear voices and decide to sneak up for a closer look. I'm curious if they are Dane or Saxon.

I'm surprised, almost disappointed, that the longhouse doesn't look much different than the houses at our hamlet. The roof is made of sod, and the walls are formed of thatched wood, covered in a layer of mud. A wooden fence encircles the house. A loud and strange wail echoes over the fields. "What's that?" I ask.

"A howl," Wulf answers.

"A what?"

"It's a dog. Sounds like a hound. The hunters use them to track down fox and rabbits. They have an incredible sense of smell."

Godi had two dogs at the hamlet, but they didn't sound like that. They barked and barked often. They had long white muzzles and pointed ears, and their tails curled up over their backs. The dogs really belonged to Godi's wife, Astrid, and they didn't do much that I know of, expect to follow her everywhere she went. In Norseland, they were used to hunt the big creatures like bear and elk, but there aren't any of those animals in Iceland. It's said that Odin's wife, Frigga, has a chariot drawn by dogs. Frigga is the goddess of marriage and fidelity, and the men joked that Astrid kept the dogs so Godi's eyes wouldn't wander.

I can see the creature now. The dog is brown and has a long snout and droopy ears. I hope she can't smell us. And now I see the faces behind the voices. Three children, dressed in baggy wool clothes and carrying wooden buckets, are leaving the small barn. They are Grim's age and younger, and break into a race towards the house. They look Dane. The smallest one, a girl I think, falls to the ground and drops her bucket, spilling whatever contents were in it. She's crying, and her siblings help her to her feet. The children rush into the farmhouse along with the howling dog.

Wulf motions for us to leave. "Do you still want to take the farm?" he asks. Quibly doesn't answer his question but quietly gets up on Hester. The reality is, warriors have children. But where are the Saxon children who used to do the chores in the early morning? I must stop Ivar the Boneless.

As we ride, Wulf teaches me some simple Saxon words. I learn how to say king, castle, and sword, and to how to ask, have you seen Norse children? Quibly, of course, learned a few curse words and how to ask for an ale. Quibly practices them out loud, yelling them at Wulf as he tries to imitate his accent. With all the sadness, I forgot how funny Quibly could be.

I can finally pronounce Lindisfarne, as well as the names of some of the bigger shires in the kingdoms. Wulf believes we are not far from a place called York. The Danes call it Jórvík. It was one of the first settlements they conquered, and it's where they launched many of their raids from. Wulf believes Ivar will go there, most likely to prepare for his attack on Wessex. I pray, however, he hasn't left Lindisfarne yet. It will be much easier to rescue Grim at a monastery than in a place where armies prepare for battle.

South of here, in the Kingdom of Mercia and on the edge of Wessex, is Lundenwic. Wulf explained that *wic* means to trade. Lundenwic is the largest trading settlement in England and was sacked by the Danes a few winters after they took York. It makes sense the Danes will make their push into Wessex from there.

And finally, there is Winchester. This is the place where the nobles of Wessex live. It's where Wulf grew up, and where his uncle lives and rules the kingdom.

We are riding on the sand just above where the waves roll onto the beach. Quibly is falling behind, but Hester keeps plodding along. Maybe a break from plowing the fields is all the horse needed to live a little longer.

Wulf pulls his horse to a stop. I do the same with Sassa. "There!" He points ahead. At first, I only see a rocky knoll protruding all alone at the end of a distant bay. Now I see the structure perched on its top.

"Lindisfarne," he says.

The knoll is steep and round, and at least ten masts high. It's steeper than a horse could ride. The monastery on top looks nothing like Papar's longhouse at the hamlet. It's more how I imagined the giants' ice citadel to look, only this one is made of stone and not frozen water. It's as big as all the kots in the meadow put together.

"Do you think they have food there?" Quibly asks as he brings Hester to a stop.

I tell him, "It's Lindisfarne." Quibly says some curse word in a bad Saxon accent. Wulf laughs and shakes his head.

"How is it that monks have the riches to live here?" Quibly questions.

"They have more silver and gold than they could carry in a horse cart," Wulf answers.

"You mean they *had*," Quibly says. "How did they protect

their treasures?"

"They didn't."

"What do you mean, they didn't?"

"The monks have the ear of God. They can store the treasures of the kingdoms in the open, for no man will dare take them," Wulf says.

"No Saxon man, you mean," Quibly counters.

"Yes, I suppose you are right. This is the first place the Danes attacked. News of what happened rattled all the kingdoms. If the people only knew that it was just the beginning. Maybe then, they would have united together."

The Saxons treat their monks like we do our seers. They believe the monks have a special connection to their god and, therefore, leave them alone. No man wants to anger the gods. Only our seers didn't have riches. I'm not aware of Papar having any treasures. Although, I never searched the back wall of his longhouse.

We take the horses into the forest and approach the hill from the canopy of the trees. As we get closer, the trees get much bigger. I have never imagined living things so large, not even the gods. I bring Sassa to a halt and stare in wonder at the one standing commandingly in front of me.

"Yggdrasill," Quibly says under his breath.

"Drasil—?" Wulf tries to repeat back.

"The tree of life," I say. "It connects all nine realms together. The gods visit it every day. Its branches reach far into the heavens, and creatures live within its trunk, including a dragon."

"Well, this is just a good, old oak tree," Wulf says. "I fell off one just like this and broke my arm."

I imagine Wulf as a child, in the gardens of his castle and dressed in his fine clothes. The Thralls shout for him to get down from the tree, for fear they will be punished for not tending to their young prince. But the defiant boy ignores their pleas and only climbs higher.

"We should keep going," Wulf urges.

I take one last look at the ancient tree. I wish Erik were here to see it with me. I thought a lot about him today. I always dreamed of seeing Norseland under Erik's command, and this place reminds me of those dreams. I hope he's on his way. The thought of harm coming to him, especially from my actions, makes me feel sick. But I remind myself that Erik is a great warrior. I should be more worried about Wulf. Erik is unlikely to be happy when he hears of Wulf's real past. Quibly needs to know. I'll ask Wulf to tell him tonight. I squeeze my legs, and Sassa springs forward as if wanting to get to Grim as much as I do.

We are close now and need to be quiet, and decide it's best to go the rest of the way on foot. We tie the horses and tread softly to the edge of the forest. We once again have the advantage of surprise. This time I won't fail Grim. We are at the center of a half-moon shaped bay, and Lindisfarne is on the far tip. Despite not having an army to protect it, the monastery has a natural defense. Unless you scale the cliffs, there looks to be only one steep, winding path up. Something is not right. There are no ships in the bay. "Are you sure this is Lindisfarne?" I ask, begging for the answer to be no. I strain my eyes to look for any sails on the horizon.

"I'm quite sure, Livvy," Wulf answers.

"They're not here," I mutter. My weapons and my pack

suddenly feel heavy. My knees want to buckle under their weight. I drop to the ground and put my head between them.

"This looks to be a good spot to wait for Erik," Quibly sighs.

I'm tired of waiting. We need to know if we just missed them or if they were ever here. The Shockheads could have lied about Ivar. They've done much worse. "I'm going in," I declare. I pick myself off the ground and start marching towards the knoll.

"We're not waiting?" Quibly questions.

"Nope!" I shout. I don't turn around.

The boys catch up, and we walk three across, our feet sinking into the muddy grass.

CHAPTER 29

We wind up the rocky path that circles up and around the lonely hill. The monastery above is eerily silent. The only sound is the crunching of pebbles beneath our feet. I've heard stories of warriors pouring boiling water and scorching sand over castle walls to defend an attack. But if an army is lurking in the walls above, I doubt we look like much of a threat.

We climb the last full loop up the stone stairs with our weapons in hand. Now the only sound I hear is Quibly gasping for air. We reach two adjacent doors as high as the walls they block entry to. A cross is engraved on each one, and large iron handles protrude beneath them. There is no damage to the wood or the hinges. Battering rams weren't necessary to get through these doors. Maybe a quiet knock was all that was needed to seal the fate of the monks praying inside.

"Now what?" Quibly asks between breaths.

I pull on a handle, and the heavy door creaks open. "We go inside," I whisper. The boys look unsure. "We're Norse. We'll be fine."

Quibly points to Wulf. "What about him?"

"I speak Norse just fine," Wulf says.

"You? You sound nothing like a Norseman," Quibly mocks.

A faint voice speaks from the other side of the door. We

all step back and raise our weapons.

"It's only a child," I whisper.

"The child just threatened to kill us," Wulf says.

"He's Saxon?"

"He or she."

I pull the heavy door with two hands until the opening is wide enough to fit through it. It's as dark as a winter's night inside, and a rush of cold air pushes through the opening. I nudge Wulf in the back with the pommel of my sword. "Say something."

Wulf shouts a few Saxon words. He waits a moment and then shouts a few more. The voice within answers back. It's a boy.

"What did he say?" I ask.

"Enter."

"Then let's enter." I pull the door the rest of the way open. A young boy steps forward out of the dark. His gaunt face matches his thin body. He's holding a small knife and has a leather helmet on, far too big for his head.

Wulf asks him a question. The frail boy answers.

"His name is Brice," Wulf says.

"Livvy," I say, pointing to myself. The boy smiles. He is thinner than any child I've seen. His dark hair is like Wulf's, but much longer and matted like a clump of dried seaweed. I want to hold him. "Is he alone?"

Wulf asks and the boy answers. "Yes," Wulf says.

We follow the boy in the dark through the stone halls. The walls are narrow, and the ceiling is short. Erik wouldn't fit through here without crouching. The air smells damp. It was much warmer outside. This place makes me feel like I'm in

Niflheim, not in a stone castle of the like I dreamt. It looked much more appealing from outside the walls. Quibly coughs and I can't help but do the same.

It's lighter ahead, and we soon step out into a space that's open to the sky above. The area is square, with a dirt floor, and is about ten strides across. Two small goats are lying asleep in the corner – unless they're dead. An open doorway is in the wall directly across from us.

The boy speaks and Wulf interprets. "If the goats die, they will kill his mother."

I guess they're sleeping after all. It's good the boy's mother is alive. He's too young to be orphaned. The woman must be with the men. "Ask him if Ivar and his men were here," I say.

"Yes," Wulf says after the boy speaks. "They left this morning. He doesn't know where they went or for how long. I believe him."

I ask Brice in Saxon, the phrase that Wulf taught me. *"Have you seen any Norse children?"*

"I heard them but didn't see them," Wulf says for the boy.

I look up at the tall, stone walls. The castle is enormous. Why would they leave this place unguarded? Perhaps they didn't. "We should look around," I say. "Quibly, stay here with Brice. Wulf and I will check the rest of the monastery." Quibly smiles at the boy, and the boy smiles back. Children always liked him.

We enter the doorway on the far wall. I keep my shield in front of me. I'm learning. Wulf follows closely behind with an arrow locked in his string. This hallway is no different than the first one – dark and damp. Water is seeping through the walls, pooling in small puddles on the floor. I was expecting the castle to be inviting and romantic. So far, I prefer the lonely confines of my kot.

We pass through numerous empty hallways and rooms. Small, slotted windows allow enough light in to see. It would be easy to get lost in here. Some rooms are clearly for sleeping, with benches lining the walls. Although, they look too small to fit most Norsemen I know. We pass by a large room that is brighter than the others. Four hearths are in the center, and small openings are in the stone ceilings above them. What is keeping these massive rocks from falling and crushing those below them? Cauldrons and dozens of bowls, jars, and plates are scattered on the floor. At least half are broken. I imagine they were neatly stacked on the empty shelves before the Danes arrived.

We enter a great hall that's far larger than any other room we've passed. The ceilings in it are high and curved like an archer's bow. Finally, I'm not choking for air. Benches are stacked messily against all four walls. More of the slotted windows fill the walls from the ground to the ceiling. The sun is peaking through the upper ones, bouncing off blotches of red on the stone floor.

This must be where the monks prayed and perhaps wrote on their skins. It also looks like the last place they were alive. The Norsemen don't have special rooms to talk to their gods, at least not at the hamlet. The one exception is when the seer sat on the chieftain's throne and spoke for Freya. At least, we all believed she was doing so. Karls weren't allowed in our great hall, and I never heard the seer speak myself. The only one I have talked to is Runa. What I do know is the hamlet seer never warned Godi of Ivar's attack or any of this. Either the seer was a fraud or the gods wanted us dead. It could also be there's no one in Asgard listening to our prayers.

A dark staircase winds down through an opening at the far end of the room. We decide to go down. There are torches on the wall at the entrance. They are soaked in what smells like animal fat and light quickly with a single strike of my flint. The staircase is very narrow, barely wider than Wulf's shoulders. It winds tightly down like the passage to a snail's home, hidden deep in the confines of a sea shell. My shield won't fit, and I rest it against the wall. We each take a torch and take our first step downwards.

I'm almost dizzy before the stairs finally end. We are standing at the beginning of a long hallway. Light is shining through an opening at the far end. It's much colder here, and a strong gust of air is pushing towards us. I walk slowly down the hollow with my sword aimed forward. It gets brighter as we near the end, and we silently set our torches on the ground. If a battle ensues, even a moment to drop the fire sticks will put us at a disadvantage.

We stop short of the opening and slowly peer out. There aren't any men waiting to ambush us. We step out into the open air. We are outside the monastery walls, and a large furnace and hearth are to my left. A short wall, the height of my waist, surrounds the surface on three sides. Black stones, each no bigger than my fist, are piled in the corner. Wooden boxes are stacked along the wall, and a large, flat stone sits alone in the center. The surroundings look very familiar.

We look over the short wall. We are somehow suspended above the sea, jutting out the side of the monastery wall. The way we came in is the only way in or out of here.

"What is this place?" Wulf asks.

"It's a smithy," I reply. "That large stone is the anvil stone. It's where the blacksmiths hammer their steel."

"And that's for heating iron?" Wulf asks, pointing to the furnace.

"Yes, it must be." Both the furnace and hearth are much larger than the ones Olaf had at his smithy. In the bottom of the furnace is a solid mass of iron, packed tightly into all four corners. The iron couldn't have been hammered into there. It would need to be very soft, like water filling the bottom of a jar. Iron does get softer with heat, but this amount of heat would be incredible.

"And what are those?" Wulf asks, pointing to some shiny, black stones in the hearth.

I pick one up and rub my fingers across its smooth surface. "I'm not sure."

We walk over to the stone anvil. The surface is flat and smooth, and it is well worn, most likely from years of hammering. I slide my hand across it and notice something scribed on the side. I crouch down and see the familiar symbols etched into the stone.

+ULFBERHT+

CHAPTER 30

Could it be my sword was made here? This seems impossible, but it's no more unlikely than it came from the gods. If so, there's a connection with these black stones and the steel. They aren't here to throw over the walls at the enemy.

"Let's start a fire," I say.

"Now?"

"It will only take a moment." I place a small stack of the stones in the furnace and retrieve my torch.

"What are you doing?" Wulf asks.

"I'm not sure." I place the fire against the stones. It isn't long before they burst into flames.

"How is this possible?" Wulf questions. He takes two steps back.

"There's no charcoal here. They had to burn something. Perhaps the stones came from the dwarves. They are the greatest smiths to have ever existed, you know?"

"Do you believe this?"

I give him a little smirk. "I was beginning not to."

They burn long and hot, much hotter than any charcoal I've used. We stand quietly and watch them turn white. Whether from this realm or not, their heat is sure to be one of the keys to the strength of my blade. We realize we've been gone far too long and need to check on Quibly. We retrace our steps up and through the monastery.

Quibly doesn't seem at all concerned. He and the Saxon boy are taking turns throwing stones against the wall with a leather sling. For such a small and thin child, Brice throws his rocks with tremendous speed.

"Watch this Livvy," Quibly boasts, swinging the sling over his head. We duck as the rock almost hits us.

"Sorry!" he apologizes. "That's the first time that happened. I was perfect until then." Brice is laughing. After the usual scolding, we catch Quibly up on our findings.

"Dwarves," Quibly mutters after I tell him about the special stones.

"That's what I told Wulf."

"Thank you!" Quibly says, as if somehow finally redeemed.

Wulf shows Brice the symbols on my sword and asks him if he knows anything about them or the smithy down below. "He has never been down the stairs," Wulf says. "But he's heard a man's name that sounds similar to the symbol. His name was pronounced 'Ulf-berht.' Brice has only been at this place a few weeks."

We decide to stay out with the horses for the night. It's far too risky to sleep in the monastery. I want to help Brice, maybe take him with us, but the boy says his mother is married to one of the Danes and he can't leave her. I doubt she is married on her own will.

Some of our elders had more than one wife, but most men avoided these arrangements. The purpose of marriage is to make it clear where a man's belongings go when he dies. Children can't own houses or land, but the wife could care for them until the sons were of age. Having more than one wife made passing on property complicated, and more often than not, the clan would just take it to resolve the dispute. I've never had thoughts of marrying.

We have a decision to make. We can go to Jórvík, the place the Saxons called York, or we can wait for Erik. Brice told us Jórvík is a two-day ride by horse. With Hester, it may take us three. Wulf believes Lundenwic is another two to three days from there. But we don't know when Erik will arrive, if at all. There is also a third option. Even with Erik's men, we are too small to fight this army. And without a fight, I may never see Grim again. We need the Saxons on our side.

We leave the monastery and look down below. The hill has now become an island, and we are surrounded entirely by water. We wind our way down the pathway and wade through the water and mud until we reach dry land. After wringing the water from our clothes, we decide to talk about our next steps.

"We should wait for the clan," Quibly says. "Hester isn't going to make it much farther. And there's the Dane and Shockhead army thing. I like our chances, being three of us and all, but why keep all the fun for ourselves?"

"I made an oath to Erik," Wulf says. "I promised I would help him find Ivar. Until then, Alfred has to wait—" He cuts himself off, realizing what he just said.

"Whoa, whoa," Quibly sputters. "Alfred? King Alfred? What's going on, Wulf?"

"Nothing's going on."

"And I'm as thin as a snake. Liv?"

"Alfred is not *my* uncle," I say. I shouldn't have said it but couldn't resist. I give Wulf an apologetic grin and nudge him with my eyes.

Wulf tosses his hands in the air. "Yes, King Alfred is my uncle. My father was king before him, and I was next to be king. But Alfred took it from me. He traded me to the Danes, who then traded me to the Norse."

"And you have two brothers," I say.

"And I have two brothers. Anything else, Livvy?"

"Your real name is Athelwulf."

"Thanks, Livvy. So that should cover it. Any questions?"

Quibly is staring at us with his mouth open like he just saw the goddess, Freya. "Are you two serious?" he stutters. "You're a king?"

"My uncle is a king. I'm just trying to get to Wessex."

"Because the kingdom belongs to you," Quibly mutters happily to himself. "I can't believe you're a king!"

"I'm not a king!"

"We both think you should be," I say with a smile.

We decide to go back to the giant tree to sleep. It was Quibly's suggestion. He might still believe it's Yggdrasill, the tree of life, but it doesn't matter. I want to see it again just as much. Quibly has been calling Wulf, *the king wolf,* since we left. I find it quite funny, but it's starting to irritate him. We all climb up to a large saddle in the thick branches and rest our backs against the wide trunk.

"It's beautiful here," I say.

"This is the first time I've enjoyed climbing," Quibly says. "Wulf, what was it like to be the son of a king?"

Wulf sighs and then goes on to explain he often traveled with his father to the battlefields. His closest friend was his cousin Edward, Alfred's son, who also accompanied them. They were far too young to fight and stayed with a guardian while the warriors went to battle. But his father spent as much time as he could with him, preparing him to be king. Wulf is similar to Erik in many ways. That thought lingers in my head for a while.

It is getting dark, and we still haven't agreed to a plan. We need to make a decision. "I wish we could stay here, but in the morning we should go to Jórvík," I say. "Every day that passes is a day farther they're away."

"What about Erik?" Quibly questions.

"Brice can pass a message on."

"I don't know, Liv. Hester may not make it that far. And we can't fight Ivar alone. You know this."

"Jórvík is halfway to Lundenwic?"

"Yes, about that," Wulf says.

"And how far from there to where your uncle lives? To Winchester?"

"On a fast horse, maybe three long days. Where are you going with this?"

"Papar once told me the Saxons believe they can choose their destinies. Is this true?" I ask.

"I don't believe in destinies if that's what you mean," Wulf says. "Men in power make choices, almost always to ensure they stay in power. The rest of us must deal with the consequences."

"Then let's choose to stop these bastards."

Wulf smiles, but in a way that really means, *what a nice but foolish thing to think*. "I'm serious, Wulf. We need to fight."

"And what do you suppose we do, Livvy?" Wulf questions.

"Erik and his men have battled the Shockheads. They know how to beat them. They can teach Alfred's men. And we can fight with them. At the least, we can warn them that Ivar is coming with a bigger army."

"My deal with Erik was to help him find Ivar and nothing more."

"But then what?"

"The way to kill a snake is to cut off the head."

"They won't leave here if Ivar is dead. There will be a flood of men to take his place. Eventually, they'll take Wessex. They won't stop until they do."

Wulf shifts his position on the branch. I don't want to press too hard, but I have a growing feeling that this is the only way to save Grim. "What would you do if you were king?" I ask. I hold my breath waiting for his answer.

"For the last time, I'm not a king!" Wulf climbs down the tree and disappears into the dark forest.

"Let's wait for Erik," Quibly suggests. "If he's not here by tomorrow night, I can go back to find him, and you can carry on to Jórvík. How does that sound?"

"Sure, Quibly," I say. "Thank you."

"Now, how do we get down from this thing?" he asks, nervously inspecting the ground below. It looks like I'll be going alone to find Alfred. I'll leave at first light.

CHAPTER 31

I dreamt again of Ivar the Boneless towering over me with his sword. This time I awoke when my shield split in half. The air is cold, yet I'm soaked in sweat. Wulf is starting a fire, and I sit up, wrapping my arms tightly around my knees.

"You were talking again in your dreams," Wulf says quietly. "It didn't sound like a pleasant one."

"It was just a dream," I say, trying to sound indifferent. Quibly is lying on his side and is dead to the world around him. I'm quite hungry and need to eat something soon. Hester is standing with his eyes closed. I wonder if Quibly would care if we ate his horse.

"I didn't sleep much myself," Wulf says. He strikes his flint above the small pile of twigs and moss, and the flames roar to life. "I would try to unite the kingdoms," he says. Wulf puts some larger branches on the fire. I move in closer to warm up. "If I were king, that's what I would do. The Saxons are losing the battles at sea and in the rivers. They need better ships. But first, they need to rise up together and fight their enemy."

I stand up and give him a hug. I knew Wulf would want to fight. What king or chieftain wouldn't? Since Erik found us on our row boat, I would be lying to myself if I haven't had feelings for both boys. Erik understands me in ways which Wulf cannot. But I can also say the same of Wulf. I clear my head and listen to the fire crack and pop. Quibly is now awake and rolls onto his belly.

"Let's ride to Wessex," Wulf says. "As long as my brothers are safe, I will talk to my uncle. I won't kill him if he doesn't try and kill me."

"Okay, what did I just miss?" Quibly asks, sitting up straight and suddenly wide awake.

The sea is again to our east, and the horses carry us along the rocky coast. Sassa is in front. She gets very annoyed if Wulf's horse attempts to pass her. Hester is content to stay a hundred paces behind.

Brice promised to tell Erik that we're heading south to Wessex through Lundenwic. He also promised to keep it a secret. It was a risk we had to take. Erik will find us. I know he will. He has Sven with him, the greatest navigator in all of Midgard. Between the two of them, they could find a mouse hiding in a field of barley.

We agreed to stay clear of Jórvík. Ivar the Boneless and his army are likely there. It's much closer than Lundenwic and is the largest settlement in the north. But if we are going to help the Saxons, we need to get ahead of the enemy. It's going to take more than a few Norsemen to defeat this army, and I'm taking a big risk that getting to Alfred and the last kingdom of the Saxons is the right decision. If I'm wrong, this whole journey will be for nothing.

My stomach hurts. It's not the feeling of hunger that

bothers me. I've felt much worse pain. Rather, it's my fading strength that worries me. I can't fight if I'm weak. Quibly isn't complaining but is very grumpy. He gets this way when he misses a meal. But going days without food turns him into a troll. For all of our sanity, we need to find something to eat soon. Hester may be our best option. Sassa could probably carry us both if she had to. Quibly is getting thinner by the day, and I don't like how he looks.

Hungry or not, the land here is beautiful – the rolling hills, the farms nestled amongst them, the craggy cliffs, and the thick, towering forests. Yet, we are under the same sky as Iceland. Odin's wagon still shines in the night, and the sun still moves across the heavens during the day. Somehow this sky connects us, no matter what island we were born on. The peacefulness is interrupted as Quibly shouts his Saxon curse words. Wulf joins him. And to think that the three of us are trying to save England!

We ride all day, only resting when the horses need it. We talk about the symbols on the anvil stone and the mysterious man who goes by the same name. Quibly's theory is Ulfberht is actually Motsognir, the father of the dwarves, disguised as a man. He thinks since Motsognir knows where all the hidden doorways to our realm are, that he's secretly in Midgard to make weapons for our warriors. The dwarf's *scheming plan* is that our warriors will take these magical swords to Valhalla with them when they die, and then somehow the swords will be used against the gods.

For a boy who never listened to the elders' stories, Quibly is quite good at making up his own. I do want to meet the maker of this steel, whoever it is, and learn how Ivar's weapon, mine, and the anvil stone, all bear the same name. Maybe it has something to do with my destiny.

We spot a small animal scampering in circles up a leafy tree. It isn't long before its skin is off and we're roasting it over a roaring fire. It's not much food for three of us, but it's something.

"Do you think the Danes brought the Berserkers with them?" Quibly asks, staring intently into the fire. Or maybe he's looking at the rat-like creature, imagining how good it's going to taste.

"The witch's army, as you call it?" Wulf asks.

"They killed my mother and father," Quibly says.

Wulf rotates the animal on the spit. "I spent many days with Runa. You agree that she is a seer, a witch as you call her? She talks to the gods and has potions and can cast spells?"

"Yes, she is a witch. And not a very nice one," Quibly grumbles.

"You see, I never saw her that way. I saw a lonely, old woman who picked berries and herbs from the forest, and traded with merchants for things she couldn't find. Yes, she talks to the gods, but don't we all at one point or another. She just did a little more often. She has no one else to talk to."

"She put us to sleep," Quibly argues. "For a long, long time."

"Doesn't ale and mead put you to sleep, too? Livvy, do you still have the herbs that Runa gave you?"

"Yes, some."

"Can I see them?" I take off my pouch and pass it to him.

Wulf takes out a few of the black seeds and rubs them between his fingers. "This plant grows in the west of Iceland. I brought these up for her from a merchant myself. Healers give them to warriors before binding wounds. The herbs reduce the feeling of pain. But in larger amounts, they make you feel invincible. Think of them as six or seven jars of ale packed into a little seed."

"Why didn't you tell me this before?" Quibly questions, his eyes wide.

"It wasn't a pleasant experience. Trust me," I say.

Take them when your fear is at its greatest. Why would Runa give them to me? Wulf returns the pouch, and despite Quibly's protest, I empty the contents into the fire. If the Berserkers need these herbs to muster the courage to fight, then maybe they can be defeated after all.

The rain begins to fall. We take cover under the canopy of a giant tree, along with our cooked rat. I eat my portion slowly, savoring each bite. Tomorrow, we will have to hunt again. I don't have the patience to search the bushes for berries, and Wulf doesn't know which fruits are made of poison anyway. As a noble, he had Thralls who did all the growing and gathering for him.

Tomorrow, we'll ride all day. We must get to Winchester quickly. Alfred and his army will need time to prepare for the coming onslaught. I curl up against the tree and close my eyes. The day begins to fade away.

At first, I hear the snapping of a twig in my dreams. Then another. Now I hear my mother's voice whispering in my ear. "Wake up," she tells me. I forgot what she sounded like. It's like the voice of a goddess. "Wake up," she says again. I fumble for my sword. I can't find it. I slowly open my eyes. An arrow is pointed at my head.

I count six warriors – four boys and two girls. They are no older than us and are armed with strange-looking bows. Wulf and Quibly are both awake, with their hands up by their chests. My sword is within reach, but I'll have no chance of striking before an arrow goes through my skull.

I study the face behind the wooden dart in front of me. She is taller than me. Her hair is brown and long, and her eyes are focused, but she doesn't look afraid. The girl's skin is pale, like the color of the fog that's settled around us. Her bow is attached to a wooden shaft. I've never seen one like it. I can feel her desire to release the arrow.

One of the boys shouts at Quibly. He's Saxon and the tallest of the group, with long, black hair, and a wide face. With his worn tunic and pants, he could be mistaken for a Karl. But I doubt he's a farmer or smith. He looks to be their leader.

Wulf responds calmly in his Saxon tongue. The tall boy repositions his arrow from Quibly's head over to Wulf's and shouts again. Wulf answers in a slow, determined manner. The boy shifts back to Quibly and asks him something. Quibly looks at Wulf and then back at the boy. He blurts out one of his Saxon curse words and shrugs.

The Saxon leader begins to snicker, and the others join him, except for the girl in front of me. Her finger is resting against a steel pin sticking out of the wooden shaft. It must be the means to release the string. Why doesn't Wulf have one of these weapons? I don't trust this girl with the brown hair. She may kill me by accident.

"You call me donkey ass?" the boy barks in Norse.

His accent is stronger than Papar's was, but I can understand him well enough. I chuckle, intentionally loud, looking straight into the girl's eyes. She's close enough that I could kick her bow with my feet. At the right moment, I may need to, and I play out the move in my head.

"I did?" Quibly questions. "I thought I called you horse droppings. I'm still working on my Saxon."

"This boy funny. Godwine, shoot him." A stocky boy with black hair, a long nose, and broad shoulders, edges his bow closer to Quibly's head.

"As I said, they are friends of the Saxons," Wulf says in Norse.

"We are going to Wessex," I say, sitting up straighter. "We have a special message for the king."

"You have message for King Alfred?" the leader boy asks. "I think, no."

"The Danes brought a new army to England," I continue. "Hundreds of ships. They're in England now and are on their way to Wessex. We are here to warn the king."

"You and funny boy not Saxon. Godwine—"

"He is the nephew of King Alfred," I say quickly, nodding at Wulf. "His name is Athelwulf. We *are* going to see the King of Wessex."

The boys and girls look at each other and to their leader, taken back by what this stranger just said. "You lie," the leader boy says, moving his attention back to Wulf. "King Alfred have no nephew with this name."

I hear a branch break and turn to see another boy emerge from the shadows, sitting still on a black horse. Unlike the others, who are wearing brown tunics and black boots, he is in leather armor. He jumps off his horse and slowly approaches.

"Wulfric?" he questions, stepping out in front.

"Edward!" Wulf shouts.

CHAPTER 32

Wulf and Edward embrace like long lost friends. I quickly realize that's exactly who they are. Edward is the name of the boy Wulf mentioned in his childhood stories – his cousin, the son of King Alfred, who went to the battles with him as a young child.

They do look remarkably alike. They have the same square jaw and same black, wavy hair. Edward is slightly shorter in height and smaller in stature, but it is clear they come from the same bloodline.

The cousins ramble on together in Saxon, and his companions lower their weapons. I pick up my sword and stand. The girl with the brown hair steps back, and although the arrow is no longer pointed at my head, her finger still rests on the steel pin. I don't blame her as I would do the same. She is really beautiful. In some ways she reminds me of Thoren.

It is some time before the cousins stop talking. Edward calls us to come closer together. He speaks in Norse. "Wulfric is the eldest son of my Uncle Athelred, the King of Wessex before my father." To my surprise, his Norse is very good. "My name is Edward, and I am both pleased and honored to meet each of you. These are my closest friends. They are also fiercely loyal servants to the king."

I look at Wulf and whisper, "Wulfric?" How many names

does he have?

We each introduce ourselves. The girl with the brown hair puts her arm around Edward. Her name is Wynn. She is much more relaxed now. The tall boy's name is George, which is one of the funniest names I've ever heard. He is clearly Edward's next in command. Godwine, with the long hair and broad shoulders, is showing Quibly how the bow weapon works. Quibly is quite excited and claims that I will make him one when we get back to Iceland. Our home seems an eternity away right now, like I lived there in another lifetime.

Edward explains that King Alfred and a small army are hiding in a swamp close by. Alfred was spending the winter in a place where the nobles went hunting for large animals. With a surprise attack, the Danes killed most of the Saxon army. Alfred escaped with a small number of warriors, and they fled to the marshes. They built a small fortress there from which to regroup. They haven't yet found a safe route back to Winchester, but are sending scouts and messengers to as many Saxons as they can reach, hoping to build a united army against the invaders.

Wulf's brothers, Athelwold and Athelhelm, are apparently alive and well, living under King Alfred's roof in Winchester. Wulf took a deep, slow breath when he heard this news. I don't know if he believes him. I will also experience this feeling when I see Grim. It's been many weeks now since I last saw my brother at the feast, wrestling with the noble children and without a worry in Midgard. I miss him.

Edward says we can get to this hide-out by nightfall. He expresses how thrilled King Alfred is going to be to see that Wulf is alive. Apparently, Edward doesn't know what happened many years ago.

The Saxons retrieve horses from the forest, and we follow our new *friends* on narrow trails that wind through the trees. They laughed when they saw Quibly mount the plow horse, but he was quick to scold them, telling that old Hester is having his second chance at life.

Along the trails, Edward tells us story after story of King Alfred's battles to keep the Danes out of Wessex. Alfred learned the language of his enemy so that he could negotiate treaties when necessary, and required all of his top commanders to do the same. Although the agreements inevitably collapsed, Alfred was buying time to unite the Saxons of England and build his army. Edward portrays his father as a man with both a great sword and a great mind. Yet, the king has been holed up in a swamp for over six months. I'll reserve judgment for when I meet him.

I am riding behind the other Saxon girl. She goes by the name Lark. She is a stout girl, almost plump, but a warrior nonetheless. She seems to be under Wynn's command, as if destined to take an arrow or sword to save her master's life. She is always fussing over her, like a mother over a baby. Wynn seems more than capable of fighting her own battles. The Saxons must have another class besides Jarl, Karl, or Thrall.

We cross over rivers and down endless paths the Saxons say are made from animals claiming their hunting grounds. Wulf and Edward are riding side by side and have been talking the entire time. Sometimes they speak in whispers and other times loudly with laughter. Of course, I can't understand a word they are saying other than the occasional mention of the kingdoms or shires that Wulf told me about. I wonder if Edward is aware that his cousin is the rightful heir to the throne of Wessex. This reunion tonight is unlikely to be as joyous as this one. We may be dead before midnight.

We must be getting close as the ground has become muddy and the horses are beginning to tire as they plod through it. Tall grasses, which start green and end gray, reach up beyond the horses' knees. Hester is way behind, but the other animals refuse to stop or slow down. They must think they'll get stuck if they do.

Finally, we find harder ground. George, riding in front, halts the winding line of animals. We wait patiently for Quibly to catch up.

"Wait here," George orders. The boy with the long hair ties his horse to a tree and disappears over a grassy knoll. Edward explains that the fortress is ahead, and they must first be certain the enemy has not attacked while they were gone. And then they must signal our arrival such that we aren't mistaken for the enemy and consequently shot with arrows.

Wulf is noticeably focused. At least I notice. He doesn't look afraid or worried. He's planning his next moves in the fast-approaching confrontation. I'm sure he's thought this moment through a thousand times or more, but it has come upon us rather suddenly. Thankfully, his brothers are alive, unless Edward told him a lie. My greatest concern, however, isn't for Wulf. This encounter must go as I planned if I'm going to rescue my brother. Without Grim, nothing matters.

George returns, announcing that all is good, and we proceed forward. I discretely remove my sword from its sheath and set it on my lap. A structure made of logs comes into view. Temporary or not, this does not look like the home of a king.

The logs lie flat and are stacked taller than our heads, but not by much. Small openings are spaced evenly across the wall in front of us, assumingly to shoot arrows from. The rectangular longhouse could maybe sleep forty, but no more. The army hiding here is *very* small.

Four warriors stand alert outside, all with swords drawn. I was beginning to wonder if Erik was right that Saxons like to fight from afar. But these men are dressed in armor and look very prepared for close combat. At first, the warriors simply acknowledge that we've arrived, then it's clear they count more horses returning than had left. One man rushes inside through a doorway. I make eye contact with Wulf, glancing down at my sword. He gives me no signal as to what his next move is.

A warrior rushes forward and takes the reigns of Edward's horse. Alfred's son dismounts, just as a man emerges from the structure. He is no taller than the warriors next to him, perhaps even shorter. The man is wearing a red cloak which looks as if taken from Godi's grave. A long necklace with a large medallion hangs below a short gray beard. The man doesn't hesitate but marches towards us. He stops short and fixes his eyes on Wulf.

"Alfred," Wulf says calmly, like he had breakfast with the man this morning.

CHAPTER 33

The King of Wessex doesn't reach for his sword, but stands calmly, like a stone pillar protruding unyieldingly from the sand on a stormy beach. There is a commanding presence radiating from this man. It is more than his red cloak that reminds me of Godi.

Edward and his father speak together quietly. I'm sure Edward is telling him how wonderful it is that his lost nephew has returned home. But more importantly, Wulf brought his Norse friends with him, and they warn of an imminent attack from the enemy.

They finish talking and Alfred approaches. He stops at Wulf's horse and gently strokes its black head. Wulf dismounts, his hand on his knife. I hope he doesn't draw his weapon. If he does, I don't know what I'll do. We need Alfred, and I'm not coming all this way to die at the hands of a Saxon. Wulf walks up to his uncle and briefly pauses before embracing him.

"Athelwulf," Alfred says, before wrapping his arms around his nephew. I keep my eyes fixed on Wulf's knife.

Alfred steps back and swiftly pulls his sword from its sheath. I tighten the grip on mine and raise it up. Sassa lifts her front legs off the ground and neighs loudly before slamming them back to the ground. She knows a battle is coming. Quibly jumps off Hester with his battle ax in hand, and I join him. The

Saxon warriors charge towards us, the clanking of their iron echoing off the trees. Alfred is my only hope. My heart is racing. I need to stop Wulf.

Alfred throws his arms in the air and shouts at his men. They hesitantly slow up and stop. I take two steps forward. Alfred and Wulf are only a giant lunge away. Alfred kneels, just as my foot comes off the ground. I stumble forward and regain my footing. The king turns his sword around, extending the pommel towards Wulf.

"What's happening?" Quibly whispers.

"Shhh," I scold.

Wulf takes the sword and gazes down at his uncle. Alfred removes his red cloak and lowers his head. Like the others, I stand frozen. Wulf raises the weapon in the air, gripping the pommel of the weapon with both hands. Wulf won't do it. Will he?

"Wulf's going to kill him," Quibly says. "We're dead."

Wulf thrusts the sword down. I want to scream, but the sound doesn't come out.

The sword is quivering side to side, its blade stuck deep into the ground, not far from the king's head. Alfred looks up and slowly gets to his feet. He pulls the sword from the earth and returns it to its sheath. He pats Wulf on the back and embraces him once again. The Saxon men have now surrounded us.

"Uncle," Wulf says in Norse, turning toward us. "I would like you to meet my dear friends. This is Quibly, the strongest warrior I have known."

Quibly stands up tall, a smile beaming from ear-to-ear.

"And this is Livvy. One of Iceland's greatest shield

maidens. I may ask her to marry me one day."

I want to smile, too, but am still absorbing what just happened. The gods, at least one of them, was listening after all. And although Wulf is undoubtedly joking about the marrying, I don't find it funny at all.

"A shield maiden?" Alfred questions with a hint of curiosity. "I have only heard tales. It is my honor to meet a great warrior."

"To health and happiness, King Alfred," I say.

"Please, just call me Alfred. You can call me king when we get to Winchester and the queen is within earshot. Please, you must all be hungry. Come inside. We will drink wine and feast on boar. We have plenty to talk about."

We follow him inside. The longhouse is spacious and tidy. Weapons cover three of the four walls – shields on one, swords, knives, and axes on another, and bows and quivers on the last. Near the farthest wall, a wool blanket hangs from the ceiling, concealing whatever lies behind it.

In total, there are thirty-something Saxons. The men are Alfred's age or younger, except for one old man who is huddled under a blanket in the corner. Other than me, Wynn and Lark are the only girls here. This is hardly the army I had expected to find. I hope the one back in Winchester is considerably bigger. If not, we are doomed.

A large, round table is in the middle of the room, with a fat animal cooked a golden brown, lying in its center. My mouth begins to water. I haven't had a full meal in days. Quibly mutters one of his Saxon curse words under his breath. The air is very warm, and two fires are roaring on opposite sides of the room. Skins are stacked high in a corner. For a temporary shelter built in the mud bogs, it is surprisingly inviting.

We gather around the table. I placed my shield against the wall but keep my sword at my feet. Edward, Wynn, George, and four men join us. Edward looks both concerned and upset. I'm certain he will demand answers when he is in the private company of his father. We are not in the clear yet. Alfred takes his seat directly across from me.

The men seem to relax after drinking a few horns of wine and filling their bellies with meat. Quibly doesn't say much, but that's understandable, as his mouth has been stuffed with food the entire time. I also eat until my belly is full but sip the wine slowly. Until my brother is back safely, I won't take any chances.

The men are in awe that another relative of the king is in their company, and they almost bump into each other to serve the lost nephew. Despite him insisting they call him Wulf, they address him as Athelwulf. At first, he is a bit frustrated but eventually gives up fighting it.

Alfred tops up our horns and raises his in the air. "Skal," he says, with a smile. "I believe that's how you say it?" We nod in approval.

"Skal!" we shout together.

Alfred is not the man I was expecting him to be. I'm not sure exactly who it was I was expecting, but I think someone bigger and more intimidating. He is much smaller than Erik, Tore, and Bjorn. He listens more than he talks, and unlike Quibly who's already half-asleep, he's intensely focused on every word spoken. I remember Wulf once said that Alfred was as clever as he was strong. To have survived for this many years against the Danes, I don't doubt it.

"Please, tell me how you made it from this distant land to England," Alfred says, leaning forward. "Did you sail on one of your great dragon ships?"

"The mightiest ship in Midgard," Quibly boasts.

"Midgard, yes, the realm of us humans," Alfred affirms. "Please, tell me everything and how I can be of your service."

We spend the evening and into the night recalling the adventures of the last two months. We warn Alfred that Ivar the Boneless and a united army from Norseland and Denmark have landed in the north. They are likely in Jórvík now, preparing for an onslaught on Wessex. We also tell him of Erik, and how he's hunting Ivar and seeking revenge for the deaths of Godi and our clan. But most importantly, we insist we can help them. We want Ivar and his men defeated as much as the Saxons do.

"This army, under the command of Erik, do they know how to build your dragon ships?" Alfred asks.

"Yes," I answer quickly, seizing the opportunity. If Alfred wants to build ships like ours, then he may be motivated to seek our help. "Sven, the great navigator, rides with Erik. His family has crafted generations of these mighty ships."

Wulf asks his uncle, "What are your plans to return to Winchester? I want to see that my brothers are well."

Perhaps this was a test for Alfred, but the king shows no signs of concern. Just as Edward told us, Alfred explains they have been in the swamps for months. They are close to having a route to Wessex secured but are waiting for a small army to leave, at a place they call Ethandun. They expect the Danes will be there another month, at the most. In the meantime, they are getting word to the Saxon farmers, craftsmen, and seamen, who have so far escaped the Danes' wrath, that the King of Wessex is alive. Alfred's hope is to summon them to war against the Danes when the time is right.

"A united England is the only way to defeat the Danes," Alfred says, offering more wine. Quibly gladly accepts.

"A united England, with our clan as your ally," I suggest.

"Perhaps so," the king says with a smile. "It is late, and it is never wise to be too tired. The men will prepare your beds. I have some work to attend to, so I wish you a pleasant sleep."

Alfred goes behind the hanging wool blanket, and his men scatter the skins on the dirt. I still have a lot I want to talk about, but it will have to wait until tomorrow.

Lark asks for Quibly's help, and he goes with her. Soon he is carrying the old man in the corner to a resting place on the ground. I assume he is waiting to die in battle so that his god will accept him into his realm. Why else would he be here?

After tucking the old man under his skin, Lark wraps her hands around the bulk of Quibly's arm, assumingly admiring his strength. I smile at her blatant flirtation, but Quibly is enjoying every bit of it. The girl squeals as he picks her up and spins her around. Thoren hit him in the face when he tried that with her. Edward and Wulf leave the longhouse together. How Wulf answers his questions could decide our fate.

A glow roars to life behind the wool curtain at the end of the room. Lying on my skin, I see Alfred between the slits where the two pieces come together. He is sitting at a table facing towards me and is looking down, holding something in his hand. Whatever it is, it sparkles like the sun off the snow on a bright winter day. I try to make out what this object could be, but my eyes won't stay open.

I awake and it's dark. Everyone is asleep. Wulf is back and lying next to me, his hand on his knife. I don't know where Quibly is, but I can hear him. I sit up and notice the light still glowing from behind the hanging wool. I peer through the slit. Alfred is still awake, bent down over the table. He looks up and his eyes meet mine. Before I can look away, he smiles and waves at me to come over.

I think of taking my sword, but I need to gain his trust. I quietly stand and step over a number of sleeping bodies. I pull the wool aside and step into the small chamber.

"I see we both have trouble sleeping," he whispers. "Please sit with me."

A stack of thin parchments lies on one end of the table. I don't know what they're made from, but the top one is covered with symbols. Another stack lies on the table's other end. I now see what sparkled in Alfred's hand. At the end of a small stick is an object shaped like a water drop. An image of a man, made from gems of blue, green, and white, is encased inside. Symbols, the color of gold, encircle the base of the object. I can't take my eyes off it.

Alfred sees me studying it. He sets it in front of me and points to the symbols. "The words here read, Alfred ordered me made," he says with a smile. "I only asked for a reading stick, but this is what he made me. Beautiful, isn't it?"

"Yes, it's one of the most beautiful things I have ever seen."

"It helps me follow the words when reading. I guess my finger would be good enough, but I like to hold something.

Strange, don't you think? I am translating these words from an ancient language into Saxon."

A feather, dipped in ink, rests on a small piece of wood. I've seen many like it at the monastery in the hamlet. "What do these symbols say?" I ask.

"Come around and I will read this to you." I do as he asks and stand next to him on the other side of the table.

Alfred picks up the stick and moves it along the symbols. "When you go to battle against your enemies and see horses, chariots, and people greater than you, do not be afraid of them, for God is with you."

These words sound no different than those told by our elders. With Odin on our side, we were told we could not lose a battle. Men may die, but Odin will always prevail.

"These words were written by man, but God said them," he says. "We write them down so we will never forget them." Alfred stands. "Livvy, did Athelwulf tell you what happened when he was a boy? Before he left England?"

I decide to hide nothing. "If you mean that you gave him to the Danes so that you could become king, then yes."

He doesn't seem surprised by my response nor does he show any sign of remorse. "Can you read?" he asks.

"I know of no Norseman or woman who can. But I had an old Saxon friend who was going to teach me one day. Ivar the Boneless killed him."

"I am sorry to hear about your friend. But have peace knowing that he is with God. I believe we can trust each other." He picks up the pointing stick and extends it towards me. "This is my gift to you. My only condition is that one day you learn how to read these words. They can help both the weak and strong win battles without bloodshed."

I take the stick in my hands. It's heavier than I was expecting. "Why would you give this to me?"

"It's just an object. I can't take it with me when I die."

"You can't?" I question.

Alfred grins. "Not where I'm going." I recall that the monks at the hamlet didn't believe in being buried with their possessions.

"You came all this way to warn me," he says. "This is my gift in return."

If this object can help build trust between us, then I would be foolish not to take it. And it must be worth a small fortune. "I accept," I say, trying to sound less excited than I am.

"Excellent. Now I can finally sleep."

"May I offer a suggestion?" I ask.

"You may make any suggestion you like. Just know that I have no obligation to follow it."

"Yes, of course." I clear my throat. "The Danes and the Shockheads will attack Winchester sooner than later. We can't wait another month. We should leave at once. And we need to get word to Erik."

"And may I also make a suggestion?" he asks. I nod. "There may be a time when you will be forced to choose between kingdom and family. If that time comes, seek wisdom in your decision. The greatest warriors are called upon to make the greatest sacrifice."

My destiny is to save Grim, not to get this far and somehow sacrifice him. Alfred may feel justified betraying his nephew for the better of his kingdom, but more likely it was driven by greed. But regardless, I need him.

CHAPTER 34

I slept well, better than I have in days, maybe weeks. The smell of something sweet and smoky fills my nostrils. Everyone is outside, except the old man who is lying in the far corner. He's staring at me. I jump up and grab my sword, checking my surroundings as I rush to the door.

I reach down and feel that the gold pointer is still hidden in my skin bag. Last night I detached the stick and concealed it in my sword's sheath. It occurred to me as I lay in bed that the gift could be a trap – Norse wanderers caught stealing a gem from the mighty Alfred. But a king hardly needs a reason or excuse to sentence Quibly or me to death. The Danes, after all, have committed countless atrocities against the Saxons. Unless it's a way to justify the execution to his nephew. I push the door open, squinting my eyes from the sudden brightness. The sun does come to England after all.

"The shield maiden awakes!" a voice bellows.

It sounds like it came from Wulf's cousin. A crowd is circled around a fire and sipping from wooden bowls. Wynn slaps Edward across the shoulder and stands up. She picks up a bowl and comes my way.

"Don't mind him," Wynn says as she approaches. "He slept the entire day after our wedding." She leans in and whispers, "And most of our wedding night. Come sit down, Alfred has summoned us." Wynn takes my arm in hers, and we walk to the fire. Wulf and Alfred aren't here that I can see. I sit next to Quibly and Lark.

"I tried to wake you this morning," Quibly says. "You reached for your sword without opening your eyes. I thought it best to let you sleep."

"Thanks." I don't know if I believe him or not. I take a sip of the soup. It's salty and oily, and tastes as good as it smells. "Where's Wulf?" I ask.

"There," Quibly points. Alfred and Wulf are emerging from the dark trees. The king is wearing leather armor and an iron chain mail. His boots reach up to his knees. Wulf is wearing the same clothes he's had on for the last week. The two nobles stop a few paces in front of us.

Alfred waves George over, and after a few brief words, the tall boy shouts some Saxon words. The men begin to assemble, and George leaves to summon the others from around the camp. Before long, the Saxon king raises an arm in the air. Wulf is standing quietly at his side. He looks at me and winks. The Saxons sit on the ground and fall silent. Quibly and I do the same.

"First, I will speak in Norse and repeat in Saxon," Alfred says, looking at Wulf and then at me. "God, our Father, has given us another sign. He sent my nephew back to me. He was lost but now is found." Wulf is standing tall with his arms behind his back. The two have agreed on something.

"Last night an angel came and spoke to me," Alfred continues. He looks into my eyes. "She warned me that unlike in the heavens, time does not stand still. Our enemy will soon be at our castle's gates. We will return to Winchester and protect our people from the Danes. But we will not stop there. The time has also come to unite England. Whether from the north, east, west, or south, we must bring all Saxons together. The time has come to fight!"

All the Saxons stand and shout their approval, their weapons raised in the air. I'm taken back to the night of the feast when Godi spoke of going back to Norseland to fight the Shockheads.

Quibly wraps his arm around me and pulls me in. "You did it," he says. "I don't know how, but you did it. And what's an angel? Not a troll, I hope."

Wulf explained once that angels are immortal creatures who serve the Christian God. He also mentioned angels who revolted against the gods and were banished from the heavens. I forgot what he called them, but one day the angels on both sides are to fight in a great war, and our world would be changed forever. This story, of course, is not so different than ours of Ragnarok, when Loki and the giants rise up against the gods. Wouldn't it be strange if our stories came from the same place? As far as one of the angels speaking with Alfred last night, I'm not so sure.

I look over at Quibly. "Papar is in the sky and is watching over us."

He looks down at me and then at the army surrounding us. "He may be," he nods. "He just may be. When we find Ivar the Boneless, I still get to hold him down, right?"

"That was the deal."

"Good, just checking. Odin and Thor will be proud, and I will feast with the gods in Valhalla."

"Yes, you will," I assure him.

The men eventually disperse, and Alfred approaches Quibly and me. "Please come inside," he says.

Wulf, Edward, Wynn, and George are already in the fort, sitting quietly at the round table. The old man is still in the corner, huddled under a wool blanket. We join them and take our seats on the wooden chairs.

Alfred takes a long breath. "I am not your king, but I am the only king of England still alive. I don't expect you to serve me as your king, but I demand trust. That is the only way we will defeat this enemy."

I feel again for the gold pointer. "You have my trust," I promise with a nod.

"And mine," Quibly says.

"Good," Alfred continues. "Edward and Wulf will take a few men to find your chieftain and bring him and his army here. Livvy and Quibly, you can stay and train with my army. In one week, we will attack the Danes who are camping at Ethandum. Our victory will not only clear our passage to Winchester, but it will show all Saxons, farmers and warriors alike, that the pagan armies can be defeated."

"What do you mean by pagan?" Quibly asks, shifting in his chair.

Alfred pauses, looking deep in thought. "It is the wrong word. Viking means to raid, is that right?" Alfred asks.

"Yes," Quibly answer. "And with it, all the property and slaves they can take."

"It will be written, that today marks the end of these raids. I will write it myself and will send this message to all of England. The raids, these vikings, will end. And from now on, we will call the armies from the Northlands, *Vikings*. Does this word seem appropriate, Quibly?"

"Yes, why not? Or we just call them bastards."

"Perhaps we will call them both," Alfred says. "The sun is rising, and we must begin our preparation."

Outside, Quibly pulls Wulf and me away from the others. "It should be me who rides for Erik," he whispers. "He will not believe you, Wulf. He will sense a trap. *Livvy and Quibly are with the Saxon king, come with me?* Would you believe this?"

"My uncle wants you both here," Wulf says. "And he is willing to fight Ivar and his army. This is what we wanted, wasn't it?"

"What if Alfred is sending you off to get killed?" Quibly questions. "How well do you know your cousin?"

"We were best friends as children."

"And now that you're back, who becomes king when Alfred dies?"

"This is not the time to discuss this," Wulf says.

"You were the one to say men would do anything to stay in power," Quibly says, continuing to press.

"I trust him, and you need to trust me," Wulf says. "And Erik will believe me. I will make him."

"This is the best way," I say. I look into Quibly's big eyes and wrap my arms as far around his belly as they will go. "It can't be by chance that we have come this far. And I need your help. You know more about fighting than I do."

"I'm not so certain of that," he says with a smile. He looks at Wulf. "If Tore rips you into two pieces, you can't say that I didn't warn you."

"You can sleep like a drunk knowing that my two parts are not on your hands," he says, slapping Quibly on the back.

By midday, Wulf and Edward have their horses prepared for their journey. They plan to head towards Jórvík and look for Erik there. There's a good chance they'll be captured or killed before they ever find them. It doesn't need to be spoken. Jórvik belongs to the *Vikings* as King Alfred now calls them. And although Wulf can speak Norse, he does not look Norse. If they are captured, and the enemy learns they're Saxon nobles, they'll be tortured with the blood eagle, just as Godi was.

Quibly and I take a break from practicing in the shield wall. The Saxons are strong for their size. I reach Wulf just as he mounts his black horse.

"I was thinking of taking Sassa," Wulf says with a grin, just as the horse kicks up his feet.

"Then I would have to kill you," I say, trying to sound serious.

"She loves you and would probably throw me to the enemy for taking her away from you."

"If she follows my orders, then, yes, she would." This time I can't conceal my smile. "I will see you in a week, no more. And don't come back without Erik."

"Do you think Thoren will be upset to see Quibly with Lark?"

I look back to see the two throwing axes at a tree. "Nothing would surprise me anymore. I wonder how Thoren's arm is healing. We're going to need her out there."

"I meant what I said when I introduced you to Alfred."

I've listened to those words a few time in my head. *This is*

Livvy

Livvy. One of Iceland's greatest shield maidens. I may ask her to marry me one day. But before I can ask if he means the shield maiden or the marrying part, he squeezes his legs and snaps the reigns. Within a few breaths, he's gone.

CHAPTER 35

"Up!" Quibly shouts. "Attack!" he shouts again.

We run forward, our shields locked tightly in place. Quibly is at the front of the arrow formation, and I am to his right. The strongest warrior is always at the point. He will be the first to make impact, and if he collapses, the entire group will fail. And in most cases, this means death. But if he holds his ground, the formation of only ten or twelve warriors will break through almost any shield wall. And more often than not, when the wall fails, it's every man, *or woman*, for themselves. And this is just how the Norse like it.

We hit the shield wall at full speed, and just like the last five times, we break through with ease. George leads the next wave of warriors and rushes through the wall behind us. Wynn and the archers aim their arrows through the collapsed defense.

"Good, we try again," Godwine says as he pushes his black hair away from his face. "This time, I take the point."

"Yes, please! I will watch your form," Quibly says as he plops himself onto the ground. Although Godwine is much lighter than Quibly, he is solid and fearless. I'm sure he will do a fine job at the point.

Despite their first encounter, when Godwine almost shot Quibly with an arrow for calling George names, the two have become good friends. They stayed up late drinking ale every night since Wulf and Edward left five days ago. Yesterday, Godwine was teaching him how to flirt with a girl in Saxon. I would be shocked if anything they said actually worked. I step back from the training and watch the Saxons repeat the exercise.

"We are almost ready," Alfred says, as he comes and stands next to me, admiring his men at work.

"Your warriors are fearless," I say, watching the shields collide. "They could almost be mistaken for Berserkers."

"Berserkers?" Alfred questions curiously.

I explain to him about the warriors with the red eyes who fight like wild beasts. I tell him of the black seeds that give them their powers, but I keep it a secret that I ate them once. I've shared nothing of Grim with any of the Saxons. My brother's life is my greatest weakness, and I see no advantage in exposing my real motives for being here. The least I share of my past, the better.

"How do you suggest we defeat these Berserkers?" Alfred asks.

"Quibly slowed one down by throwing a large stone at his head," I say with a smirk.

"Slowed him down?"

"They feel invincible and have no fear of death. Some believe they're beasts from another world. Perhaps from the realm of the giants. But beasts or men, they have a weakness."

Alfred waits for me to continue, looking at his warriors fighting on the muddy field. I recall the advice the seer gave me when I asked her how the Berserkers could be defeated.

"They'll only think of killing what is in front of them," I say. "Actually, they won't be thinking at all. Our warriors are taught to be aware of their surroundings at all times. Berserkers won't remember their lessons. We attack them like a pack of wolves attacks a bear. Distract them with one warrior and slice them down with another."

Alfred looks back at his men as they make another charge. "I have not seen this wedge formation before."

"It is one of ours. Quibly taught us."

"What do you call it?"

"The boar snout. At least that's what Quibly calls it."

Alfred quietly watches his men before speaking. "Fitting name, but your boar snout has vulnerabilities. It is weak from an attack from the sides, and retreating is almost impossible."

"Our warriors don't retreat," I say.

"Good."

"Good?"

"We will use their strength as a weakness," Alfred says. "George! Let your men rest. Bring the others to the round table."

"Come with me," Alfred says, wrapping his arm around my shoulder. "We will devise a new attack. And later you can tell me about this realm of giants."

I roll my eyes, revealing that this realm may be more tale than truth. I don't doubt there is another realm besides ours, but I've only seen men kill each other. If giants, dwarves, or trolls do exist, they must be shy creatures hiding in the shadows.

As I take my seat next to Wynn at the table, I see the old man's face for the first time. He is sitting up against the wall below the swords, knives, and axes, and is drinking from a wooden bowl. His gray, wirily hair extends past his shoulders, blending into his thick beard. The old man's gaunt face is a pale yellow, as is his eyes, and his shoulders are drooping as if they've been pulled from their sockets. Although he is thin and wrinkled, he looks more alive than he did earlier.

The men are standing and pouring themselves a drink of ale. Lark is helping cook a deer that was killed this morning, and Quibly is glancing her way. At any other time, I would be certain he was looking at the food, wondering how soon it will arrive at the table. Today, this is not the case.

Wynn leans over and whispers in my ear. "I'm with child." She takes my hand and squeezes it under the table. "Shhh, only you and Lark know."

"That's great!" I whisper with a forced smile, concealing the thoughts that jumped into my head. "Does Edward know?"

"Not yet. I wanted to be sure before I told him. He's going to be so happy. Naturally, he wants a boy, but I'm secretly praying for a girl."

I turn my attention back to the old man. I've never been comfortable talking about babies, and Grim is the only one I enjoyed holding. But more important than my feelings, war is no place for a woman carrying a child, and to war is exactly where we're going. Wynn lets go of my hand as the men take their seats at the table.

We spend the evening devising a battle plan for Ethandun. We are going to be severely outnumbered, so we need to take them by surprise. Alfred's observations are right. The boar snout attack is built to break through a horizontal shield wall. The common defense is to strengthen the point of impact with the strongest men. But the charging warriors have their shields aimed forward. If we create a counter-attack to leverage this weakness, it can help shift the odds in our favor. And the gods know we're going to need all the help we can get.

After a long evening of planning, we take to sleep on the skins. Alfred, as he does every night, lights the candles behind the curtain. I fall asleep watching him write his symbols through the glowing slit between the hanging wools.

I'm awoken by shouting. If we're being ambushed by the Berserkers, we're as good as dead. Images of the night of the feast flash through my head. I grab my sword and shield, and rush with the others towards the door. I look for Quibly, but it's too dark to identify anyone. I trip over someone or something and almost fall to the earth. It must be the old man. Perhaps he died in the night and won't get to fight his final battle.

Outside, there are no Berserkers swarming our fort, at least not yet. I was expecting them to be chopping the Saxons down like twigs, just as these beasts did to us the night of the feast. I dart behind a tree, shielding myself from the risk of incoming arrows. The Saxons are storming into the forest, shouting in words I don't understand. *What are they doing? Do they wish to die?*

Quibly pushes up next me, just about knocking me over. I almost swing my sword at his head.

"The Saxons are fleeing," he says as he raises his ax up by his head. "What do you want to do?"

"We fight," I say. I don't need to think about it, as I've already imagined this situation, and countless others, awake and in my dreams. If we're captured, I'll say we were taken by the Saxons as slaves. Then I'll find a way to kill them and escape when they least expect it. If we run, the enemy will chase us down, just as wild animals attack on instinct when their prey runs. This decision is an easy one.

The Saxons, however, begin to emerge from the thin forest,

dragging a man behind them. At first, I assume he's one of theirs, but then I see they're pulling him by his feet. Even from a distance, I recognize the long hair and inked face. How did they find us? If the Shockheads are here, then so is Ivar the Boneless.

CHAPTER 36

I look down at the man's face. The muscular warrior is bigger than any man here. If it wasn't for the arrow in his chest, there is no way the Saxons could have taken him alive. He recognizes at once that I am Norse, and the anger in his eyes turns to confusion. He pulls and twists at the ropes binding his arms and legs.

There were two Shockheads, at least that's all the men saw. The other one escaped in the dark. Alfred sent a few men to find him. But even if they do, the Norse armies will know we are here.

"Are you traitor or slave?" the Shockhead mutters in Norse through his clenched teeth.

"It doesn't matter," I answer. "You are the one who's going to die." The Shockhead grimaces as he looks at the broken shaft still impaled in his body.

"Fairhair took my clan's land, and the Danes killed my people," I say, leaning down and whispering in his ear. "Tell me, is Ivar the Boneless with you?"

The man spits in my face, and I stand while wiping it off with my sleeve.

"Ivar will find you, and you will pray to the gods that you die before he rips your ribs and lungs out," he growls.

"We will find him first," I say. I leave him to the Saxons to do their interrogation and go outside with Quibly. The Shockhead won't live long, but with Valhalla so close, he won't risk angering the gods either. I doubt he will give them any useful information.

"They're going to find us," Alfred says. I turn to see him coming out of the fort. "We need to go."

"To Ethandum, while we have the advantage of an ambush," I say as a statement more than a question.

Quibly clears his throat. "We can't go to war without Erik," he says. "We don't have enough men, Livvy."

"If Ivar is here, they're marching to Wessex. If we don't stop them, the kingdom is sure to fall. And if it falls—" I hold my words back. *I will never see Grim again.*

"Livvy is right," Alfred says. "If the kingdom falls then I have failed Wessex. No—I have failed all of England. The stories will not be written that the King of Wessex died holed up in a swamp with his ink and skins. It is time to fight."

Quibly gives me a look that says, *here we go again.*

"We can't live forever," I say to him with a shrug.

"Well, at least you have Sassa and your magic sword. All I have is Hester," he grumbles.

"Your sword has magic?" Alfred questions.

"It was made by the same iron that slayed Sigurd's dragon," Quibly says. "A witch gave it to Livvy. Well, at first she gave it to Thoren. Okay, she didn't really give it to her, but she told us where to find it. It was in a grave. And Ivar has one just like it. Then Livvy found the anvil stone at the monastery, so now we don't know where it came from, but I think Motsognir, the dwarf lord, is up to no good. You see, when the end of Midgard comes, the dwarves will join the giants—"

"Quibly," I interrupt. "You're rambling."

"Dwarves are evil creatures," he sulks as if that was the point of his entire rant.

"You mentioned a monastery, where you saw an anvil stone?" Alfred questions. "Was there something special about this stone?"

"We found a smithy at Lindisfarne, and there was a forging stone that has the same markings on it as my sword. I think the sword may have been made there, but how it found its way to Iceland is a mystery."

"You found a sword made by Ulfberht?" Alfred asks in disbelief.

"You know this man?" I ask.

"Know him? He's inside."

The great steel maker is inside? When did he arrive? Before I ask who it is, the Saxons come through the door carrying the Shockhead by his arms and legs. We watch as they lug him into the forest, his torso barely off the ground.

"Let's go talk to Ulfberht," Alfred says as he leads the way into the fort. "I'm fascinated as you are about this sword of yours. I want to know if it's better than the one he made me."

Alfred has one? How many of these swords were crafted? We enter through the doorway, and I search the dark room for the blacksmith who made my sword, Alfred's, and the one Ivar carries. But unless Lark or Wynn has a secret craft, there is no one else here.

"Ulfberht, have you met our Viking friends? You aren't going to believe what they came into possession of."

A frail voice comes from the dark corner of the room. "I've seen it." The old man shuffles slowly out of the shadows into the light cast by the moonlight through the open doorway.

"You feeling any better?" Alfred asks.

"No, I'm not feeling any better. Stop asking," he grumbles.

"The priest prayed for you and anointed you with oil. If it's God's will for you to live, then you will live," Alfred says without empathy.

The old man swipes his hand at the ground, dismissing the Saxon king as he nudges forward. He stops in front of me, his old eyes level with mine. "What I want to know is why Athelwulf would give you his sword?"

Wulf's sword? I turn my head to locate the pommel of the weapon sticking out of my sheath. This can't be Wulf's sword, he would have told me. We found it in a grave with a dead man. "I'm afraid you are mistaken," I say.

"I have made many mistakes in my life, but this isn't one of them," he says. "I made that sword. It belongs to Athelwulf." He reaches his quivering arms forward. "Let me see it."

I do as he says, pulling the sword off my back and placing it in his hands. His tired, yellow eyes light up, and a faint smile emerges from his cracked lips. He studies the weapon, looking first at the pommel, then at the cross-guard, the length of the blade, and finally the engraving.

"It took me over a month to craft this steel. One of the finest I ever made." He hands the weapon back to me and slowly sits down at the table.

"I don't understand," I say, thinking of any reason as to how Wulf's sword found its way to a grave in Iceland when he was taken as a slave. I find Alfred's eyes, and he looks sternly into mine as if trying to read my thoughts. If Alfred traded his nephew to the Danes, he knows what became of this weapon.

And he knows that I know this.

Ulfberht mutters something in Saxon, and Alfred looks away. Lark hurries over and guides the old man back to his bed, just as George and Godwine come clanking through the doorway covered in sweat.

George speaks in Saxon, huffing between breaths. "In Norse," Alfred commands.

George mutters to himself in frustration. "There is no sign of other Viking," he says. "It is too dark to see anything."

"Tell your men to go to sleep," Alfred says. "Tomorrow, we will march to Ethandun."

George speaks slowly and carefully. "My king, we don't have enough men to win battle."

Lark returns with Alfred's robe, and the king drapes it over his shoulders. "You are not the first one to tell me this," Alfred says. "God parted a sea with the staff of Moses. He collapsed the walls of Jericho with the sounds of trumpets. If it is his will that we defeat this heathen army, then we will prevail."

Lying on my skin, I sharpen my sword – or is it Wulf's sword? The room is dark, and the candles aren't lit behind the wool curtains. I didn't notice the engravings on Alfred's sword, but I wasn't looking either. I must talk with Ulfberht before we leave for Ethandun. It will take a day to reach the camp, and he is in no condition to make such a journey, nor will he be of any help in battle. I must know how these weapons are forged. In the right hands, an army with these weapons will be unstoppable. He must also tell me where to find these rocks that burn with such heat. Blacksmiths don't share their secrets readily, but Ulfberht is an old man. I will convince him.

Although I won't sleep well tonight, I feel strong and rested.

But as hard as I try, I still can't see Grim in my thoughts, and it frightens me that I think less and less of him. Like those of my mother, my memories of him are slowly vanishing. I know my destiny, my purpose, is to fight for him. But I may be fighting to avenge my little brother and not rescue him. This thought is unbearable, and I put my attention back to my weapon. When the sun rises, we will march to battle, and despite all the impending death, I can't help but smile.

CHAPTER 37

"Livvy." It's a faint whisper. I recognize the salty smell of his hair at the same moment I do his voice. "Livvy, it's me."

My sword is lying out of its sheath, next to my sheepskin, but I don't need to reach for it. I open my eyes, and he's kneeling next to me, his hand gently touching my shoulder.

"We're back. We're here to fight with you," he says. Erik's long, blond hair is hanging past his scruffy beard and resting on my chest. Although it's still dark, his big smile is as clear as if it were midday.

"Hi," I whisper back, disguising my excitement to see him. I now see what the girls at the hamlet saw while they huddled together like bees attacking a lonely flower. Erik does look like a descendant of the gods. He moves his fingers softly across my cheek, and I almost lose my breath.

"I've been searching for you for days," he says. "I thought I might have lost you. But the gods told me that my destiny was to defeat this army with you by my side."

"Where's Wulf?" I ask, gazing into his blue eyes.

"I'm right here!" a voice growls. Wulf is standing above us, gripping a long arrow with two hands. He smiles at me before thrusting the arrow down.

I sit up in bed, gasping for air. The boys aren't here. I pick up my sword and stare into the darkness. It's the first night in days I haven't dreamt of Ivar pounding his sword against my shield, but this one was worse. Quibly is next to me, and he rolls onto his side while muttering something to himself.

I get up, making my way around the sleeping bodies, and step outside into the cool, damp air. Two men are stoking the fire with branches, and another two are standing guard at the edge of the forest. The sun will rise soon.

"You are up early." I turn to see Ulfberht sitting against the wall of the fort, with a thick sheepskin draped around his body. "Please sit." He pats the spot next to him, inviting me to join him.

I take a seat, wrapping my arms around my legs to fend off the chill. "You were up before me," I say.

"I'm always up," he replies. "I haven't slept in months, maybe years. I'm sick and can't work. So I just wait."

"You're waiting to die?" I ask.

Ulfberht laughs, then coughs. "Yes, I suppose I am."

"In Iceland, where I'm from, my father was a blacksmith," I say. "I became an apprentice after his death. I helped make a sword once but never on my own. Mostly I made arrow tips and shoes for horses."

Ulfberht smiles. "You appreciate the effort that goes into making a fine weapon, then?"

"This sword is the most magnificent weapon I have ever seen. Wulf told me that a warrior fighting with this blade will never lose a battle."

"Well, you are still alive, aren't you?" he says with a grin. "Maybe it's true."

"Yes, I suppose I am." The fire is now roaring to life, and the crackling of wood cuts through the silent darkness as its moisture tries to escape. This is as good a time as any to ask.

"Will you tell me how you forged this steel? I would like to learn the secrets of your craft and use it against the Danes."

The old man stares at the fire before slowly getting to his feet. "All the monks who worked with me in the smithy are dead. The Danes threw most of them over Lindisfarne's walls into the rocks and sea. I was in Winchester making jewels for the king and his palaces at the time. It was on that day that I started fearing your gods more than my own."

Ulfberht steadies himself against the walls of the fort and wobbles towards the doorway. "The secrets of my craft are in your hands," he says, before disappearing inside.

I sigh as I get to my feet and make my way to the stable to feed Sassa. I wasn't able to convince the old man after all. He's going to die soon, and I don't see the benefit of him holding his craft a secret. He must not trust me. I am a *Viking* after all.

It is late in the day before we begin our journey to Ethandun. We spent the morning practicing our battle plan. The rest of the day was spent sharpening the swords and axes, and preparing the horses. Other than weapons and a day's rations, we didn't need to pack much. For me, the only things I'm bringing are my shield, sword, two knives, and the gold pointer given to me by Alfred. Ulfberht is the only Saxon who stayed behind. If we don't return, he said he would somehow make it to Lindisfarne so that he could die there and not in a swamp infested with insects. I hope he makes it, even though his fate will be certain if he gets there. And it won't be a pleasant one.

Our plan is to make it to the Dane camp by nightfall and attack at first light tomorrow. Immediately before dawn, the men will be in their deepest sleep, yet we'll have just enough light to mount our attack. This timing is no different than when the Danes attacked the hamlet the night of the feast. If we're lucky, they will also be drunk and confused.

We're back into the thick of the bog, and the horses are struggling with each step. In some places, the slop is up to their knees. As if we need another challenge, the clouds have descended from the sky, and we're in their cold and wet center. I'm in the middle of the file of horses and can't see the beginning or the end of our small army.

But I can hear Quibly. He's riding Hester and has already fallen way behind. He's shouting his Saxon curse words and drawing laughter from the men. If the enemy can't see us, they'll hear us. I think of scolding Quibly and the others. Although we're still far from Ethandun, that doesn't mean the Danes and Shockheads won't be lurking in the shadows, ready to mount their own ambush. But the men need to keep their spirits high, so I hold my tongue.

Alfred and George are at the front, and we're following them like a procession of ants that have found a large breadcrumb. We could be going back to Lindisfarne and I wouldn't know it. I'm riding alongside Wynn. Lark is on a smaller horse immediately in front of us, her shield and sword drawn. If we're attacked in this mud, it won't matter what weapons we have in our hands.

I wonder if Lark is more alert knowing her master is pregnant. Wynn seems unconcerned that the child living in her will likely never take a breath, yet alone grow up to inherit a kingdom one day. Edward is Alfred's first born and will rule the Kingdom of Wessex when his father dies. His son, that is if Wynn is having a boy, will do the same when Edward dies. If they all die tomorrow, then I don't know who's left to rule. It won't matter anyway. I watch Wynn riding in silence. Her husband is missing, and we're going to war. It's largely my doing that Edward and Wulf went to look for Erik and his men. I muster the courage to say something other than that of battle preparations.

"We won't likely survive tomorrow," I say. That didn't sound compassionate, and from the look on Wynn's face, she didn't take it that way either. "You may be carrying the future King of Wessex," I continue. "Are you certain this is a good idea—you going to war?"

"There is no kingdom if the Vikings kill us or take us as slaves," she answers, turning to me. There is no fear in her voice. "We have no choice but to fight. I am fighting so that my son or daughter can live."

"Would Edward let you fight if he were here?"

"Not if he knew I was with child," she says without hesitation. "But I wouldn't tell him. We need every sword tomorrow, and I can fight as well as any man."

"You're a shield maiden," I say.

"A shield maiden?"

"We call women warriors shield maidens. Thoren, Erik's cousin, is the greatest shield maiden I have ever met. She fought in many battles and killed many men. She even fought Ivar the Boneless with this sword. She didn't win but she survived. I think you would like her."

"At least I will get to fight side by side with another shield maiden," Wynn says with a smile.

"If you see a giant warrior with a red beard, who looks more like a troll than a man, he's mine," I say.

"Ivar, I assume? It sounds like you have a history with this man."

"Let's just say he took something from me, and I'm getting it back."

CHAPTER 38

After making it out of the swamps, we hugged the trees for the rest of the day. We are as close to Ethandun as we want to be for the night. Any closer, and we risk being seen by the guards. We eat well, and the men even drink a little wine, but we don't risk lighting a fire. We are fortunate that the rain has held off. George and Godwine return from scouting the Dane camp just as we finish eating. After sharing the details of what they saw, Alfred summons us together below the canopy of a towering oak tree.

"My brothers," he begins. He speaks first in Saxon and then in Norse. "Tomorrow we fight for England and for the survival of our faith. We must stop the great heathen army. Our Lord tells us through his prophets, that if we believe in him, our hands will be lifted up in triumph over our enemies. The Lord will destroy our enemy's horses and demolish their chariots. He will destroy the cities of their land and tear down their strongholds. He will destroy their witchcraft and their idols. He will take vengeance in anger on all people who have not obeyed him. Tomorrow will be the first day of the united kingdoms of England."

Alfred looks towards Quibly and me. "And maybe a kingdom of Iceland as well." I nod my approval and grab Quibly's hand. "Your children and your children's children will know this day as one of the greatest in our history!" Alfred shouts. "Sleep well. We march at midnight!"

I didn't sleep, and I don't think Quibly did either. I laid my head on his shoulder for most the night, silently staring up at the stars in the black sky. We didn't need to talk. We've hidden nothing from each other since we played together as small children, and we can speak without words. No one knows me better, not even Grim.

We eat the last of our meat and bread, and begin our short ride to Ethandun. We've prepared as much as the days would allow. George and Godwine marked the path last night so we wouldn't get lost, but the sky is clear, and there's plenty of light being cast down by the stars. I locate Odin's wagon. The gods, on both sides, will get a nice view of the battle. The unknown is whether or not they'll interfere.

Our men do their best to keep their steel from clanging as our horses plod through the night. Sassa is anxious. She can smell we're going to war. If there is any proof that magic lives in Midgard, it's with her. I called her Sassa as a reason to hear my mother's name out loud, but now I wonder if she has returned to live in this animal's spirit.

I stroke Sassa's head and whisper to her softly. "I need you. Don't tell anyone, especially Quibly, but I need your help. I don't know if I can do this. I miss Grim. Please give me courage." Sassa pushes her head against my hand and neighs softly. I sit back up in my saddle as all the horses come to a stop. We've arrived.

I sit motionless, listening for any sounds of the enemy. A creek is nearby, and the leaves of the trees are rustling in the wind. The sun will rise soon.

We dismount our horses, and George motions us to put our shields on the ground. We follow him to a grassy knoll covered in yellow wildflowers.

"Do you think Ivar is here?" Quibly whispers. He is by my side with his battle ax in hand. His knuckles look white.

"I hope so."

"I'm not sure I'll be able to hold him down." He looks apologetic. Of course, I never expected Quibly to get that close to Ivar. But it was a promise we had made to each other before we began this journey. He gets to hold him down, and I severe his head. I stand up on my toes and kiss him on the cheek.

We crawl up the knoll on our bellies. We are soon peering down on the Dane camp, only a few hundred paces away. At least twenty white tents are pitched tightly together in the middle of a flat grassland, thick with golden weeds. It reminds me of the barley fields that surrounded Papar's monastery – the ones I often crossed to teach my spiritual guardian the Norse tongue. I wonder if he's watching me right now. I think he is.

There aren't as many tents as I was expecting. This is good. Two fires are smoldering at the center of the camp. They haven't been attended to for some time. There are no warriors in sight. Could it be that the Danes are drunk and deep in their dreams? I look up into the night sky, hoping to see Papar looking down on me. The Saxon god must be on our side.

The orange glow that proceeds the sun's rise is beginning to peek over Midgard's edge. The time is now. We slither back down the hill and retrieve our shields. As planned, we'll sneak into the camp and spread out to the doorways of the tents. We can't bring the horses as we need to get in unseen. For an ambush, the bows and arrows will be of no use either. We'll attack with steel and strike without mercy. If we're lucky, we'll kill half of them before they awake. After that, may the gods, on either side, look favorably upon us.

We stay low, quickly moving through the tall grass towards the tents. Wynn is on my left, and Quibly is on my right. If Erik and Wulf were here, it would be a perfect morning.

We are halfway to the camp, and there's still no signs of the Danes stirring. I can smell the smoke from here. A flock of birds flies out of some shrubs ahead. We stop and crouch, as surprised by them as they are of us. We look to Alfred. He waves his arm, giving us the signal to carry on.

I look towards the tents just as they emerge from the earth. I stand frozen as their screams shatter the silence. "Berserkers!" I shout.

Their bodies are covered in fur and their heads with the faces of wolves, just as at the night of the feast. They race towards us with their axes and swords swinging at empty air. We may have them outnumbered, but we aren't favored to win this battle.

I can feel our men backing away. This is my destiny, and retreating is not an option. "As we trained!" I yell as loud as I can. Our men aren't moving, and the Berserkers are closing in quickly. Even Quibly looks as if he's turning to run.

Then I hear Alfred's voice. "For England!" he shouts. "Attack!"

He charges forward, and I don't hesitate, shouting as I raise my sword high in the air. Quibly and Wynn are right behind me. The others quickly follow, likely on instinct more than will. It doesn't matter. We finally fight!

I am matched up with Wynn, sprinting at full speed. We

make eye contact as we close in on the warriors. They are giants and running at the speed of horses. I remind myself they are human. These beasts are only men under a spell, which gives them weakness as much as it does strength.

A Berserker locks onto me, and I onto him. His red eyes are peering through me. I see the monks getting slaughtered in their beds. Godi is lying lifeless on the commanding stone on the flats by the sea. There are flies everywhere, swarms of them, picking at the flesh of our dead. Runa whispers in my ear. *A lone wolf will have no chance, but together they can outsmart the beast, tearing it apart.*

My father's shield is in position, and I grip my weapon hard, ready to strike. The Berserker has a sword in one hand and an ax in the other. I can see his breath. He's three strides away, just where I need him to be.

I cut hard to my left, locking my eyes onto the Berserker hurtling towards Wynn. I feel her brush behind me as we switch targets, just as we practiced a dozen times. I swing my sword hard, aiming high for the warrior's neck. My steel makes contact before he can change course. The ax flies from his hand, grazing my ear, as he falls dead to the ground.

I turn quickly towards Wynn. Her opponent is on the ground, and he roars as he jumps to his feet. I storm at him, ramming my shield and all my weight into his back. He stumbles forward into Wynn's awaiting weapon, collapsing to the ground.

Quibly is standing above a body, his battle ax hanging by his side. His red cheeks are dripping in sweat, and he's gulping for air. Across the field, the Saxons who didn't strike first are left defending themselves against men bigger and stronger. The

Berserkers roar, overpowering the shrieks of the Saxons as our men begin to fall. We run to help.

George is holding his shield up with two hands, his sword on the ground. A Berserker is towering above him, striking blow by blow into the splintering wood. Godwine is almost there, yelling as he closes in. The shield splits in two. The Berserker plunges his sword downwards. I turn away as Godwine's weapon hits his mark, but it's too late. George is gone.

I locate Alfred. He's in battle, retreating as he defends each incoming blow from a Berserker's swinging sword. Alfred falls to the ground as the warrior kicks the king's shield away. I rush towards him, but I'm not going to make it. Just like on Westman Island, when Ivar the Boneless stood above Thoren, I'm watching helplessly. The Berserker thrusts his sword in the air, and Alfred closes his eyes, as if at peace that he will soon see his god.

With both hands, I throw my sword end over end towards the warrior. I remember Thoren telling me never to let go of my weapon. I hold my breath as the steel slices through the air.

The Berserker drops his sword and falls to his knees. Alfred rolls out of the way as the man collapses forward, my sword sinking farther into his chest as he hits the ground. I rush to retrieve the weapon as Alfred crawls to his feet.

We turn back to the battle.

We stop and look at each other and the dead bodies surrounding us. We lost nearly half our men, including George, and many others look fatally wounded. The wolves may have won this fight, but it came at a price. Godwine screams at the top of his voice as if to tell the gods and giants that we have arrived.

"We did it!" Alfred proclaims. "Thanks to God, who gave us this victory!"

The men cheer as my eyes meet Quibly's. We both look towards the camp at the same time. The rising sun is bouncing its light off the white tents. I squint, only to see it's not the tents redirecting the sunlight. The Dane army is lined from one end of the camp to the other, two rows deep. There are at least a hundred men.

CHAPTER 39

"Shield wall!" I scream. The others spin and turn, casting their eyes on the ominous sight in front of us. Their joy gives way to fear.

"God help us," Alfred utters. He says it more in disbelief than in fear. Quibly and I knew the Berserkers would be just the first wave, but it's the size of the next one I never imagined. We're outnumbered five to one.

"Shield wall!" Quibly hollers, reinforcing my command. The Saxons scuttle together and clumsily find their positions.

The Danes' wall hasn't moved. Maybe running is the right thing to do. But Wynn grabs my hand, telling me without words that we aren't going anywhere. This time, I don't pull away. Instead, I squeeze hers tight. She shouldn't be here, but I know I would do the same if I were her. I wish I had the chance to know her better.

I hear a familiar call and twist around to find her. Sassa is racing towards us, her lead rope dangling from her neck. I break away and run towards her, jumping onto her back with both my sword and shield before she comes to a complete stop. "Thank you, girl," I cry out as I take the reins. "You just couldn't let me fight alone, could you?" She gallops to the front of our army. It's as if she can sense the fear in the Saxons' stomachs, and she's here to urge them to carry on.

The Danes' wall parts, and a man emerges from its center. He moves towards us as the shields close behind him. "Saxons!" he shouts in Norse.

Ivar the Boneless steps into focus. He's here! His red beard is still tied in a braid, hanging down over the steel mail that covers his chest. He stands a head taller than the men behind him and is carrying a single sword in his hand – most likely the steel that bares the same mark of Ulfberht.

"England is mine!" he bellows into the sky above him. "Your god has forsaken you. Bow to the gods of Asgard, and I promise to kill you quickly!"

Ivar tortured Godi. He tied Papar to a tree like an animal. He took my little brother from me, whom I'll never see again. I may have failed Grim, but my destiny isn't complete.

"I'll see you in Niflheim, you coward!" I scream across the field. My voice echoes back, trailing into silence. I don't know if I startled her, but Sassa rears back, lifting her forefeet off the ground. I hold on tight as she returns to the earth.

"Slave!" Ivar hollers back. "Odin continues to give me gifts! Thank you for bringing the Saxon king to me. As a reward, I'll kill you last!"

"You know this man?" Alfred questions as he comes to my side.

"He is Ivar the Boneless, son of Ragnar Lothbrok. The man I'm going to kill today," I say.

Quibly also comes out from behind the wall. "And I'm holding him down while she does it," he says.

Alfred looks at me as if he somehow understands the motivation behind my words. "May our gods be united on this day," he says.

I repeat his words in my head. My thoughts race back to the cave in Iceland, to the place where I met the old seer. *It was prophesied that a shield maiden will unite the gods. This is your fate. It's you I have waited for.* I look up into the black sky, wondering if all the gods are watching me now.

"England will know your courage and bravery for generations to come!" Alfred shouts to his men. "It's God's will that we are here today. His plan is perfect. We fight for God, we fight for England, and we fight for each other!"

Without hesitation, our men charge forward in the shield wall, yelling as they run towards the Danes. For a moment, I think I hear my brother's name being called. I snap the reigns and kick my feet.

"For Grim!" I scream as Sassa and I sprint towards the enemy, ahead of the others. The Dane wall opens at its center, but Ivar doesn't retreat behind the safety of the shields. Good. Today may be a perfect day after all.

I keep my eyes fixed on Ivar as I close in. He's wearing a fur coat with a bear's head, just as he did on Westman Island when he drove his sword into Thoren. I switch grips on my weapon.

Arrows fly over me. I lower my head against Sassa's mane right before she collapses forward. I tumble downwards, losing both my sword and shield as I hit the earth. Sassa is lying on her side in front of me, her eyes staring into mine. Her chest is gasping for air, but she's making no effort to get up.

I crawl to my feet, scrambling to locate my weapons. I hear Ivar's laughter. He's close. The Saxons have stopped. What are they doing? They need to fight!

I find my weapons in the grass and jump up to face the

enemy. Ivar is less than ten strides away. The Danes have broken from the wall and are rushing together like a swarm of wasps attacking a rotting animal. A horde of arrows fills the sky. I thrust my shield over my head before I realize what's happening. The arrows aren't coming *from* the Danes – they're being shot *at* them. Warriors rush out of the forest from my left and right. At first, I think I'm dreaming. Steel against steel and screams flood the field. The Saxons rush into battle.

I charge at Ivar with everything my legs will give. The hulking warrior chops down Godwine before I get within striking distance. I swing my sword hard, aiming for his arm. But the force of his blade against mine almost rips the weapon from my hand.

I look up at the massive warrior. He rears back with his sword but halts before striking, as if teasing with my life. I step back and prepare my next move.

"What a shame I have to kill you, slave," Ivar roars. "After you burned my boats, you forced me to kill your brother. That is your fault."

"You're lying!" I scream.

Ivar laughs and strokes his long, red beard. "Grim," he says. "That's your brother's name, right? And you're Livvy, the *poor* orphan girl. Oh, you didn't think I wouldn't find out after you offered to trade the priest for a slave boy?"

I lunge forward, swinging wildly at the heinous beast, but his defending blow knocks me flat on my back. He steps onto my shield, crushing my chest below it. I can't breathe.

"Little Grim begged me to stop," Ivar chuckles, pushing down harder. "I almost felt embarrassed for him." My ribs are snapping under the weight. It can't end like this. I twist and kick my legs, but he only pushes down harder. "It's time to see your brother," he snickers, heaving his sword up.

His weight comes off my shield, and I hurl it aside, grasping my sword with both hands. I swing it towards him, throwing my arms across my body. Shards of steel shatter into the air as my blade strikes his. I quickly roll to my feet, expecting to be standing helplessly without a weapon But it's Ivar who's holding onto nothing more than a cross-guard and pommel, his blade lying in pieces on the ground. My sword is unbroken. I point my weapon towards his throat.

Ivar laughs, tossing what's left of his weapon aside. "Father Odin doesn't want me to kill you," he says.

"I'm the one holding the sword," I say.

"You can't kill me, just like I can't kill you. We are the same."

"I'm nothing like you!"

"Don't you see it? The gods want you to help me purge Midgard of the Saxon filth. Why else would they bring you here? They chose you like they chose me."

"Yes, the gods chose her," Alfred announces as he approaches. Wulf, Erik, and Thoren are by his side!

Warriors slowly amass and surround Ivar and me, their bodies covered in sweat and blood. Sven, Tore, Gunner, Edward, and Wynn look on, as well as countless faces of men and women, both young and old. Most of them are carrying nothing more than spears and chopping axes.

"Your fight is hopeless!" Ivar growls. "My brothers will come after me. Ironside, Snake-in-the-eye, Ubba, and Halfdan will avenge me like I avenged my father."

"They may try," Alfred says. "But we will fight. The

united kingdoms of England will always fight."

"Then what are you waiting for?" Ivar barks. "Send me to Valhalla. Let me feast with the gods!"

"You are not a warrior deserving of Valhalla," I say. With a sudden swipe, Ivar grabs the end of my blade with both hands. He clenches his teeth as I try to yank it back. The steel slices deep into his hands as he pulls me and my weapon towards him. I release my grip, and he thrusts the blade into his chest. Ivar collapses to the ground.

Thoren rushes over. "Why did you let him do that?"

"He just grabbed it." We both look down at the man who destroyed our kingdom – at the man who took my brother from me.

"Finish—me," Ivar groans.

"I would be glad to," Thoren says. She stands over his chest and points her weapon at his neck. "Any last words?"

"Last words? I will drink with the gods before the sun sets."

Thoren pushes the tip of the blade against his throat. Ivar spreads his arms wide and closes his eyes. But instead of ending his life, she slowly pulls the weapon back. She picks up a shard of steel from Ivar's broken sword and rubs it between her fingers. "You're not going to Valhalla if you take your own life," she says. "The gods are clear on this." She drops the shard onto Ivar's chest and watches as he leaves this realm.

Thoren wraps her arm around my shoulder. "If I killed him, I'd have to feast with the bastard for a thousand years. The Valkyries had a plan. Thank you for doing your part." She pulls me in for a tight hug.

"Your shoulder is healing," I say.

She rotates her arm in a circle. "Strong enough that I may want my sword back." She picks up my weapon and hands it to me. "But not until you're dead," she says with a smile.

I go to Erik and throw my arms around his neck. "Thank you for coming," I say. "These are good people. They fought hard today."

Erik leans down and kisses me on the cheek. "Good to see you, Red. You can thank Wulf for getting us. We would have been here sooner, but he and Edward insisted we mobilized as many Saxon farmers and seamen as would come. Hardly a man or woman said no."

I hug him once more and look up into his blue eyes. "You do look like a descendant of the gods," I say with a smirk.

"Really? You are the first to ever say that," he says with a laugh. "Wulf wouldn't stop talking about you the entire way here. It was quite annoying. He loves you. And I think you love him, too."

I go to Wulf and kiss him on the lips. "Is this true?" I ask. "What Erik said?"

Alfred puts his arms around us both. "Athelwulf, if my memory hasn't failed me, you said you were going to marry this girl one day."

"I said, I *may* ask her to marry me one day," Wulf says with a grin.

"Everyone, I would like to introduce you to Alfred, King of Wessex," I announce. "Or should I say the King of England. Alfred, this is my family."

Wait, where's Quibly? I don't see him anywhere! "Quibly!" I shout in a panic. I yell his name again, searching the crowd of faces around me.

"I'm here, Livvy!" his voice shouts back.

The crowd parts and Quibly appears. But he's not alone. There are children with him— "Grim!" I scream.

"Disa!" my brother shouts as we run into each other's arms. I lift him off the ground and squeeze him as my eyes swell up in tears.

"Are you okay? Are you hurt?" I cry as I set him down and hold his face in my hands.

"I'm hungry," he says. "Do they have honey and buttermilk here?"

"And who might you be?" Alfred asks.

"My name is Grim. I'm from the hamlet."

"It is my great pleasure to meet you, Grim from the hamlet. My name is Alfred. Where we are going, you can have all the honey and buttermilk you can eat."

"And where are we going?" Grim asks.

"To the largest castle ever built."

Grim's eyes light up as he smiles from ear to ear.

Quibly walks over to Ivar's body. "I guess I'm not holding him down," he says. He carefully looks him over. "Thank Odin!"

CHAPTER 40

"What's his name?" I ask quietly.

"Athelstan," Wynn answers, swaddling the baby in her arms. "Would you like to hold him?"

"Yes, I would." He reminds me of Grim when I held my brother for the first time. The same day my mother died. "He looks just like his father," I say.

"Edward got his wish for a boy. But now that I see him, I couldn't imagine another."

"But can you imagine that he'll be the king of England one day?" I ask, bouncing him gently.

Wynn rolls her eyes. "It's your child who should rule the throne."

"We've discussed this a hundred times. Alfred is a great king, and Wulf has no intention of contesting him. We must stay united if we're to banish the Vikings from England. Ivar's brothers won't leave here on their own. And besides, I'm not married!"

"You still haven't set a day?" Wynn questions, shaking her head.

"Wulf would already be married if he had it his way, but the thought of all the attention and preparations makes me sick. And besides, I don't want to take away from Quibly and Lark's day."

"Athelwulf is a wonderful man, Livvy. Be careful not to

lose him."

"It would be so much easier if we were in Iceland. I don't want to sound ungrateful. It's just the castles, the food, the servants, are very—overwhelming."

"Have you heard from Erik since he returned?" she asks, with a hint of suspicion.

"Yes, he's sent word, as any *good friend* would. Erik and Thoren have retaken Iceland from the Danes. They're rebuilding the hamlet before sailing for Norseland."

"You don't still dream of going there?"

"To Norseland? Not at all."

It's not a complete lie. I still long to sail Midgard's seas in search of the rainbow bridge. Norseland would be just a single stop along the way. Wulf, of course, doesn't believe in the nine realms, but as I keep telling him, how do we know what's out there if we don't look?

I leave Wynn and the rock walls of the castle to start my day. First, I go to the stables. There are over a hundred horses here, but only one that I visit every day. I pull the apple from my pocket and step into her stall.

"Sassa," I say as I give her the fruit and rub her head. "You're getting stronger every day. You'll be out there saving England again before you know it." Sassa took an arrow deep in her leg. They wanted to put her down, but I wouldn't allow it. Alfred was kind to pay a farmer to look after her until she was strong enough to be sent for. I will repay the king in full and then some.

Hester, too, is somehow still alive. He doesn't like the stalls and prefers to wander the fields, and Quibly is happy to let him do it. He says Hester has earned his right to do whatever he wants in his old age. I couldn't agree more.

I make my way to the shipyard at the river to check on the boys. There are at least twenty hulls under construction. The masts will go up in another week. It's going to be a magnificent fleet. The boys are eating lunch, and I try to sneak up on them.

"We see you, Livvy!" Sven shouts. "Get over here!" His cheeks are as rosy as ever, and his belly is getting fatter. The boys are eating well.

Gunner ducks under Sven's waving arms. "Bjorn wants to know which boat is your favorite," Gunner says. Despite being the shortest Norseman I know, the Saxon girls adore him. His long and wavy blond hair doesn't hurt his chances.

"And Bjorn asked you this?" I question.

"Not in the words that you and I speak, but yes he did."

Bjorn shakes his head, looking down at his closest friend. "Come on, brother," Gunner moans. "You want to know, too. And we both know she'll pick mine."

"My favorite is the one that will sail faster than Erik's," I say.

"Then it's mine you have chosen," Gunner boasts. Bjorn frowns and punches his friend in the shoulder.

"Hey, keep your beastly paws off my coat!" Gunner growls, pretending to inspect his fur for damage.

Sven offers me some bread, and I join them on a shaven log under the sunny skies. Alfred convinced Sven, Gunner, and Bjorn to stay in Wessex and help him build a great fleet of ships – a navy as Alfred calls it. I'm sure the convincing had a lot of silver involved. The men at first refused his offer, citing their loyalty to Erik. But eventually Erik *ordered* them to stay. He argued the Saxons needed better ships to fight the Danes and

Shockheads with, a fact that no one would refute. But I believe the real reason was to give his friends hope of a better life. Their families at the hamlet are gone, and England offered a new beginning. The others left with Erik and Thoren, including Tore. Quibly protested for days, trying to convince the giant of a man to stay, but Tore was convinced his destiny was to go to Norseland and rid Midgard of every last Shockhead.

"I'll let you boys get back to work," I say as I stand to leave. "Where's Quibly, by the way?"

"He went to the forest to chop down some more trees," Sven says. "The boy is stronger than a plow ox." I'm happy Quibly found a job he loves. He was always great with axes.

I make my way to the upper field to meet the warriors for our training. Today, we're working on swords and axes. Wulf's brothers, Athelwold and Athelhelm, are already on the grass fighting. They are always first to arrive and last to leave. In a few more springs, they'll be great warriors.

I pull out my sword and race onto the field, joining them in their battle. I sharpen my blade every day. I've been working with the smiths to forge one for Grim, but we haven't been able to make one as strong or light as Alfred's and mine. And Ulfberht is gone and his secret with him.

I head back to the castle to the inner courtyard. Tonight, we are having a feast to celebrate the birth of Athelstan. Grim and Brice have been counting the days for at least a month. After we ambushed the Shockheads at Lindisfarne, we brought Brice and his mother back with us. The two boys have since become the best of friends, not unlike Quibly and me when we were the same age. Grim is now proficient in Saxon and speaks it more than he does Norse.

I've been learning Saxon myself, both to speak and to write. As I promised Alfred in exchange for the gold pointer, I've started reading his ancient stories. I plan to write down some sagas of my own. I don't want Grim, his children, or his grandchildren, to forget where we came from.

As I don't have anything to give to Edward and Wynn tonight, I decided to scribe Athelstan a story. It reads of a young prince who is to inherit the throne one day. He grows up believing that to rule the kingdoms is his birthright, and he lives a comfortable life inside the walls of a beautiful castle.

But one day, the prince is told in a dream that the kingdoms were given to him as a gift, and if he doesn't use his power for good, the gift would be taken away. At first, he ignores the dream, for this can't possibly be true. The kingdoms are his right to rule as he chooses. But the next night, he has the same dream and a very restless night's sleep. This continues for weeks, until finally he talks with his mother and asks for her help. She tells him to walk outside the castle walls and talk to the peasants, as this is a proven cure for such an ailment. The prince does as his mother says. Sure enough, each day that he walks outside the walls, he has a peaceful night's rest. When he doesn't, the dream returns.

Eventually, the prince inherits the kingdoms as a young man. Through years of talking to the common men and women, and not just the nobles, he learns to be a king for all people. He learns that power comes from giving and not taking, and becomes the greatest leader the land has ever known.

I sit down in the courtyard to finish my story. I pull out the pointing stick which Alfred gave me. Thoren said I was foolish for not trading it. She says I could probably get a new dragon ship in return, and what am I going to do with a stick and a jewel?

"Livvy!" Quibly shouts as he comes bounding into the courtyard. I jump at his sudden entrance, reaching for my sword. I accidently drop the pointer onto the rock floor.

"I broke it," I sigh as I reach down to pick up the two halves of the stick.

"I'm sorry, Livvy, I didn't mean to—"

"Look at this," I say. Inside the hollow of the stick is a thin sheet of white wool, rolled up tight. I unwrap it and begin to read the words written on it.

"What does it say?" Quibly asks.

"It's instructions." I read the words from the beginning to the end. "It tells how to forge a steel sword."

"Ulfberht made the jewel for Alfred, did he not?"

"Yes, he did." I smile as I recall Ulfberht's last words to me. *The secrets of my craft are in your hands.* Grim may get his sword after all.

"Now you can give Wulf his sword back," Quibly says.

I haven't told Wulf that Ulfberht made this sword for him. And Alfred, for whatever reason, has kept my secret to himself. It's not like I haven't tried to get the words out. But each time something pulled at me to stay quiet. As foolish as it seems, it's as if someone or something is telling me to hold onto it.

I look over and Quibly is staring at me like he's caught one of the children with their fingers in the honey jar. "He still doesn't know, does he?"

"I'm only borrowing it."

Quibly closes his eyes and shakes his head. "And after all these years, I thought I knew you."

"I will tell him."

"Uh huh. Sure."

"I will! Now then, what's so important that you come charging in here like a wild beast?"

"Just wanted to see if you were hungry."

"You are lucky I love you, belly and all, otherwise I would kill you."

Quibly turns and hurries away, with a pretend look of fear on his face. "You would have to catch me first." He stumbles on nothing that I can see and grabs the back of his leg as he hobbles out the door.

The feast is wonderful. Grim and Brice ate at least three bowls of meat and are now wrestling on the grass. Wulf and I sit on the ground and watch the others.

"Quibly and Lark have been dancing all night," Wulf says.

I look towards them and smile. They do look happy. I take Wulf's hand in mine. "I found instructions inside the jewel that Alfred gave me. They tell how to make Ulfberht's swords. Every last detail."

"That's amazing, Livvy! You can finally make Grim his own. Then you can make me one. Care to join me for a dance?" Wulf pulls me to my feet.

"As long as I get the next one," a voice behind me calls out.

"Erik, Thoren—Tore!" I shout. We all embrace and then laugh as we tell each other, "To health and happiness."

"What are you doing here?" I ask excitedly.

"I met a man in Iceland whom I'd like you to meet," Erik says. "Leif, this is Livvy and Wulf whom I've told you so much about."

A tall, lanky man with a neatly trimmed beard extends his hand. "Hello, it is very nice to meet the shield maiden who saved the realms," he says.

"I did no such thing!"

"That's not what the saga says," he says with a smile.

"We're joining Leif on an adventure and would like you both to join us," Thoren says.

"An adventure?" I ask.

"Leif has learned of a distant realm called Vinland. It is weeks away by ship, but it's a land unlike man or woman has ever seen. Grapes grow like weeds, and the trees reach up to the stars. There is more game in the forests than all of Midgard could hunt in a hundred years."

My heart is beating fast. "Is this true?" I ask Leif.

"I wouldn't say the trees touch Asgard, but yes, it's beautiful."

I look up at Wulf, pleading with my eyes for him to say yes.

Quibly spots us and rushes over. He hugs each of his friends.

"I heard you are getting married," Thoren says to Quibly. "Lark is a very lucky girl."

"I am the lucky one," Quibly boasts. "Not only can she cook, but she can hunt. Every day is a feast!"

"When we go to Valhalla, I will feast with you for a thousand years," Thoren says, before kissing Quibly on the cheek.

"I'm looking forward to it," he says with a smile. "So

what's going on?"

"We're setting sail to Vinland," Wulf answers, wrapping his arm around me.

I turn and jump into Wulf's arms and kiss him on the lips. "Thank you," I whisper.

He looks at me with those beautiful green eyes. "How do we know what's out there if we don't look?"

"Where is this Vinland?" Quibly questions. "We don't have to walk there, do we?"

We laugh and join the others, united not as Norse or Saxons, but as friends sharing a common sky. We dance until the sun rises. And next week we'll sail west, and if the giant serpent doesn't eat us first, perhaps we'll see the rainbow bridge along the way.

Author's Inspiration

T. Karr traveled the world looking for the perfect story and found its beginning in the small hamlet of Seydisjordur in Eastern Iceland.

Visit www.goldencirclepress.com to learn more.

GOLDEN
CIRCLE
PRESS

Made in the USA
San Bernardino, CA
28 June 2017